*"I need an*** [***Dani,"***]

Adam said. "I've never been to the theater. I can't tell one wine from another. Hell, I don't even know which fork to use first at a dinner party."

"Is all that so important to you?" Danielle asked.

"Yes. I want what's best for my sister."

"I can't see how I fit into all this."

Touching Dani's arm, Adam pointed out a random woman in the party crowd. With her stylish black dress and long blond hair, she exuded class, charm, confidence. "Do you know that woman?"

Dani realized he was indicating her sister. "Yes. Why?"

"Then you'll help me?"

"Help you do what?"

"Make me over into the kind of man a woman like that would want to marry."

Dear Reader,

Each and every month, to meet your sophisticated standards, to satisfy your taste for substantial, memorable, emotion-packed novels of life and love, of dreams and possibilities, Silhouette brings you six extremely **Special Edition**s.

Soon these exclusive editions will sport a new, updated cover look—our way of marking Silhouette **Special Edition**s' continually renewed commitment to bring you the very best and the brightest in romance writing.

Keep an eye out for the new Silhouette **Special Edition** covers—inside you'll find a soul-satisfying selection of love stories penned by your favorite Silhouette authors and by some dazzling new writers destined to become tomorrow's romance stars.

And don't forget the two Silhouette *Classics* at your bookseller's each month—the most beloved Silhouette **Special Edition**s and Silhouette *Intimate Moments* of yesteryear, now reissued by popular demand.

Today's bestsellers, tomorrow's *Classics*—that's Silhouette **Special Edition**s. And soon, we'll be looking more special than ever!

From all the authors and editors of Silhouette **Special Edition**s,

Warmest Wishes,

Leslie Kazanjian
Senior Editor

PAT WARREN
The Evolution of Adam

Silhouette Special Edition

Published by Silhouette Books New York

America's Publisher of Contemporary Romance

To my aunt, Julia Kitchens,
for all the warm memories of my youth
and for the love and friendship of today.

SILHOUETTE BOOKS
300 East 42nd St., New York, N.Y. 10017

ISBN: 0-373-09480-9

First Silhouette Books printing September 1988

Printed in the U.S.A.

Books by Pat Warren

Silhouette Special Edition

With This Ring #375
Final Verdict #410
Look Homeward, Love #442
Summer Shadows #458
The Evolution of Adam #480

Silhouette Romance

Season of the Heart #553

PAT WARREN

is a woman of many talents, including a fluency in Hungarian. She has worked for a real estate firm, a major airline and a newspaper, where she wrote the "Pat Pourri" column. Growing up as an only child in Akron, Ohio, she learned early to entertain herself by reading books. Now she enjoys writing them. A mother of four—two boys and two girls—Pat lives in Arizona. She and her husband, a travel agent, have toured North America, Mexico, Europe, Israel, Jordan and the Caribbean. When she can find the time, Pat also enjoys tennis, swimming and theater.

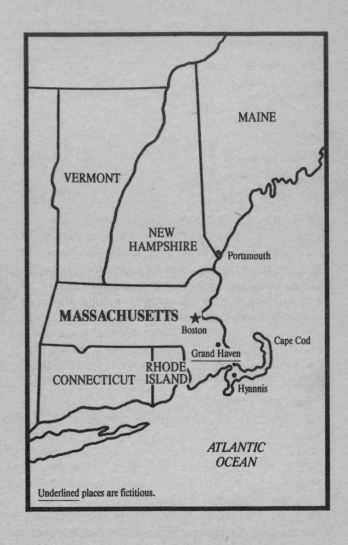

MAINE

VERMONT

NEW
HAMPSHIRE

Portsmouth

MASSACHUSETTS ★

Boston

Cape Cod

Grand Haven

CONNECTICUT | RHODE
ISLAND

Hyannis

*ATLANTIC
OCEAN*

Underlined places are fictitious.

Chapter One

The party was in full swing. Standing in the living room doorway of her mother's oceanside home, Dani looked about at the wealthy and prominent Hyannis crowd doing what they did best: socializing. How had she let herself get roped into attending still another of these stuffy affairs? she wondered, stepping inside the vast, beautifully decorated room. Even at twenty-seven, she found it hard to refuse a parent's request, she decided with a sigh of resignation.

"Danielle, I'm so glad you're here," purred a low voice behind her. "We don't see nearly enough of you." Antoinette Fischer patted her bright red French twist and regarded Dani through false eyelashes. "How did Arlene manage to pry you out of that gymnasium you're so fond of? No basketball game tonight?"

Dani gave her mother's closest friend a smile and ignored the faint disapproval in her voice. Neither Toni nor her mother could understand why Dani had chosen teaching athletics at an elementary school over a line of endeavor that was more socially acceptable—at least to them.

"She caught me on a free evening," Dani said, returning the older woman's hug. She knew that despite her constant nagging, Toni, who'd never had children of her own, was very fond of both Dani and her sister. "How are you, Toni? You look terrific." And she did; clever make-up camouflaged the years, and expensive attire cloaked the results of a few excesses.

"Thank you, dear." Toni looked pointedly toward the far corner of the room. "Did you see? Howard's here. Why don't you go over and talk with him, make the poor boy's day? He's started jogging recently and would love for you to join him, I know."

Dani followed her gaze, trying to keep her face expressionless. Toni's nephew, Howard DeBries, was another reason she should have ignored her mother's pleas and stayed home in her comfortable beach house. An up-and-coming stockbroker, Howard was dull and endlessly boring, with an odd laugh that could only be classified as a giggle. She'd dated him a few times, more to please Toni and appease her mother than because of any real interest on her part. "A little later," Dani answered, hoping to find a way to avoid Howard altogether.

Toni patted her arm affectionately. "Mingle, dear. You need to mingle more. You're much too solitary for your own good."

"I will," Dani answered, trying not to look relieved when Toni sailed off to join a group of her friends. Three times married and divorced, Toni was an inveterate matchmaker who hadn't yet given up on romance. Which was fine, if only she'd confine her efforts to her own love life.

Glancing about the crowded room, Dani thought again how much she disliked these parties. With good reason. She didn't belong, hadn't for years, by her own choice. From her looks to her life-style, she was different.

A person could rub shoulders with more designer clothes at one of these soirees than Yves Saint Laurent did on a good day, she thought. It was likely that the money spent on jewels worn in this room alone could amply feed the citizens of a third-world country for a week. It wasn't that Dani couldn't afford designer dresses, or even good jewelry, for she had some of both. It was just that she felt no compulsion to frantically buy more and more, always trying to outdo someone. In fact, she often wondered why these many smiling women did.

The biggest smile of all belonged to the hostess with the mostest—Arlene Winthrop Ames. Her mother. Not that Dani or her sister, Sabrina, was permitted to call her "Mother." Everyone called her "Arlene." Everyone, including the help. Certain women are immediately recognized worldwide by just their first names—Liz, Barbra, Sophia. In Boston and Hyannis, everyone knew Arlene without benefit of surname. It was something Arlene took pride in, though Dani couldn't imagine why.

She spotted her mother across the room, looking petite, chic and vivacious. A party girl through and through—that was Arlene. How she'd given birth to a tall, athletic, somewhat introspective daughter with freckles on her nose and brown curly hair was a mystery to Dani, one she was fairly certain her mother often puzzled over, as well.

Deciding that she couldn't stand just inside the doorway all evening, Dani walked over to the hors d'oeuvres table. At least she was hungry, so the evening wouldn't be a total loss. Looking around, she heaved a sigh of relief that Arlene had locked up her twin white poodles, Pierre and René. Although Dani was an animal lover, she considered her mother's two dogs spoiled and obnoxious.

As she filled her plate, several of Arlene's friends stopped to greet her and ask the inevitable where-have-you-been-keeping-yourself questions. The price you pay for being the maverick of the family, Dani thought as she found an empty chair off to one side and sampled a stuffed mushroom. As she ate she scanned the room, noting that there were few newcomers and spotting no one who caught her interest. Finishing, she stood and was about to get herself a drink, when her gaze settled on a man she hadn't noticed before.

He stood at the far end of the table, appearing a shade uncomfortable and oddly out of place in this elegant setting. It was his size, more than anything else, that set him apart. Tall men always caught Dani's eye, and this one had to be three or four inches over six feet. The tweed sport coat he wore looked too snug over his broad shoulders and his tan slacks, which hugged muscular thighs, didn't quite match his jacket. He wore no tie, and his white shirt was open at the throat.

Dani set down her plate and saw him give a quick smile to the passing waiter who handed him a drink. Nice smile, almost shy, she thought. It softened his angular face. His hair, bleached golden by the sun and worn just below his short collar, looked wind tossed and unruly even indoors. That was it. He looked as though he'd be far more in his element outdoors, in blue jeans and a sport shirt. Or perhaps bare chested. Not the usual sort Arlene had at her parties. He seemed alone. Who had invited him? Dani wondered.

As she was about to turn away, his eyes met hers. They were dark brown, intelligent and sharply assessing as he looked from her face down to her toes and back up again.

He didn't smile, just continued to stare into her eyes. Dani felt her heart thud in a surprising response. There was curiosity in his gaze, an inherent sensuality and a disturbing intensity that had her breaking the look and turning away to search the crowd.

That was one man who definitely wouldn't bore you, Dani thought. Then Howard caught her eye from across the room, and she gave him a quick wave. Hoping she could avoid him a bit longer, she headed instead for Arlene. Visiting with her mother would be far more interesting than listening to Howard extol the wonders of jogging.

She found her mother talking animatedly with her sister, Sabrina. As Dani approached, she thought for perhaps the hundredth time how much alike the two of them looked. Both were no taller than five foot four, slender and small boned. Arlene's blond hair was intricately styled and accented with ornate combs. Sabrina wore her fair hair soft around her face and straight down to the middle of her back. Arlene was clad in a vivid green silk jumpsuit, while Sabrina had on a black linen dress, simple yet elegant, probably one of her own designs. Her eyes were a darker green and more compelling than Arlene's, but equally large and luminous. The two women were like peas in a pod, Dani thought, and not just in looks.

"Welcome home, Sabrina," Dani said, moving close for a warm hug. Although they had little in common, she loved her sister and knew Sabrina cared for her, as well. They just marched to different drumbeats.

"Thanks. It's good being home," Sabrina said.

Since the opening of her haute couture shop in Boston last year, Sabrina had taken to flying to Paris with increasing regularity, trying to establish connections in that fashion mecca. She'd returned only last week from another such trip.

"How'd it go?" Dani asked.

Sabrina shrugged offhandedly. "So-so."

Turning, Dani embraced her mother. "Nice party."

"I'm so glad you came, Dani," Arlene said, "even though I know you hate these things."

"I don't *hate* these things."

"You'd rather be bowling and you know it," Sabrina said with a laugh.

"Bowling? Is that the new 'in' thing in Paris these days?" Dani asked with a teasing smile.

"Hardly. Frenchmen are more imaginative than that." Sabrina took a sip of her white wine. "But I go to Paris to work, not to play."

Dani studied her sister for a long moment. Only a year older than she was, Sabrina nevertheless had tiny lines around her eyes, new since Dani had last seen her. Sabrina had been tiny and cute as a baby, then small and lovely as a child. Now she was delicate and beautiful, a natural to work as a designer.

Dani had never been little *or* cute, she thought as she recalled their childhood. She'd been tall and gangly and awkward from day one. Now she was slim, almost boyish, a natural to teach athletics. She knew she was attractive, but in a different, quieter way. Strangers would seldom think she and Sabrina were sisters, yet they were attuned to each other and shared a strong bond. Lately Dani couldn't help wondering if something was bothering Sabrina.

"Sure you go to the romance capital of the world to work," Dani teased her, trying to keep the mood light. She'd talk with Sabrina later. "Arlene, do you believe that Sabrina's working while she's away or is she hiding a new man in her life from us?"

"Oh, I'm sure not," Arlene protested. "She'd have told me."

Dani raised a questioning brow. "Sabrina, are you still telling Arlene *everything*?"

"Absolutely," Sabrina said with a wink.

"Oh, you two," Arlene admonished them. "Dani, you look very nice. That's a lovely outfit."

Dani suppressed a smile. Arlene meant well, but she was painfully transparent. Dani knew her mother wouldn't be caught dead in her daughter's off-the-rack knit suit. "Did you think I'd show up in shorts and gym shoes, Mom?" She saw Arlene frown; whether at the question or because she hadn't addressed her by her first name, she wasn't sure.

"Of course not. You *can* look lovely if you want to."

Dani glanced at Arlene's elaborate hairdo and Sabrina's careful makeup. "Most of the time it's too much bother." Then she caught sight of the tall man she'd noticed earlier. He was standing by the open terrace doors, sipping his drink and studying the guests milling about. Curiosity got the better of her. "Who's that man over there? I haven't seen him here before."

Arlene turned her head, squinting for a better look. "Oh, that's Adam Kinkaid. He's working with your father on that new shopping mall complex. He's the builder, I think. Carter had me invite him to a party I gave last month."

Sabrina strained her neck to see. "Mmm, he's awfully good-looking." She added with a touch of disdain, "In a rugged sort of way."

"What's wrong with rugged?" Dani asked. "Rugged is more appealing than these lawyers and bankers and stockbrokers with their Brooks Brothers suits, soft hands and perfect diction."

"Lawyers, bankers and stockbrokers all make more money than most so-called rugged men," Sabrina commented.

"There's more to life than making money," Dani countered.

Sabrina smiled as she looked at Dani. "Such as?"

"A walk along the beach, a conversation by the fire, a—"

"A roll in the hay?"

"Sabrina, really!" Arlene scolded, pursing her lips, while Dani burst out laughing. "I've spoken with Mr. Kinkaid. He's certainly attractive, but he has a lot of rough edges."

"I like rough edges in a person," Dani asserted, deciding that Sabrina had loosened up a bit lately. She must get her alone soon and find out just what had happened on her last trip. "Shows character. If you ask me, he looks to be the most interesting man here tonight." Then, hearing a familiar voice, she glanced toward the doorway and smiled as she caught sight of a tall, dignified-looking man who was just arriving. "With one possible exception. There's Dad. I haven't seen him in ages. See you two later." Quickly she made her way over to Carter Ames.

Adam Kinkaid took a sip of his Scotch and berated himself for not having worn a tie. He owned only two, which, as far as he was concerned, was at least one too many for all that he ever wore them. He'd attended one of Arlene's parties last month and should have remembered that everyone came dressed to the teeth. Why, he couldn't imagine, since it was pretty warm, even with the terrace doors open. It was only the middle of April, and already the evenings were no longer cool.

Evidently—though her house was well built and obviously professionally decorated—Arlene, like most owners of the stately homes on the Cape, didn't believe in air conditioning. Old charm and old money here, Adam thought as he looked around. The beautiful people—no doubt about it. There was an unmistakable air of elegance, an atmosphere of confidence, an aura of wealth. The women looked as though they'd stepped out of *Vogue*, the men out of *Gentleman's Quarterly*. Their taste in clothes wasn't really his cup of tea, but he couldn't help admiring them.

He recognized a prominent judge, a female newscaster from New York, a retired senator, a fashion model, some high-powered attorneys and several prestigious bankers and stockbrokers who controlled millions daily. The movers and the shakers, pillars of the community, older men of power and position, younger men on the way up to join them. This was his second glimpse into this special world, and he'd thought a lot about these people since he'd attended the first function. Yes, this is what he wanted for Bonnie.

A smiling waiter dressed in an elegant tux and white gloves interrupted his musings by handing him a fresh drink he hadn't asked for. As he nodded his thanks, Adam was impressed. Arlene thought of everything, even instructing the waiters to remember the guests' drinks and bring them refills at the proper moment. Style and class. And he needed both. For Bonnie.

In the past he hadn't had the opportunity, the time, the money or the patience to work on acquiring style and class. Taking a swallow of his drink, he scanned the glittering assemblage again. This was what he had missed, and this was what he wanted for his sister. The good life, social position, someone from a good family to marry, acceptance by the right people. Then, perhaps, she could forget the hard times they'd been through. Adam badly wanted her to become one of these beautiful people, to be happy and secure.

Yet his being invited occasionally to one of these parties and standing around on the fringes of the crowd, an awkward stranger, wasn't enough. He needed an entry into this world so he could bring Bonnie in when she finished school and was ready. He had to be more than the man who constructed shopping malls for these people. He had to become one of them. But how? he wondered, frowning.

His roving glance found Arlene, deep in conversation with a young blond woman who wore a black dress that made her tanned skin look like warm honey. Even from where he stood, he could see that her jewelry was very real and very expensive. Beautiful, classy and rich—chances were that if he could get close to a woman like that, she'd draw him into this moneyed crowd.

But how in the world could he get to know her or someone like her? His hair was shaggy, he had calluses on his hands, and a total of two ties graced his wardrobe. She wouldn't give him a second glance with all these guys around in their white slacks and navy blazers with the gold buttons, their fingernails buffed and their hair-salon cuts. He could match most of them dollar for dollar in the wallet, but he was no match for their fancy manners and finishing-school ways.

But he could learn, Adam thought. He had the time, now that he had a huge staff and good people managing his company, though he still kept very much involved. He could discover what a woman like that cool blonde enjoyed doing, then learn to do it. A crash course in class. That's what he needed. But there weren't too many Ivy

League schools that provided summer courses in the social amenities. If only he knew someone who could teach him. Adam set his glass down on an empty tray. Damn, but he had to find a way.

Turning toward the arched doorway, he spotted a familiar face. Carter Ames wasn't nearly as stuffy as his name suggested. He was an astute business man who had his carefully manicured fingers in many corporate pies, including shopping centers, apartment buildings and office complexes. Ames Enterprises was also well diversified—real estate, oil, precious metals—with holdings all over the world. Carter employed a very successful architectural firm that in turn had recommended a very reputable construction company to Carter. Adam Kinkaid's company.

He and Carter had hit it off from the first. Adam found Carter to be a workaholic, much as he himself was, innovative in his thinking, surprisingly knowledgeable about the building end of things, with a quick wit and genuine manner. There was only one thing he didn't understand about Carter: he and his former wife, Arlene, were good friends despite their having been divorced eight years ago, and they often entertained together.

Adam couldn't fathom amicable divorces. He didn't believe in divorce, which was why, at thirty-one, he'd never been married. All too often, the one led to the other. Besides, he'd never met a woman who could put up with him, keep him interested, keep him faithful. And he wasn't sure he ever would.

As he watched Carter greet several friends, he saw the tall, dark-haired woman who'd first captured his interest when he'd arrived rush into Carter's arms for a big hug. The older man returned the affectionate gesture, kissing her cheek, then leaned back to talk to her, a smile on his face. Adam stood still for a moment longer, wondering who the slim, attractive woman was.

Earlier as he'd studied her he'd thought that she looked to be about the only one in the room he would feel comfortable introducing himself to. She appeared natural and unpretentious, and she had wide, very blue eyes with laugh lines at the corners. In those eyes he saw intelligence, humor and a flash of vulnerability. She was obviously a good friend of Carter's. He decided to join them.

"Of course I haven't been avoiding you," Dani was saying, her arm still around her father. "You're the busy one, forever jetting off somewhere."

"You know I always manage to put in an appearance at Arlene's parties. She expects it."

"Mmm, don't I know. Not my favorite way to spend a Friday evening."

"Nor mine. How have you been, Dani? You look wonderful." Carter hugged her to him.

"I'm fine," Dani assured him, thinking, still a handsome man at fifty-nine, as pride in her father welled up in her. Although they weren't as close as she would have liked, because he was so absorbed in his work, she knew his feelings for her ran deep, as did hers for him. She'd inherited from him her height, her dark hair, the blue of her eyes, and perhaps her aversion for the limelight. Carter Ames was definitely a behind-the-scenes power broker. "How are *you*?" she asked.

"Fine, too. Busy traveling, endless meetings, speaking engagements..."

"And you love every minute," Dani said, knowing it was true, glad he sounded content.

Her father's smile was suddenly boyish, as if he'd just been found out. "Yes, I do." Appearing to have become aware of someone alongside them, Carter turned from his daughter, then beamed a welcoming smile. "Adam, it's good to see you."

"And you, Carter." Adam returned the greeting, shaking hands. "I was hoping you'd be here."

"No problems on the project, I hope?" As Adam shook his head, Carter nodded and drew Dani closer. "Good…. I'd like you to meet my youngest daughter, Danielle. Dani, this is Adam Kinkaid. He's building Ames Plaza for us, and doing a hell of a fine job."

Dani watched Adam's gaze move to her, his face breaking into that quick smile she'd seen him flash from across the room. He reached for her hand.

"Happy to meet you," Adam said. So that's who she was, he thought. Yes, there was a resemblance. Yet whereas Carter definitely belonged in this setting, his daughter looked slightly out of place in the crowd of carefully made up, bejeweled, overconfident women. She wore the merest trace of pink on her lips, a thin gold bracelet on her slim wrist, and a somewhat shy smile. He would have thought Carter's daughter would be more fashionable and livelier, like Arlene.

Dani's hand felt lost in his big, callused palm, yet she found she liked his touch. Looking up, she broadened her smile. "Nice to know you, Adam. I've been by the plaza and wished I could ride the elevator up to the top of those big orange girders. I'll bet the view's outstanding."

"Twelve floors up there's a bit of sway with the wind, but yes, the view's pretty spectacular." She probably was just being polite, Adam thought. He'd never met a woman that daring. He found he didn't want to relinquish her hand.

"And Dani would go up, too," Carter told him. "She loves challenges."

She became aware her palm felt damp, then slid it from his grasp. "You're making it sound as if I climb Mount Everest when I get bored, Dad."

"I'm surprised you haven't," Carter said affectionately.

"In that case," Adam said, "stop at the site sometime. I'll take you up."

"Do you mean that?"

"I always mean what I say." He stepped closer to her. "Do you live here with your mother?"

"No, I have my own place not too far from here, in Grand Haven."

"It didn't occur to me until just now," Carter commented, "but you two are almost neighbors. Adam recently built himself a house on Oceanside, right on the water. Number 140, isn't it?"

"I know! The big stone structure at the end of the block. I'm at 112. I wonder why I've never seen you around."

"He's probably not home any more than I am. Right, Adam?" Carter asked, taking a drink from a passing waiter.

"My work does keep me pretty busy. I don't take enough time to play."

Dani looked up at him, way up. The feeling was a nice one. After a long day at work, she'd worn flats tonight, for comfort as well as to play down her five-feet-eight-inch height. While being tall served her well on the basketball court, at social events the added inches from heels put her eyeball to eyeball with most men—something that intimidated all but the very secure. Adam Kinkaid was even taller than her father, and she had a hard time picturing either of them being easily intimidated. Like her father, he appeared to be a hard worker. She liked that too. Nine-to-fivers had rarely appealed to her. "A group of us play volleyball on the beach most every Saturday morning," she said, snapping out of her reverie. "You should join us sometime."

Adam looked at her with measuring eyes. She wore a yellow knit skirt and matching sweater, the sleeves pushed up on her slim arms. Her manner lent the simple outfit a stylish air, but her clothes couldn't hold a candle to what the other women at the party had on. Carter was always impeccably dressed, and Arlene was a fashion trendsetter. Yet their daughter chose casual clothes over designer originals, a house on the beach over this mansion and appeared intrigued by the challenge of riding to the top of his building in a wire-cage elevator. Interesting. Was Danielle Ames a rebel, or just someone with a mind of her own? Suddenly he was curious to know more about her.

"So you're the athletic type?" he asked.

Just the image she wanted to convey, Dani thought wryly, keeping her expression bland. "You could say that. I'm athletic director at an elementary school in Boston."

"No kidding! I—"

A newcomer interrupted him. "Danielle, I've been trying to get your attention all evening."

Turning her head, Dani found Howard giving her a mock scowl.

"Are you hiding from me?" he asked, ending the question with a small giggle as if the thought was ludicrous.

"No, of course not, Howard." Sighing inwardly, she introduced him to Adam, wishing Howard had a better sense of timing.

As soon as he acknowledged her father and shook hands with Adam, he turned back to Dani. "I believe this is our dance," he said, his round face beaming.

She hadn't even noticed that the small band had started a medley of show tunes. It would be unpardonably rude of her to refuse Howard, she decided resignedly. Planting a smile on her face and nodding to Carter and Adam, she took Howard's arm and let him lead her to the terrazo area by the open terrace doors, where several couples were already dancing.

Adam watched her leave. "She's very attractive," he said to Carter. "I'm surprised she prefers teaching to—" he waved his arm to include the room and everyone in it "—all this."

Carter's laugh was slightly hollow. "You mean surprised that she's not following in her mother's footsteps? I'm pleased she's her own person. Dani doesn't give a damn about money or social position."

Adam nodded knowingly. "That's because she's always had both."

"Maybe," Carter said, sipping his drink. "But Dani's had to fight to be what she is today. She honestly enjoys helping other people."

Adam watched Dani as she followed Howard around the dance floor. Every inch the poised woman, she was masking her obvious reluctance to be with the persistent man in the red bow tie. Smart, personable, caring and well-connected—Dani didn't seem crazy about the life-style she'd been born into, but she *had* learned all the right moves from the cradle to the present. To top it all off, she was a teacher and lived scarcely a block from him. Yes, she was the perfect one to help him, he decided. Perhaps with a little nudge from her father she'd be willing to work with him.

Smiling, Adam turned back to Carter. "Carter, I have a favor to ask of you," he said, placing a friendly arm across Carter's shoulders and leading him over to a quiet corner.

* * *

With a puzzled frown, Dani searched the crowd for Adam Kinkaid. She'd just had an odd conversation with her father, and she still wasn't quite sure what he wanted her to do.

Carter had rescued her from Howard and his ramblings on the joys of jogging, and she'd hugged her father gratefully. Then he'd told her he'd be enormously pleased if she'd do him a kindness. Carter had always taken her side the many times Arlene and Sabrina had launched campaigns to get her to do something she didn't want to do, and for that reason alone she had trouble refusing him anything. But this request was a little bizarre.

Her father had mumbled on somewhat disjointedly about how Adam had started out as a poor boy from the wrong side of the tracks, and now that he was enormously successful, there was only one thing missing in his life. He wanted to help his sister, Bonnie, and he needed Dani's assistance. When Dani had asked Carter what she could do for Bonnie Kinkaid, he'd been somewhat vague. Nevertheless he'd elicited a promise from her that she'd do all she could to help. Maybe it had something to do with getting his sister into athletics, she conjectured.

Craning her neck, Dani spotted Adam by the terrace doors. As she walked toward him, she saw him study her approach. "I understand you'd like to talk with me," she began.

"Yes," he answered, a slow smile appearing on his tanned face.

Dani found herself getting lost in his dark gaze. Adam Kinkaid was quite possibly the most appealing man she'd met in years. And when he smiled... The evening suddenly offered some interesting possibilities, she mused.

"Do you think that if I grabbed us each a drink, we could go out onto the terrace?" he asked. "It's pretty warm in here."

"A glass of wine would be nice," Dani said.

Adam motioned to a passing waiter for two glasses of wine, then took her elbow and steered her toward the terrace. They strolled over to the waist-high ledge. The cloudless evening sky was filled with stars and in the distance below, the tireless sea rolled toward the shore. Flames danced in glass lanterns at intervals along the bricked wall, adding a shadowy glow.

When Adam had discussed his idea with Carter, he'd been surprised and pleased that the older man had gone along readily, even somewhat enthusiastically. Now here Dani was, willing to listen, and Adam wasn't quite sure where to begin.

"What made you decide to teach?" he asked. "I'd have thought you'd...I don't know—do charity work or something."

She gave him a tolerant smile. "The idle rich? No, I leave that to Arlene. She adores hostessing charity luncheons and giving fund-raising balls. My sister works, too, designing clothes for her own company. And I don't have to tell you my father works rings around most men."

"But you can't make much money teaching kids to play basketball and field hockey."

She set down her wineglass, her expression a shade cooler. "I don't do it for the money. There's a lot of satisfaction and pleasure in teaching. Do you build your skyscrapers just for the money?"

"Not anymore. I did in the beginning. Not all of us can afford the luxury of choosing an occupation that satisfies us regardless of its pay scale."

If he'd said that to put her in her place, Dani thought, it hadn't worked. She wasn't about to apologize to him for having money, since she'd had no choice in the matter. She took little interest in the family business, knew only that her share of the dividends was reinvested regularly, that her capital was never touched and that the total was by now surely sizable. Money simply didn't interest her. She was aware of it as she was of the color of her eyes, something she'd known forever.

She knew that all over the globe, Carter and his vast army of men in three-piece suits, striped ties and wing-tip shoes watched over the family's interests. Making money simply for the sake of stockpiling more money seemed somehow obscene to Dani. But after years of trying to make her opinion heard—without results—she had found her own way of dealing with the issue. She ignored it. Undaunted, Carter had set up a trust fund for her, which for the most part she pretended didn't exist and instead lived off the money she earned. Still, she wished Adam hadn't implied that she lived such a pampered life.

"Not everything has come easily to me, Adam," she said, thinking how long and hard she'd fought with Arlene about teaching. People always assumed the wealthy had no problems.

Adam sat down on the ledge, raising one knee and angling his body so he could look at her. He wondered how he could make her understand. He'd never been good at talking about himself, his life, his plans, to anyone else, especially a woman. But this woman was the key. "More easily than to some."

Dani sighed, wishing he'd get to the point. "My father mentioned that you had a problem, that something was missing from your life."

"No, not missing from my life. I'm content with my work—deeply satisfied with it, in fact. It's Bonnie, my sister."

Like pulling teeth, this process, Dani thought. And she still didn't know the problem. "All right, what's missing from Bonnie's life?"

He waved his arm at the room they'd just left. "That's what's missing, what I'm not able—at the moment—to give Bonnie. Social connections, knowing the right people, beautiful manners, an involvement in culture."

"It's not all it's cracked up to be. Honest," Dani told him, surprised at his odd revelation.

"That's easy for you to say—you've always had it."

And I turned my back on it as soon as I was able, Dani thought. But obviously she could never explain all the whys and wherefores of her choices to this man, whom she'd just met. "Let's just say it's a life-style I'm not terribly comfortable with." She watched as Adam gazed through the archway at the room beyond, his face wistful.

"But Bonnie would love it. She'd thrive in it, meet the right man, one who would always take care of her, see that she never lacked for a thing. Equally as important, they'd be socially prominent, travel abroad, mix with the rich and famous."

Too much, she thought. The man has delusions. "Adam, I think you watch too much television. Trust me. It's not like that. Life isn't like *Dynasty* or *Dallas.* You've achieved something on your own, something you can take pride in, not something you inherited. Half the men in that room would probably trade places with you."

"Do you know I've never been to the ballet, that I don't know one wine from another? I can't discuss the right books intelligently. Hell, I don't even know which fork to use first at a dinner party. And to you and the people in there, those things are all second nature."

Crossing her arms over her chest, Dani regarded him. He was really serious. "Is all that so important to you? Have you been miserable up to now, not knowing all that?"

"Yes, there's a reason it's very important, and no, I haven't been miserable not knowing. If it were only me involved here, I would never bother to learn. I like the simple things, beer instead of Scotch, steak instead of sautéed medallions of veal, bowling, a movie now and then, a walk along the beach...."

Bowling? Dani had to smile. "Me, too, Adam. My favorite food is peanut butter."

His dark eyes filled with disbelief. "You're kidding?"

"Why would I lie to you?"

He ignored her question. "But that's not the life I want for my sister. My mother's got a heart condition. She won't always be around. Bonnie can't look to her big brother all her life. I want her to have status, to marry well, to be happy."

"Have you talked this over with Bonnie?"

"She's only nineteen, a kid."

"Some nineteen-year-olds have pretty strong feelings about the direction they want their lives to take, in case you haven't noticed."

"Not Bonnie. She listens to me. She knows I want only what's best for her. And what's best for her is in that room."

"I wouldn't be too sure about that." He certainly was single-minded, she thought. Poor Bonnie.

Adam brought his attention back to Dani. "I don't go after something, or someone, without the odds on my side.

Right now they're not, and I know it. I also know they can be. *You* can help me improve my odds."

"I still don't see what you want from me."

"I need an entry into that world, Dani—your world. It appears you have little interest in it, but I have a great deal. I need to win over a woman who fits in, who's comfortable in this crowd, one who'd pull me in. In time I'd get to know her friends, and I could introduce Bonnie gradually to all the right people. But I've never learned the social amenities, the skills I'd need to attract a woman of that sort. I don't have a lot of women friends, just ... women I've known. I don't know about old-fashioned courting, the proper behavior, the right words."

This whole conversation was getting stranger by the minute, Dani marveled. He just didn't want to believe that the world he craved admittance to was no longer her world. "I can't see how I fit into all this."

Adam stared inside, searching for the right words. Then his gaze landed on the stunning woman he'd noticed before, the one in the stylish black dress and the long, blond hair. A tall man whispered in her ear, and her bright laughter rang out as her green eyes sparkled with amusement. She had class, charm, confidence. Just what he had in mind. Touching Dani's arm, he pointed her out. "Do you know that woman?"

Dani realized he was indicating her sister, Sabrina. "Yes, why?"

He looked back at Dani, his eyes earnest and imploring. "Then you'll help me?"

"Help you what?"

"Make me over into the kind of man a woman like that would want to marry."

As Dani's mouth dropped open, her wineglass slipped through her fingers and shattered on the terrace floor.

Chapter Two

Dani used the time it took a white-jacketed server to clean up the glass fragments to compose herself. It took every second.

She hadn't been quite sure where her conversation with Adam Kinkaid was headed, and she certainly would never have guessed. He wanted her to help make him over to suit his preconceived notion of the perfect male—not for himself but to help his sister climb the social ladder. No wonder her father had been vague. Ridiculous! Of all the wacky, off-the-wall ideas. She'd have to dissuade him somehow.

"Did you want another glass of wine?" Adam asked.

Dani shook her head.

At last the waiter left, and Adam touched her arm, turning her toward him. "Are you all right?" he inquired, and saw her slow nod. "Now then, where were we?"

Dani cleared her throat. "I seem to remember you'd just announced that you wanted to marry my sister."

"Your sister? That blond woman is your sister?"

"Sabrina Winthrop Ames, in the flesh."

He gazed back into the room, narrowing his eyes. Small wonder Dani had been shocked. Yes, the blonde did look a great deal like Arlene. All the better. "No, I don't want to marry your sister. I just want you to help me become the kind of man she—or someone like her—would find attractive enough to marry."

"What makes you think you aren't?"

Adam let out an exasperated sigh and sat down again on the ledge, drawing Dani down beside him. "I don't mean just male-female attraction, though that's part of it. Maybe the right word is *acceptable*. I know that most socially prominent people stick with their own kind, marry within their own circle. I can't do anything about my background, but I can alter my present and guide my future. And Bonnie's."

Dani shook her head. "I think you're making too much of this, Adam. If Sabrina, or any other single woman in there, found you attractive, interesting, fun, your background wouldn't stop her from pursuing a relationship with you. Contrary to popular opinion, people with money are still people with feelings."

"All right, let's test that theory," Adam said, warming to his subject now that he saw he had her undivided interest. "Does someone like Sabrina play tennis or prefer miniature golf? Does she have a beautifully decorated apartment where she gives intimate little dinner parties, or does she live in a rustic house on the beach and eat hot dogs? Does she go sailing, or does she camp out under the stars? Does she run into New York to see all the latest plays, or does she rent movies for the VCR and snuggle up in front of the television with a bowl of popcorn?''

He watched Dani chew thoughtfully on her lower lip, considering his remarks, as he continued, ''Does she go dancing at the latest 'in' spots? Does she attend opening night at the opera? Does she know her way around some of the capitals of Europe the way she knows her own backyard? Does she set fashion trends or follow them religiously, or does she not give a damn what people think about her clothes choices? Did she get that tan on the Riviera, or tending flowers in her own garden?''

Leaning closer, he saw the truth on her face. He moved in for the kill. ''In other words, how much would we have in common? What would we talk about, do together? Have you ever seen her date someone dressed the way I am tonight? Or would she be embarrassed to be seen with me?''

Dani sighed. ''She wouldn't be embarrassed, but . . .''

''But she'd think of me as an offbeat diversion, not someone who'd fit into her life seriously. What would Mama say if she brought me home with serious intentions? That she was going through her bohemian phase and it would pass?''

''It's hard for me to guess,'' Dani said, hedging. ''My sister and I are very different. Her circle of friends do prefer a lot of the things you mentioned, but that doesn't automatically make them snobs. It has to do with the way they were brought up, the things they've been exposed to since birth.''

Adam nodded, satisfied that she was beginning to see. She even seemed a little defensive. ''My point exactly. Background. And I don't have the right one.''

''But Adam, you are what you are. You can't just decide you'll like opera by attending a performance, or that you'll like tennis better than miniature golf, or that you'll learn which fork to use first and thereafter choose formal dinner parties over hot dogs on the beach. There's nothing wrong with your preferences. Why change them for anyone, much less for some nebulous woman you think is the key to social acceptance?''

"Because she *is* the key. I don't have to learn to love those things. I just need to learn them, to become acceptable to that group in there. Not just acceptable on the fringes, but totally acceptable, even sought after. Then I can introduce Bonnie to that world."

"What happens to you after that? Do you go back to bowling and camping, or do you stay with sailing and the ballet?''

Adam ran a hand through his hair, and rubbed the back of his neck. Dani was not exactly a pushover. He had to make her understand, because she was his answer. "I can roll with the punches, decide that later.''

Dani stood and turned to gaze at the winking stars. The salt spray from the sea drifted to her, tangible in the humid air. Another wave rolled in, powerful, patient, then receded, revealing tiny land crabs scurrying for shelter before the next big pull. She felt a little like one of them, drawn in, with no place to hide from Adam's strange request. The time when she could have walked away easily was long past—even if she hadn't promised Carter she'd help. Adam had her.

She understood all too well the need to belong. She was the family misfit—and this man, with the intense brown eyes, had spotted it immediately, thereby establishing a connection. Although Dani loved Arlene, she'd never been able to relate to her. It was the same with Sabrina. Adam had analyzed her sister with eerie accuracy without ever having exchanged a word with her. Dani was perhaps closest to Carter, yet her father's zeal for business to the exclusion of almost everything else was one she could never share. So that left her as odd man out. Which was why she knew how Adam felt.

Dani watched a night bird light on a wisteria bush that bordered the terrace wall. Cocking his head at her, he whistled a plaintive tune, reinforcing her mood. Basically she didn't agree with Adam's premise that he had to make himself over to become acceptable. But she empathized with his desire to protect his sister from knowing the sad feeling of being on the outside looking in—if indeed she wanted in. If he'd asked Dani to help him gain acceptance for himself, she would probably have walked away. But his obvious love for Bonnie, she couldn't ignore. Still, would Bonnie want this life?

Turning, she looked up to see a breeze ruffle Adam's sun-bleached hair. He watched her patiently. Swallowing, Dani leaned against the ledge. "I understand that Bonnie's attending a good college now. Isn't she meeting people there who could draw her into the kind of life you want for her without your having to go to all this bother?"

"Unfortunately not. Last I heard she was dating a guy who sounds like a real loser. She's made a few friends, but she's no more comfortable with those people than I am. It's not as easy as you might think to fit into a world you've never known. You can help change all that. For me and for Bonnie."

"I think I will have that other drink," Dani said.

He had her. Adam was sure of it. He went to the arched doorway and grabbed a glass of wine for Dani from a passing waiter, skipping the round himself—he was euphoric enough without another drink. Then he walked back and handed her the wine, waiting impatiently as she took several sips.

"If I were to agree to this mad little project," she began, "and that's still a big *if*, what would I have to do?"

Adam pulled himself up onto the terrace ledge, trying to keep a victory grin off his face. "I'm afraid you'd be working with some real raw material here," he confessed. "But I learn fast." As he gazed off into the distance, his busy engineer's mind formulated a logical plan. "For openers, I'm not very comfortable at dinner parties, since I'm pretty much a meat-and-potatoes man. I get confused with all that silverware, all those wineglasses. Sometimes I'm not even sure what I'm eating."

Dani laughed. "Sometimes I'm not, either. That part's no problem. I'm pretty much a seafood-and-salad person, but I can cook. I suppose I could have you over for dinner and take you step-by-step through the formalities."

Adam's smile was instantaneous. "That'd be great. Now, let's see. How about sailing? Don't Sabrina's friends sail?"

"Probably, but although I've been out a few times, I can't teach you to sail. I'm not that good."

"All right, another sport, then."

"Which ones do you play?"

"I played baseball for a while, a sandlot league. And I play basketball with the guys after work once in a while. Those aren't exactly high-society games."

"No, I guess not. What about tennis? Have you ever played?"

"Never had a racket in my hand. In the South Boston neighborhood I grew up in, any guy caught playing tennis probably would have had his face rearranged on his way home."

"So you were a tough street kid?"

"More or less," he answered, thinking that the only place she'd run into kids like that had been in the movies. "Do you think you could teach me tennis?"

Despite his size, Adam Kinkaid had a little-boy appeal. She ran her eyes over his powerful shoulder muscles, his lean, hard torso, then back up to his dark eyes. "I guess you've got some coordination if you climb around on those girders twelve stories up and manage not to fall off."

"Do you belong to a tennis club?"

Dani thought of Easthope Country Club and barely suppressed a grimace. "My folks do. But there are public courts available."

"I'd really like to try the country-club atmosphere. Aren't there some special rules of etiquette you need to know to play there, beyond the rules of the game?"

There certainly were. Dani sighed. "I'll check into it. What else?"

Adam crossed his long legs at the ankles and leaned back. "Books. A list of the current ones I should read would be helpful. Music—the kind I should be listening to." He glanced down at his clothes. "I probably could use some wardrobe pointers. I'm not much for dressing up."

Dani wasn't either, but she didn't suppose he wanted to hear that. He looked just fine to her—more than just fine. But, then, he wasn't trying to appeal to her but to someone like Sabrina. She'd have to keep that in mind. So far his requests were uncomplicated and quite easy for her to deliver on. She really couldn't come up with a solid reason to refuse him. What harm could there be in giving the guy a few hints on the social graces?

Slowly she took another sip of wine, then set down her glass. "I don't know how much help I'll be, because, as you may have gathered, my life isn't that of a socialite."

"But you were raised that way."

"Yes, I was." And I hated most of it, she thought. There'd been ski trips, shopping jaunts to New York, vacations in London or Paris and parties. Always parties. Her life had been predictable—and boring. Trying to remember her father's enthusiasm for this escapade—and wondering about it—Dani hoped she wasn't biting off more than she could chew. "All right, I'll do it."

Adam pulled her into a quick, hard hug. He'd always been good at persuasion. "Great." Leaning back, his arms still around her, he smiled down into her eyes. "Thanks, Dani."

Suddenly his scent surrounded her, musky and very male. It wasn't often she felt small, but with this big man's strong arms around her she did. The warmth of his touch flowed through her cotton sweater, making her shiver, making her aware. What am I getting into here?

Gently she eased back from him. "Better save your thanks until we get some results."

His smile was confident. "We will. I think you're probably a hell of a teacher, Dani."

In basketball, yes. In social strategy, that remained to be seen. Distancing herself a step or two from him, Dani clenched her hands, aware they were a little shaky. The cool night air was making her tremble a bit, that was all. "Well, where do you want to begin?"

"Up to you, coach."

"Okay, how about dinner, then. Perhaps a French menu?"

"Sounds good to me. Tomorrow's Saturday. That too soon?"

He wasn't wasting any time, was he? Well, why not? If their first lesson didn't work out, she could always call the whole thing off. "That's fine. About seven?"

"I'll be there," Adam said, smiling. He glanced toward the doorway. "I've taken enough of your time tonight. I think Howard's trying to get your attention again. I take it he's a close friend?"

Looking past Adam's broad shoulders, Dani spotted Howard waving in her direction. She gave him a weak smile. "Not exactly," she said, resigning herself to the inevitable. "More a friend of the family." She sighed. "He jogs."

She raised her eyes to Adam again, comparing the two men. No contest, she thought. "I suppose I'd better go talk with him. I'll see you tomorrow night." Squaring her shoulders, she marched through the doorway toward Howard the Jogger.

Adam shoved his hands into his pockets and stood quietly for a moment, his eyes on Dani's retreating back. She was his ticket and Bonnie's to the inner circle. And wrapped in a pretty nice package at that, he thought, watching her lithe, fluid movements. She had grace and style and warmth. What had started out as a feeble idea was now a full-fledged plan. He grinned and went inside. Damned if he wasn't looking forward to Lesson Number One: the dinner party.

The dinner took Dani all day to plan, shop for and prepare. By six o'clock she had things under control. With a weary sigh she picked up her watering can and bent to water the plant that occupied the far corner of her kitchen.

"Honestly, Oscar," she complained to the overgrown philodendron. "I haven't fussed this much since Arlene brought her bridge club over, and I wanted to impress their socks off." She snapped off a dry leaf. "Do you think it's worth it?" The tall plant seemed to weave in the soft breeze coming in through the screens. "No, me either."

She walked over to the window and rained water on the wide fern perched on the sill. "What about you, Clara? Aren't you shocked at my sudden domestic streak?" A leafy wave was her answer. "That's right. A clean house, flowers on the dining room table, cold soup, a fish course, a fowl course, a rich dessert and enough wine to fill the bathtub. By evening's end, Adam Kinkaid should be confident enough to dine with the Queen Mother." Or Dani's own sister, as the case might be.

Moving mechanically about the kitchen, Dani watered her Chinese evergreen and her new coleus, lost in her thoughts. For at least the dozenth time that day, she wondered what Sabrina or Arlene would think of her latest undertaking. That she'd lost her mind, she decided, putting away her watering can and moving to the bathroom for a quick shower. And it wouldn't be the first time they'd think one of her projects odd. Nor would it probably be the last. Carter had always tried to be supportive, though, which was why she'd gone along with his request. She'd had a few words with him before she left the party, and he'd assured her she could really help Adam, whom he seemed oddly fond of. Dani wished she felt as certain.

She removed her sticky clothes, then jumped under the lukewarm water and spread bath gel liberally on her sponge, then on her body. Was Adam the prompt sort or often tardy? Would he come in shorts, the preferred attire of most of her neighbors, or make another halfhearted stab at dressing up? Would he bring wine—something they certainly didn't need more of—or a six-pack?

She turned off the jets, grabbed the big fluffy peach-colored towel and inhaled its clean fragrance. Dani didn't surround herself with the trappings of luxury, but huge, sweet-smelling towels, very soft percale sheets and delicate silk underwear were the few indulgences she allowed herself.

She rubbed herself dry, then reached for her bath powder, her mind running through a checklist of last-minute things she had to attend to. Set table, make sure wines were chilled. It had really been a long time since she'd entertained on this scale—most of her friends preferred the more casual dinners that living oceanside lent itself to. But, once learned, formal entertaining wasn't something one forgot.

What to wear? she wondered, moving into her bedroom. She gazed into her closet and yawned. This was silly. She and Adam weren't on a date. She reached for a pair of white slacks and pulled them on, then added a purple cotton sweater that, she decided, set off her tan nicely. She slipped on white sandals, ran a brush through her short curls and surveyed herself in the mirror. A touch of blush wouldn't hurt, she decided, and a little lip gloss, perhaps a dab or two of her favorite scent. She always wore cologne, even when she was home alone, she reminded herself. No big deal.

She heard the doorbell, and her heart skipped several beats. No big deal and definitely not a date, she scolded herself. Taking a deep breath, she went to answer the door.

Daisies. He stood there wearing a Mickey Mouse T-shirt, blue jeans and a silly grin, holding a bouquet of slightly wilting spring daisies. Dani smiled, not quite sure why the unexpected gesture warmed her so. Had she thought that just because he needed some tips on social etiquette he was totally without charm?

"I picked these up," Adam said hesitantly. "I wasn't sure if..."

He was nervous, and the thought somehow put her at ease. "They're lovely." She drew him inside. "Thank you so much."

Dani gestured toward the living room. "Please, make yourself comfortable. I'll just put these in water." She left for the kitchen. If she was quick, she could grab the dining room table's centerpiece, which she'd picked up from the florist earlier, and throw it into a cupboard. She'd put his bouquet on the table and he'd never be the wiser, she thought, smiling.

Adam stood gazing about Dani's living room, totally surprised. He knew houses, and although this one was smaller than his, it was rock solid. The large window that faced the sea offered basically the same view his place had. It was the room itself that caught him unaware. Danielle Winthrop Ames, for all her blue blood and bulging bank accounts, apparently preferred confusion.

Comfortable furniture, upholstered mostly in blue and beige fabrics, was haphazardly placed about, more for convenience than for artful arrangement. One whole wall was lined with bookcases whose shelves were stuffed to overflowing with all manner of books, magazines and artifacts. Plush pillows were casually heaped in front of a well-used corner fireplace. Plants of all sizes and shapes were everywhere—on the mantel, in hanging baskets, trailing off tables. A silver heart-shaped balloon on a stick with the slogan "Hang in there!" was stuck into the base of a massive dieffenbachia. It was a room filled with contrasts.

An expensive-looking stereo, almost buried under stacks of records, played something soft and low, while a Baldwin piano dominated the opposite corner. Everything was clean and obviously costly, yet carelessly cluttered. Not what he'd expected to find, Adam thought, rubbing his chin. The rich could afford to be eccentric, he decided, thinking of his own neat and orderly home. Still, the room had a comfortable appeal.

He heard Dani's voice and went to see what was keeping her. He found her in the dining room with her face buried in the vase of flowers she was placing on the table. A smile played at the corners of her mouth as, eyes closed, she sniffed appreciatively. He thought it odd how much the small gift seemed to please her. She must have had many wealthy dates bring her far more expensive things. He hadn't intended to bring her anything, thinking that instead he would offer to pay for the meal and her trouble, but he now was glad he'd changed his mind.

"I thought I heard you say something," he said.

"Mmm, I was probably talking to Oscar," Dani answered. "Come into the kitchen and meet him." She led the way and introduced him to all her plants, saying a few words to each.

Adam didn't bother to hide his amusement. "You talk to them?"

"Certainly. They thrive if they know you care."

"Right." Adam decided in that moment that she was delightful. "Your home is very comfortable."

"I like it," Dani said, taking a bottle from the counter wine rack as he came up behind her. "After being raised amid *House Beautiful* perfection and forced to be neat and tidy every waking moment, I could hardly wait to get my own place and be as informal as I wanted." She gave a small laugh as she uncorked the wine and poured. "Perhaps I've overdone the clutter a mite."

He laughed with her. "No, I think it's very much *you*."

Handing him a glass, she teased him, "You think I'm a little cluttered?"

"I meant casual, which is very relaxing. And you're very nice to do this for me." When she didn't comment, he studied the contents of his glass. "What are we drinking?"

"Your first lesson in wines. Are you familiar with any?"

"Yup. There's this great little Italian joint in Boston that serves cheap Chianti that hits the spot with a plate of spaghetti and fresh bread."

She gave him a look of mock despair. "I can see we have a long way to go. This is a wine from France. It's generally accepted that the French make the finest wines in the world. Probably a combination of the right soil, sunshine and centuries of experience, along with an inbred love of the grape."

"I'll bet a few livers have been sacrificed in the process."

"Undoubtedly. This one's from Bordeaux, an area about the size of Rhode Island that, experts say, produces the cream of the crop. It's a claret from the Médoc district, a moderately expensive French sipping wine."

Such a big deal about a glass of wine, Adam thought, frowning, wondering how he'd remember everything she was telling him. "How do you know all this?"

Dani shrugged. "My father goes to France regularly and has been bringing a variety of wines home for years. He's always told us the wine's history, so I've picked up a few facts along the way."

"You always had wine with dinner when you lived at home?"

Yes, during the approximately six times a year when all four of us ever sat down together to share a meal, Dani thought. But that was another story. "Not always. I haven't found a wine yet that complements a peanut-butter-and-jelly sandwich."

"Is that really your favorite food?"

She cocked a brow at him. "If you're going to challenge everything I tell you, this meal may take till next Saturday night."

"Sorry. Go ahead."

"They say to fully appreciate wine, you should sniff the bouquet." Bringing the glass close to her nose, she demonstrated. "Next, take a small sip and roll it around in your mouth so the wine hits all your taste buds." Again she showed him what she meant. "Your turn."

Adam felt somewhat silly but followed her directions. Swallowing, he had to admit the wine wasn't bad. Still, it would never replace beer. "Like that?" he asked.

"You're a natural," she told him approvingly. "Why don't you go sit at the table, and I'll get our first course?"

"Right." He drained his glass, then set it on the counter and went into the dining room.

Dani barely suppressed a laugh, thinking how her father would have flinched to see Adam toss back a special wine as if it were a shot of bourbon. This might take longer than she'd planned, she thought, following him in with a tray.

Adam watched her serve him first, then herself. The pale blue cloth was the exact shade as the simple rose pattern in the center of the white china plate. Three wineglasses of different shapes sparkled in the muted light from the overhead chandelier. Her kitchen work area had been something of a mess, but this room was furnished simply and quite elegant. The lady had undeniable class and a certain flair, even if she looked closer to Bonnie's age than his.

"We're starting with the American version of vichyssoise, a cold, leek-and-potato soup that the French originated. Have you had it before?"

Adam eyed the bowl. "No, but I've heard of it. Cold soup, eh?"

"It's a summertime dish," she said, watching him. She didn't do that much dining room entertaining, and rarely with men alone. Adam filled the chair and the room with his commanding presence, his obvious maleness. His hair fell onto his forehead, looking as untamed as he did. His dark eyes had tiny gold flecks in them that she hadn't noticed last night. His skin was tanned to an almost bronze hue. *Yes, he was very male.* Dani had to smile. "Are you always this wary? Go ahead—it won't bite you."

As he studied the array of silverware on both sides of the dinner plate, Adam looked confused. "Do we need all this cutlery?"

"Yes, we're going to use it all. The best way to remember the proper order for silverware is that you work from the outside in." She picked up a spoon. "The soup is the first course, so the soup spoon is placed on the far right. All very logical."

Adam picked up his soup spoon. "From the outside in. Like making love—you work your way from the outside to the inside, right?"

"Interesting analogy," Dani answered, lowering her eyes and dipping her spoon into the soup.

Bending to his bowl, Adam decided that he liked her with high color in her cheeks. He'd never expected to have fun while learning some of the strange ways of the elite. "You know, this isn't half-bad. Did you make it yourself?"

Not half-bad? He wasn't one to overwhelm a person with praise, was he? she thought. Maybe her next lesson should include compliments to the chef. "It's not difficult, really. Anyone who can read can cook."

When he was finished, Adam leaned back. "Where did you learn?"

"From Sarah. She's been my mother's cook for years."

"And you like her a lot."

He was pretty astute, she thought. Or she was pretty transparent. Dani pictured tiny, dark-eyed Sarah, who could work magic with food and with a young, lonely girl. Dani had learned a great deal more than just cooking from Sarah, who'd been there so often for her when her mother hadn't. "Yes, she's very special." She stood to clear their plates. "I'll be right back with the next course."

Wistful, Adam thought. She'd sounded downright wistful. She'd grown up with two interesting parents and everything money could buy, yet for a moment she'd looked vulnerable and melancholy. What memory had caused that look? he wondered. She was very different from Arlene, and probably from her sister—and not just in looks, he'd wager. Despite her cool beauty, Sabrina put him off. Too bad Dani wasn't more into the social scene. She seemed more interesting. But she couldn't, or wouldn't, help him with Bonnie other than teaching him the social graces. He would have to win over someone like Sabrina.

In moments Dani was back with the food. Adam stared at the steaming ramekin, then bent to inhale the delicate fragrance as Dani poured the next wine. "Something fishy, right?"

"You're quick, Adam," she commented dryly, taking her seat. She'd been wondering who he reminded her of, and finally she connected the memory. When she and Sabrina had been in their teens, they'd had an exchange student stay with them for a year, a bright, enthusiastic boy of fifteen from Brazil. Nearly every meal had been an adventure for Carlos, and Adam now regarded his dinner with the same curiosity.

She saw him watch her pick up the small fish fork on the extreme left, then he followed suit. "You might have had this dish before. Scallops and mushrooms in a white wine sauce. The French call it coquilles Saint Jacques, and it's quite rich, which is why I've served us only a small amount as an appetizer. Some people make a whole meal of it, but frankly, I think that's too much of a good thing."

She noticed amusement flash in his brown eyes. "I thought you could never get too much of a good thing, Dani."

His implication seemed somehow sensuous. Was he flirting with her? Hardly. He was interested not in her but in what she could teach him. "All in how you look at it, I guess." Her own fork suspended, she watched him take a bite. As he smiled, she relaxed. Why was his opinion important to her? she wondered as she bent to eat. She was the instructor here, someone doing him a favor. If he didn't like gourmet fare he could go back to greasy hamburgers, for all she cared.

"This is really good," Adam said, wondering why she was frowning. He picked up his wineglass. "And what have we here?"

"One of my favorites, Pouilly-Fumé, a light white wine that's always good with a fish course." She took a sip, savoring the chilled fruity taste.

He rolled the liquid around on his tongue as she'd taught him, then swallowed. "Nice." Not spectacular, but nice. Perhaps after all these years he'd ruined his taste buds on Chianti and beer, for he obviously wasn't getting the enjoyment out of the wines that Dani was. Setting down his glass, he crossed his arms on the table and leaned forward. "Why do they drink a different wine with each course? It seems like a lot of bother to go to for one dinner."

"I suppose it is, but if, for instance, you serve a robust wine with a delicate fish, it'll overpower the taste of the food. A really spicy dish will kill the flavor of a light wine."

"You mean the way a sexy woman can intimidate a shy man?"

She found his turn of phrase interesting. "Sort of. And a wine that's too dry will taste sour if you serve it with a sweet dessert."

Adam's brow shot up. "You serve wine with desserts, too?"

Laughing, Dani rose to clear their plates. "We are tonight."

Adam shook his head as he, too, stood. "Good thing I could walk here along the beach. I might not be able to drive ."

She ran her eyes up the broad length of him. Definitely a big man, she mused. "Oh, I don't think a few glasses of wine will put you under the table."

He stood close, blocking her way. "Think I can handle it?"

Yes, but could she? Dani's grip on the plates was shaky.

Noticing, Adam took the plates from her. "Let me help," he offered, then turned and walked into the kitchen.

Sighing, Dani wondered why this man's presence had her acting strangely. She had a lot of men friends, always had. Though there was no one special right now, she still dated frequently, worked with male coaches, often had single men from the neighborhood over. Why should Adam, someone she'd known twenty-four hours, unnerve her so easily? She just must be a little nervous about teaching him social graces that she considered relatively unimportant in the scheme of things.

She followed him into the kitchen, where she found him rinsing and stacking dishes. "That's not necessary. Truly. You're the guest."

He was making her nervous, Adam decided, as he wiped his hands on a towel. He moseyed over to study the framed needlepoint she had hanging on the wall. "Cooking is like love—it should be entered into with abandon or not at all," he read. Interesting. He glanced around the bright yellow-and-white kitchen, which, like her living room, was filled with an assortment of plants. He was getting used to the clutter, actually admiring the cozy look. "I miss hanging around the kitchen, watching my mother, talking and stealing a taste of things to come."

"Then you deserve a sampling," Dani said, removing a pan from the oven. She held up a full spoon of sauce, cupping a hand under it to catch possible drips. "Come taste this."

As he swallowed the creamy mixture, his eyes widened with pleasure. "Mmm, that's great." When he spotted two drops that had landed on her thumb where she still held the spoon, he quickly licked them off. "Good to the last drop."

Not quite sure how to respond, Dani spooned out the entrée with her back to him. She was overreacting to every little gesture tonight. He was just a man, one who apparently loved his mother and was willing to make himself over to help his sister. A man who was looking for a woman like Sabrina. Who was worlds apart from being like Dani! She'd better keep that in mind. She made a concentrated effort to bring her thoughts back to their conversation. "Your mother's a good cook?"

Adam casually leaned against the counter. "Terrific. Years ago when we had very little, she was always able to make something out of nothing and still keep the stomach of a growing boy filled. She could stretch a chicken into three meals and you still walked away full each time. And her angel food cake—it just about melts in your mouth." He moved to her side and picked up the plates. "I'll take these in."

When he was seated opposite her again, he gazed at the attractive plate. "I got this one figured out. Chicken breasts."

Dani smiled. "Very good. They're often served at those dinners you might be invited to, because they can be prepared so many different ways. These are stuffed and sautéed in wine. I've made ratatouille, a casserole consisting mostly of eggplant and assorted other fresh vegetables. And we mustn't forget the staple of French meals—crusty bread."

"Smells wonderful. I may become a believer." He picked up his second wineglass and waited for her explanation.

"The dinner wine is a full-bodied white Burgundy."

Raising his glass, Adam smiled into her eyes. "I want to make a toast. I know you had your doubts about tonight, about me and this whole project. Even though it was my idea, I had a few reservations, too. But not anymore. You're not only a great cook but a super person. Here's to you."

"Thank you, but why don't we drink, instead, to our partnership in this venture, such as it is?"

"Okay, partner. If we get nothing else out of this, we'll at least be pals, right?"

Pals, Dani thought. Just what she needed, another pal. "Right." She took a long, fortifying swallow, wondering why her appetite had suddenly fled.

By the time they'd finished the main course and she'd uncorked the fourth wine of the evening to accompany the rich chocolate mousse, Dani was feeling light-headed. Adam, however, seemed as fresh and eager as when he'd arrived. She poured the dessert champagne into his glass and watched him take a healthy swallow. Sipping, it seemed, was not in his nature.

"I have to tell you, I've never had wine with dessert, but I may take it up," he told her.

Dani tasted her mousse and set down her spoon, deciding she couldn't handle another mouthful of food. "You see? It's not so difficult being a blue blood."

"At least they eat well," Adam agreed, eating every last morsel of his mousse. Picking up his glass, he studied the pale contents. "What happens to all the half-finished bottles of wine that are left over from one of these dinner parties?"

Dani shrugged. "They're served another time, I suppose. Or..."

"Or thrown out?"

"Probably." She'd never given it much thought, she realized.

Adam nodded. "A terrible waste. Growing up the way I did, I could never do that, even now, when I can afford to." He looked at her, suddenly serious. "There are more differences between the haves and the have-nots than I'd suspected."

Dani leaned back, regarding him. *More than you know, Mr. Kinkaid.* "Want to call off the project?" It hadn't been the easiest evening she'd ever spent, and she wouldn't be heartbroken if he gave up his makeover plans.

"Not on your life. I—"

At the sound of the low, mournful wail coming from the direction of the back door, they both turned toward the kitchen. Dani jumped up. "Prepare yourself. That's my dog, home after his evening wanderings."

Adam followed her into the kitchen, and as she opened the door, a shaggy sheepdog that looked as if it had once been white bounded inside and all but knocked her over in his enthusiastic greeting.

"We have company, Mutt, so mind your manners," Dani said, trying to keep the exuberant animal from pouncing on Adam. "Sit!"

The dog obeyed, his tail whipping across the polished floor.

"Now, shake hands with Adam."

Mutt raised a sandy paw, and with a grin, Adam shook it. "Nice to meet you, Mutt."

Tongue dangling, Mutt panted warmly.

"Now, say hello to our guest."

The big dog raised his head and made a low noise in his throat that sounded oddly like a greeting. Dani patted him in praise as Adam shook his head. "How'd you teach him that?"

"It wasn't easy."

Mutt quickly dropped his manners after his performance and licked her hand.

"Is that the only word he knows?" Adam asked.

"Well, I'm trying to teach him to swear in Italian, but he's having trouble mastering the accent." She saw Adam cock his head at her, and she laughed. "Just kidding. It took him two years to learn his first word."

"Did you grow up with animals?"

"Not one of my own. Arlene likes poodles."

"And you don't?"

Not pampered poodles who eat off china plates, she thought. "Not particularly."

"This has been a great evening," Adam said, reaching for his wallet. "I want to thank you, and I want to pay you. You went to a lot of trouble and expense."

She quickly put her hand out to stop him. "No. I agreed to do this, and I don't want payment."

"But—"

"No, or we stop right now."

Again Adam shook his head. "Just what I need. Another stubborn woman in my life."

"I'm not a woman in your life—I'm your partner. Remember?"

Adam thought he heard an odd note in her voice, but when he looked at her questioningly, she merely smiled. "Right."

He let the issue drop and opened the back door to go outside. Dani followed, with Mutt trailing behind. "Beautiful night," Adam commented.

"Yes, isn't it?"

Breathing in the salty air, he watched while a big wave pounded in to shore. The night sky was dotted with stars. He felt sated, comfortable, content. Dani had walked out farther on the sand, and he joined her where she stood gazing out to sea.

"Well, coach, when's Lesson Number Two, and what'll it be?"

"We might as well get to the tennis, work off our big dinner. I can call Easthope in the morning and reserve an early court. How about if I pick you up about eight?"

"Sounds good to me." Companionably he slid his arm around her shoulders and gave her a light squeeze. He couldn't help noticing how she smelled, all wildflowers and summer sunshine. "Again, thanks."

Dani's feet had sunk into the shifting sand, and he seemed even taller. Turning her head, she found herself very close to him, her cheek brushing against his chest. It was a casual touch, yet she could feel her blood stir, and wondered if he could tell. The sensation was a nice one, and she was loath to let it go. But she had to. "You're welcome."

She began to pull away, but he drew her back and placed a quick kiss on her forehead. "See you in the morning." With a wave, he turned and jogged off down the beach toward his house as Mutt gave a quick goodbye bark.

If hard-pressed, Dani thought, she could come up with an impressive list of names of women who wouldn't want to change a thing about Adam Kinkaid. Except maybe his burning desire to make himself over for the kind of woman who likely wouldn't appreciate him. Too bad.

Moonlight fell on him as he ran, kicking up the sand. An altogether magnificent specimen, Dani decided. Raw material she was molding, albeit reluctantly. It wasn't easy making over someone for someone else. It wounded her self-esteem to have him place her sister on a pedestal and view her as a pal.

Things shouldn't come too easily in a makeover. Her perverse nature wanted him to fall on his face—not literally, but figuratively. He'd taken readily to the dinner, but anyone could eat. How would he hold up on the tennis court, never having even held a racket? If he did poorly, maybe he'd give up his scheme and realize he wasn't meant for the likes of Sabrina. And Dani wouldn't have to honor her commitment to redo Adam for another woman, spending hours, days, in his disturbing presence. Tomorrow would tell the tale, Dani thought with a smug smile, then wondered if Adam Kinkaid owned a pair of tennis shoes.

Chapter Three

His tennis shoes had seen better days, Dani decided as she waited in her car while Adam ambled down his walk toward her. Yet she had to admit that the white shirt and cutoff shorts looked wonderful against his tan. He opened the passenger door, jumped in and turned to her with a morning smile.

"Nice car," he said, admiring her red Mercedes, its top folded neatly down.

"One of my few indulgences," Dani replied, shooting away from the curb after noting there were no other cars on the road this early. "Controlled power. I love it."

Adam angled toward her in his seat. "I'd have pegged you more the conservative BMW type."

She gave him a quick smile. "Guess you don't know me too well."

"Not yet, I don't."

"That sounds ominous. I hope you don't have any big plans on changing me, too."

"So far I haven't seen anything I'd want to change."

That sounded awfully flattering, but Dani knew it wasn't so. "Sure you would. You'd like me to be a socialite like Arlene and Sabrina so I could haul you into their world."

Adam smiled at her profile. She really was a very attractive woman. Her copper hair looked the color of whiskey. The few freckles she had gave her a wholesome appearance that contrasted sharply with her full, sensuous mouth. And those wide blue eyes crinkled in laughter one moment and became dark and thoughtful the next.

"No, not everyone's meant for the mad social whirl. Your life-style seems to suit you."

And his seemed to suit him, too, Dani mused. Yet he was dead set on changing himself. He looked as though he'd be bored in the boardroom, as well as the drawing room. The bedroom was more his style. Where had that come from? Dani asked herself, her thoughts making her blush. To cover her embarrassment, she sped the car up again, her mind searching for safe conversation material.

"I brought along several rackets. One should be about right for you. You choose by weight and grip." Before she could stop herself, she launched into a dissertation on the merits of tennis rackets that would have put all but a few diehards to sleep in short order.

She was babbling, Adam thought, listening with half an ear as she rambled on. Why did she seem so nervous and jumpy this morning?

"Does everyone in your family play tennis?" he asked.

"Yes."

"But you're better at it." It wasn't a question; he just knew. Carter was undoubtedly too busy except for a game now and again. The two other ladies didn't look as if they liked to get hot and sweaty, even in an air-conditioned country club.

"Only because it's part of my work," she said.

"But you like to play the game."

"I like most sports."

"How about winter sports?"

"Especially winter sports."

"What's your favorite?"

"Ice skating." She saw no reason to tell him about the years she'd spent in training, the endless hours of practice, the hopes that had been dashed that fateful winter day at the nationals. Not quite good enough; something she'd had to learn to live with.

"Who do you usually skate with, someone special?"

Now she saw where he was headed. "A variety of people."

"Is there someone special in your life, Dani, someone whose time I've been taking up these past couple of days?" He'd gone home last night wondering that. An attractive woman available on short notice on both Saturday and Sunday. Not just attractive, but rich. Who were the men in her life—and where were they?

"No, no one special."

"Why not?"

Direct, she thought. He was certainly that. And slightly annoying. Just because she'd agreed to help him didn't mean she'd agreed to share every aspect of her life. "Why isn't there someone special in yours?"

He loved that haughty, go-to-hell look, which she'd also flashed at him Friday night when he'd suggested she could make more money working at something other than teaching. He'd be willing to bet there was a temper hidden beneath all that finishing-school decorum. And some interesting fire.

"I haven't had the time," he replied.

Dani swung into the curving, tree-lined driveway of Easthope Country Club and drew up in front of the steps that led up to the big double doors. "Ditto," she said, shifting into park. "We're here."

The doorman opened her side first and Dani scooted out, giving him a smile. As she unlocked the trunk, she saw Adam jump out and come around back. So, he was going to ask her personal questions, was he? She could play that game, too.

She helped Adam select the best racket, watched the doorman drive off with her car toward the parking lot, then led Adam along the winding walkway toward the tennis house.

"We're not going in the front door?" he asked, sounding disappointed.

"Not dressed like this. The tennis entrance is around the corner. That door is for the dining room and the social function rooms—business meetings and the like."

He knew quality when he saw it, and this sprawling stone building with the slate roof and two separate wings qualified. "Very nice," he said, looking around as they walked and noticing the spring plantings, some of which were just coming into bloom. "Do you come here often?"

"No, hardly ever." Actually, she couldn't remember when she'd last been at Easthope, and she wouldn't be here today if it weren't that Adam had insisted on a country club atmosphere, instead of a public park. She'd reserved an early court, knowing that most of her family's friends weren't too keen on wandering out on Sunday mornings. If luck was with her, she and Adam wouldn't run into anyone who knew her, and could avoid nosy questions and matchmaking attempts.

Inside, Dani stopped at the desk to sign in. The sleepy-eyed clerk looked her over as she wrote her name on the court register.

"We can skip the locker rooms, since we're wearing our tennis duds," Dani told Adam. "The courts are just down that hall through those doors."

"Uh, miss?" the young man behind the desk said, calling her back.

Dani swung around. "Yes?"

"I'm sorry, but, well, I've never seen you here before." He looked embarrassed. "Could I see some ID?"

"Sure." Dani dug into her bag for her wallet. She handed her driver's license to him, watching as he studied it.

Bringing out his ledger of approved members, he checked for her name, and when he found it, relief flooded his face. He gave her a crooked smile. "Sorry, Miss Ames, but you're not a regular, and I'd get into a lot of trouble if I didn't check."

"No problem," Dani told him, putting away her wallet. She started toward the courts with Adam beside her.

"How long *has* it been since you've been here?" he asked.

"A couple of years, probably."

"You haven't played tennis in a couple of years?"

"I didn't say that. I just don't play it *here*." She shoved open the door and went on through.

He'd puzzle that over later, Adam thought as he looked over the tennis hall. The cavernous area was glassed off from the upper level where they'd strolled. They stopped to look down on six double courts, which were separated

by netting. Only the one on the far right was occupied—
two teenagers going through the motions.

"Ready?" she asked.

"When you are," Adam answered.

They went down the stairs and out onto the court. After a few warm-up swings, Dani explained the basics of the
game—the scoring, the various serves. "I don't teach tennis at my school—it's not on the curriculum—though I've
studied how to teach the game. As you might imagine, you
can be all flash and fire on defense, but if you don't develop a really good serve, you won't score."

He stood at the serve line, looking cocky and aggres-
sive. "I always like to score."

Dani decided to ignore that. Standing beside him, she
demonstrated several serves, hoping he'd try them and flub
them all. The arrogant goon. She put on a sweet smile and
turned to face him. "Your turn."

His first ball went wide and wild. The second hit the net.
Swallowing a smile, Dani stepped up to the line.

"Watch me again." She served a hard one, showing off
a little. It seemed that Adam was bringing out the beast in
her this morning. "Try again, and put a little body English into it this time."

Adam took a few practice swings. *Body English, she
wants,* he thought. And she had a pretty good body to
demonstrate her point. He stepped up to the line, taking
aim.

As Dani watched Adam, she had to admit to a certain
admiration. What Adam didn't yet have in game knowledge and form, he more than made up for in coordination
and grace. He had the long, limber body of a natural athlete. His height gave him the advantage of reach, his
strength gave his serve enormous power, and his experience working high in the sky on steel girders gave him the

agility that enabled him to twist and turn artfully. After the bucket of balls was empty, he turned to her with a grin. Damned if he hadn't fooled her, she thought.

"Not bad," she said coolly, walking across the court to gather up the balls. She wasn't about to lavish him with praise.

Why was she so testy this morning? Adam wondered. He scooped up several balls as he admired her legs, which seemed to go on forever. Her white shorts stretched over a very appealing bottom, and her knit shirt outlined small but firm breasts that had captured his interest the moment he'd gotten into her car. But he wasn't here to develop an interest in Dani Ames, and he'd do well to keep his mind where it belonged, he told himself.

"Do you want to serve out another bucket, or do you want to try a warm-up volley?" she asked, suppressing her irritation. She was here to help him, yet she was annoyed he was good at the game without half trying. Whatever was wrong with her? she wondered.

"Let's try the volley," he answered, then headed for the opposite side of the court.

She took it easy on him at first, and he returned most of her balls without too much trouble. She demonstrated the forehand, the backhand, how to guard the back court and play the net. Then they began to actually play, calling out the scores.

As Dani watched Adam, she knew he'd master the game. Enthusiasm and a driving need to excel poured out of him. She could see it, smell it, and it was greater than she'd anticipated. He'd be good at most anything he tried, because he wanted to succeed badly, willed it to happen. Near the end of their hour, after he'd returned an almost impossible lob, she decided she'd had enough. She walked around the net to him.

"Looks like you'll be ready for the circuit in another couple of lessons," she said, putting on a smile.

"You're just a good teacher, that's all." Shifting his gaze to the next court, Adam noticed a beautiful blonde wearing a pink-skirted tennis dress smile in defeat at a handsome Ivy League type. Sabrina would be like her, he thought, playing more for the company of her date than the enjoyment of the game. She might even let the man win, if it suited her purpose. But not Dani. Though he hadn't embarrassed himself his first time out, he hadn't come close to beating her.

Dani glanced up at the gallery and saw people filing in for the next hour. "I think our time's about up."

"Just one more quick thing," Adam said. "Sometimes when I serve, the ball goes too far off either to the left or right. I want it more toward the center. Any suggestions?"

"It's probably in the way you're standing. You need to point your feet more like this." Dani demonstrated the proper stance. "And hold your body aimed in the same direction, like this." She did a practice serve that hit precisely where she'd aimed it.

"Let's try that again." Adam set down his racket, moved up behind her and encircled her in his arms.

"What are you doing?" she asked, startled.

"I thought I could get a better feel for this position and this grip if I moved with you. Do you mind?"

Did she mind? she marveled. With sweaty fingers she held the grip as he put his large hands over hers. As he aligned his body with hers, his added height forced him to bend, so that his face was very near hers. He smelled musky and blatantly male. Dani felt her heart thud in heated response.

Time seemed to stop for Adam as he held very still, breathing in the scent of her hair. French perfume or expensive soap or both. He felt his body's answering reaction to her nearness and wondered at the impulse that had led him to touch her. Perhaps it had been motivated by watching her stretch and twist and move enticingly in front of him for the past hour.

Quickly Dani got off the shot, pulling out of his arms in almost the same motion. "Time's up," she said, then walked hurriedly off the court. This had definitely not been part of the bargain. The problem was, she'd enjoyed the feeling of him up close to her entirely too much. Damn!

She was nearly outside, when Adam caught up with her. "Is something the matter, or did you just remember you left something on the stove?"

She slowed just a little as she made her way to the door. "No, I just want a shower, and since we didn't bring a change of clothes, we'll have to go home."

The doorman saw them coming and rushed to get her car. Adam watched Dani wait impatiently, jamming a pair of oversize sunglasses on her face. For the second time he wondered what was making her so edgy today. Maybe something had happened at this country club that had caused her to avoid coming here for over two years. Or maybe she regretted her decision to help him, just when they were getting somewhere. He didn't want to lose her cooperation. He'd have to try to make her see how much her help meant to him.

When the car pulled up, he hurried over to the doorman and handed him a dollar, then held open Dani's door. She'd already had the tip in her hand, and she gave Adam a sharp look. "I have to pay for some things," he stated, closing her door.

Drumming her fingers on the wheel, she waited for him to go around and climb in. She was being unreasonable and she knew it. What she didn't know was how to stop.

When they were under way, Adam said, "I need a favor from you, Dani."

Another one? Wasn't that how this whole thing had gotten started? "What do you have in mind?" she asked curtly.

"I want to take you somewhere this afternoon."

A thank-you lunch, perhaps? she thought. No, thank you. "There are some things I really have to get done before work tomorrow, Adam."

"This won't take long. I promise. I want to show you something important to me. Let's both go home, shower and change, and I'll pick you up, say, in an hour." He reached over and touched her hand. "Please Dani?"

The man was hard to resist. She felt her anger melt away, which was fine, because she wasn't certain she had a right to it, anyway. She glanced over at him and caught his eyes dark and sincere watching her. Finding a smile, she nodded. "All right, on one condition."

"Name it."

"I saw a Porsche and a Bronco truck in your drive. Could we take the Bronco? I've always wanted to ride in one."

Adam grinned, pleased at her choice. "You're on, lady."

"It's really high up here," Dani exclaimed as they pulled away from her house in the Bronco. "Like riding in a tank."

"I think the windows are smaller in my tank, and you'll notice that I unhooked the machine guns because it's Sunday."

"Cute, Kinkaid. I don't suppose you'd like to tell me where you're taking me." A long shower had cooled off both her body and her temper, which seemed to flare up more easily these days. She really hadn't had any special plans this afternoon, so she decided to relax and enjoy the day.

"To my old neighborhood in South Boston. It's pretty seedy. I'm sure you've never been there."

She had been to South Boston, and she knew it would surprise him to learn why. "I really don't spend all my time dashing between Hyannis and London."

"Where do you like to spend time?"

"Oh, I have a close friend in Connecticut—Nora—whom I love visiting. And my Uncle Troy lives in Iowa. He and his wife have four children and live on a big farm. I really enjoy them."

Swinging the truck onto the highway, Adam shot her a quizzical look. "A farm? You mean complete with animals and crops?"

"You bet. They raise corn and wheat, and they have cows, a few pigs and even chickens."

"You honestly enjoy it there?" Could it be that she would choose an Iowa farm over Paris?

"I don't know why that surprises you so. Wouldn't you?"

"Sure, but I wouldn't have thought *you* would. Why do you?"

His preconceptions of her were way off, but she had to remember he really didn't know her. "It's so peaceful there. And Troy and Lydia accept themselves and others for what they are. They're two of the happiest people I know, and their happiness is contagious."

"I wouldn't have figured that an Ames woman would prefer an Iowa farm over a more glamorous setting."

An Ames woman. Was that what she was to him?

"Maybe after I show you where *I* come from, you'll understand what I mean more clearly, understand me and my motives."

"Adam, you don't have to justify your motives to me. Nor do you owe me any further explanations. I've already agreed to help you."

"I know, and I'm grateful. But I think you agreed because Carter asked you to and because you're curious about someone like me. But I want more. I want you to *understand*."

"Why is that so important to you?"

"I'm not sure. I just know that it is."

Half an hour later Adam brought the Bronco to a halt, turned to Dani and pointed out the passenger window. "There it is."

Rundown was the first word that came to mind as she gazed at the sad, neglected house. Sorely in need of paint, porch sagging, listless curtains hanging inside the dirty windows, a weed-patch of a yard enclosed by a rickety, falling-down fence. She knew immediately what it was. "Where you grew up," she said, her voice low.

Slowly Adam nodded. "It didn't look much better when I lived here, though it was a lot cleaner. This house was probably old when my mother was a girl." His gaze swept up the street. "All these houses were old and tired even then."

Dani groped for the right words. "But you took your family out of here, Adam, and that should fill you with pride."

"Let me tell you a story," he said, stretching his arm along the back of the seat. "My father left us when I was in my teens and my sister was just a kid. My mother worked two jobs to keep food on the table and a roof over our heads. I had several jobs after school, and summers, I worked for a construction company. As soon as Bonnie was old enough she had a paper route, baby-sat, and worked in a grocery store on weekends. A lot of hard work and a lot of years later I bought that construction company from the owner, who wanted to retire. I worked even harder, because it was for me and mine. In time I was able to expand, and now Kinkaid Construction is one of the largest on the East Coast."

"My father's a self-made man, too, Adam. It's one of the things I admire most about him."

Sure, Carter Ames was self-made, he thought. How hard was it to make a couple of million when you'd inherited the first million to build on? He went on, not even acknowledging her comment. "Those were hard years, but they finally paid off. I was able to have my mother quit work, and I built her a really nice home on the other side of town. Bonnie's in her second year at a good college. The money's rolling in. But money's not enough. You can't buy status." He turned to face her. "Status is what I want for her, and now you know why."

How very intense he was, Dani thought, seeing the fire in his dark brown eyes. She was more used to placid men than those with fervor. She found she liked the change. "Yes, I see." She still didn't agree on the things he wanted for her, but she understood the reasons.

Adam pointed out the window on his left. "And there's another building that's important to me. That old high school. Not only did we live across from it, but I graduated from there."

Looking past him, Dani at last recognized where they were. The school was adjacent to the gymnasium where she occasionally did some volunteer refereeing, though she usually entered from the parking lot on the other side. The three-story building was in the process of being rebuilt after a recent fire. "Yes, I know this place. That was a terrible fire, but thank goodness no one was inside the school at the time."

"A terribly mysterious fire. The city fathers were going to tear down the remains of the building, sell the land. Not much new stuff going up around here. But that would have meant busing the neighborhood kids pretty far," he explained, gazing out the window.

She was getting the picture. "So you stepped in."

"Me and several other businessmen, many who had once called this area home. We got some bonds passed and a bank loan approved." He saw no need to tell her what almost no one knew: that Kinkaid Construction was rebuilding the school and he was donating the cost of labor, paying his men from his own pocket for this project, which was so close to his heart. It wasn't altruism, as Adam saw it. It was repayment of a debt. A man had to share with others some of his good fortune if he could, or what did it all matter?

Turning quickly toward her, he realized their faces were quite close. Her eyes were soft and warm. Maybe she did understand him a little better now.

Dani looked at him, not quite sure why her understanding was important to him, yet it pleased her that it was. She fought to keep her hand from reaching out and touching him. "That was a nice thing to do," she said, meaning it.

Adam shifted uncomfortably. "I didn't bring you here for praise or—"

"That wasn't praise. It was an honest comment." She saw him smile then, that quick flash of gentleness she'd come to watch for.

Adam started the engine. "Then I'll say thanks and feed you. You must be starved."

"Now that you mention it, I could eat."

"And so you shall. We're off to Mama's."

"Mama's?"

"The best Sunday dinners served in Boston."

"Did you call her to tell her we were coming?"

"Nah," he said with a grin. "Mama always cooks extra in case I drop in."

And now he was taking her home to meet Mama, she thought. Heavens, what was she getting into?

Adam drove down the narrow street, which was shaded by heavy old trees. As they passed by, he saw that the warm weather had enticed people outside. An elderly man rocked on a porch swing, an aproned woman watered her flowers, and four young boys tossed a ball on a vacant lot.

In ten minutes Dani and Adam were on a country road, headed north. "You're going to like my mother. She loves people, especially feeding them. Don't be surprised if she sends a covered dish of leftovers home with you. I think she's trying to make up for all the lean years, you know."

"Don't think I won't take it. Whenever someone cooks for me I'm thrilled."

Adam glanced at her quickly. "I'll have to remember that." He returned his eyes to the road as he considered how to acquaint her with his family before their arrival. The Sunday visit had been an impulse, one he was glad he'd given in to, for he wanted Dani to see his mother's new home now that she'd seen their old house.

"And wait till you see my mother around the Christmas holidays. She makes tons of cookies and passes them out to all the neighbors. She brews up this old family recipe of mulled wine that will rot your socks, and makes us all toast with it. And the tree—we still do the old-fashioned version, stringing popcorn, cranberries, nuts, plus all these handmade ornaments she's collected through the years.

Lots of fuss and bother. She starts about mid-November and doesn't finish till after the New Year."

Dani smiled at his words. "And you love it all."

"Yeah, how'd you know?"

"A lucky guess." Dani's thoughts drifted to holidays at the Ames compound, slickly orchestrated, well attended by friends and a few strays, somehow devoid of much depth. Although her memories weren't unhappy ones, stringing popcorn for an old-fashioned tree was infinitely more appealing.

It wasn't until she'd gone away to college and been paired with Nora Mason as a roommate that she'd experienced her first warm Christmas. Attending on a full scholarship, Nora was bright, funny and caring, characteristics Dani had found lacking in most of her friends. That first Christmas away from home, when she'd learned that Sabrina was joining Arlene at Aspen and Carter would be in Europe, she'd rejected both invitations and had jumped at the chance to go home with Nora. She'd gone back again and again, and those trips had changed her life.

In Connecticut she'd come to know the large, bustling Mason family—mother, father and Nora's four brothers—who, though they had precious little money in comparison to her family, were welcoming and fun loving and possessed family traditions that charmed Dani. The years of friendship with Nora had strengthened Dani's belief that the superficial life she'd been leading needed altering. After that first visit, much to her mother's chagrin, she'd changed her major and decided to follow her dream of teaching young people. She'd never regretted her choice.

Yes, she'd experienced a heartwarming Christmas like the one Adam had described. But it was only April, and she couldn't help but wonder why he was including her in visions of Christmases to come. They'd be long finished with his makeover before the first snowfall. Evidently he'd forgotten that for a moment.

They were in the country now, Dani noticed as they passed under an old wooden covered bridge. As the car emerged, she noticed in the distance a steepled white church with a black-faced clock, and several red barns dotting the hilly area. A cozy, inviting tavern sat nestled amid artfully overgrown shrubs when she and Adam broke out onto the winding coastal road.

And then she saw it, a two-story stone structure tucked into a small cove. Jagged rocks served as breakwaters for the dashing sea waves. The view was magnificent, solitary, breathtaking.

"How did you ever find this location?" she asked, awestruck by the natural, stark beauty.

"It wasn't easy," Adam said, inordinately pleased that she liked something he loved. He stopped the truck in the curving drive behind a white Cabriolet convertible, jumping out to help her down. "Looks like Bonnie is home for the weekend. You get to meet the whole family in one fell swoop." He jumped out and went around to help her down.

"Do they know . . . I mean about . . ."

"About our project?" Adam's eyes laughed down at her. "No, that's our little secret, if you don't mind."

Mind? She'd be hard put to explain it to another living soul. Letting him take her hand, she followed him up the front walk. "Then how are you going to explain me?"

"I'll introduce you as my new live-in love," he said just as the door swung open and a small woman with salt-and-pepper hair, a big smile and kind blue eyes emerged to give Adam a big bear hug.

If Doris Kinkaid noticed the crimson stain on Dani's face as Adam indeed introduced Dani as his live-in girlfriend, she was controlled enough not to let on, Dani thought with gratitude as she gave her a nervous handshake. Or perhaps she was more used to her son's off-the-cuff remarks than Dani was. But the moment passed, and inside, she met Bonnie, who was tall and slender and had hair the color of Adam's. Then Adam gave her a tour of the house, his pride evident in every room. With good reason, for Dani could tell it was designed and built with love in every brick and board.

Afterward, while Adam and Bonnie chatted on the couch, Dani helped Doris with the salad and discovered that Adam's mother could hardly be classified as a "little old lady," despite being well into her sixties. She bowled twice a week, played cards with her lady friends every Saturday night and was a voracious reader.

"I'm so glad you could join us for dinner," Doris said, handing Dani a bottle of her homemade salad dressing. "Adam usually works on Sundays. And all the rest of the week. I tell him all the time he should ease off, but he won't listen."

"My father's like that. I'm not sure some men know how to enjoy their time away from work." As she stood tossing the salad greens in the big sunny kitchen, Dani had a moment of déjà vu, so strongly reminded was she of standing and chatting just like this with Mrs. Mason all those years ago while they prepared a meal together. Although preparations had been more chaotic then, with Nora's brothers constantly strolling in to steal a taste or two, she'd still felt the same camaraderie. Odd how she'd never once shared a moment like this with Arlene, though she often had with Sarah, the family's housekeeper.

Spooning the steaming vegetables into a bowl, Doris nodded. "I guess it's up to us women to coax the men away from their jobs. Distract them, you know?"

Dani tasted a lettuce leaf and chuckled to herself. An unmarried man over thirty always came with a matchmaking mother, or so she'd learned in recent years. Twenty minutes in her home and Doris wanted Dani to keep her son from overworking himself by "distracting" him. Wouldn't it curl Mrs. Kinkaid's hair if she knew that his ambitions stretched far beyond the likes of Dani?

"I certainly hope you're better at it than my mother has been," she told Adam's mother with a smile. "And I seem to have no talent in that department either."

Doris appeared to take a moment to digest that, then gathered everyone at the big oak dining room table, where Dani was seated next to Bonnie, which gave her an opportunity to ask a few discreet questions to see for herself if Adam's assessment of his sister was on target.

"What are you majoring in, Bonnie?"

"Mmm, just a general humanities course right now. I love English literature, reading the classics. I do a little writing, mostly awful poetry."

Dani smiled. "We all go through that stage, I think. And it's usually awful. Have you made any friends at school? Usually small colleges are great places to form lasting friendships."

"Not too many. The people aren't really friendly." Dani watched as Bonnie stole a glance at Adam and saw that he was busily eating. Her eyes took on a special glow. "I know this really nice boy. His name's Jeff Hayden, and he wants to be an architect."

Adam made a low sound in his throat. "Jeff had better clean up his act, if his photo's any indication," he muttered.

"Now, Adam," Doris chimed in, "a lot of young men have long hair today and dress like that."

"Stringy hair down to his shoulders, a tattoo on his arm and leather pants, Mom?" Adam asked, raising a brow.

"Those pants are his pride and joy. They cost him a lot," Bonnie defended him. "Everybody's wearing them."

"He should have spent the money on a haircut instead. Pass the rolls, please."

Better stay out of this one, Dani thought. Adam was sure taking a hard line against someone Bonnie obviously liked. Was he always so domineering, and did both these women just let him get away with it?

"What made you decide to become a teacher, Dani?" Bonnie asked in an obvious effort to shift the topic of conversation and not rile her brother further.

"I wanted to teach children. It's something I very much enjoy doing."

"How about some mashed potatoes, Dani?" Doris offered gently. "And we have strawberry shortcake for dessert."

It was already dark when Dani and Adam left, with warm goodbyes, full stomachs and two plastic bowls of leftovers. They rode in silence until they were on the highway, headed for Grand Haven, then they both spoke at once.

"Your family's very nice...."

"I want to apologize...."

She turned to him and saw a frown on his face. "Nothing to apologize to me for." To Bonnie, maybe, but not to her.

"We're usually... less argumentative. Bonnie's really a very nice girl."

"I thought so. You've never met this Jeff."

"No."

"Do you usually judge a person by the cut of his hair and the style of his clothes?" If Adam, with his flyaway hair and his casual wardrobe, didn't get that one, he was really obtuse.

"Trust me. He's without ambition. A latter-day hippie."

Dani always distrusted people who said, "Trust me." This conversation had nowhere to go. Still... "Sounds a little judgmental to me."

"Dani, I—" They both started as they heard a terrible bang that sounded like a gunshot. "Damn!" The truck lurched. "A blowout! Wouldn't you know it?" Carefully Adam got the swaying vehicle under control and off onto the shoulder of the highway. He sighed wearily.

"I hope you know how to change a tire, because I don't," Dani said.

"I do," he acknowledged, turning off the lights and opening his door. "How are you at holding flashlights?"

"A-1."

"Great. Come on."

They scrambled outside and Adam went to work removing the lug nuts, which were most uncooperative, as Dani beamed the huge flashlight.

"I sure wish I had my power wrench with me," he said.

"I left mine home in my other jeans, too."

He glanced up at her, grinning. She was definitely adaptable, he mused. Back at dinner he'd thought she would have a less-than-favorable impression of his family, but he realized that wasn't so. She wasn't quick to judge, not nearly as quick as he, he admitted sheepishly. He'd been worried there for a while that she'd call the whole thing off because of Bonnie's idiotic devotion to that worthless boy. Fortunately Dani was smarter than that. With a final twist of the wrench he freed the nut.

Securing the jack then, he cranked it up and had the big tire off in moments. He stooped to put the spare in place. "I hope this'll do. There probably aren't too many stations open this late on a Sunday night."

"You look like you've done this a time or two before," Dani said, watching carefully in case she ever faced just such an emergency.

"Yeah, I have," he said, looking up at her, "but never with such an attractive assistant." Finished, he stood, wiping his hands on a rag.

"You have a smudge on your cheek," Dani said, using her fingers to rub off a couple of streaks of dirt. His cheek was rough from a day's growth of beard, which she found oddly appealing. "There, just like new," she said smiling. The smile slowly faded as she became aware that he was very close, very serious, his brown eyes shining in the dim moonlight.

Unable to stop himself, Adam raised a none-too-steady hand and ran it down her cheek, pausing to cup her chin. She was a freckle-faced charmer with a grease spot on her nose—which he carefully wiped off with his thumb. A teacher who taught children games, and maybe more. A little rich girl out of her element. Desire hit him, strong and fast and hot. But he knew that he must not feel it, not for this woman, even as his eyes melted into hers, as his hand moved over her soft skin.

She had rejected all that he wanted and needed in his life right now, and was somewhat critical of his plans, despite her best efforts to understand. She could never take him where he wanted to go, would never take Bonnie along. Dani was a rebel, an idealist, a misfit. And he wanted her more with every second that ticked by.

Her heart thudding, Dani took a step back, hoping her agitation wasn't written all over her face. How had she allowed this to happen? Where was her good sense, her self-control, all her defenses? What a mess!

Adam cleared his throat noisily and dropped his hand. "Thanks," he muttered quickly. Bending, he cranked down the vehicle and removed the jack. "Looks like we're ready to roll." While she got into the cab on her side, he went around to the truckbed and threw in the tools. Damn, but it was going to be a long, uneasy ride the rest of the way home.

Chapter Four

The ball whizzed past Dani's face with a whoosh, narrowly missing her.

"Hey, Dani, are you with us?" Kent asked, bounding over to her in the sand and throwing a friendly arm around her shoulders. "That's the second sure shot you missed this morning."

"I'm sorry," Dani said, annoyed with herself. She'd always enjoyed these impromptu Saturday-morning volleyball games on the beach. They were loosely organized, open to anyone who cared to show up, and drew most of the singles from the neighborhood. But this Saturday she was having trouble concentrating.

"A lot on your mind?" Kent asked.

"I guess so." She'd dated Kent for a while last year, infrequently, casually. There'd been no sparks, and they'd settled into a comfortable, caring friendship.

"I came by last night about nine, but your lights weren't on, so I figured you were out."

No, she hadn't been out. She'd been sitting in the dark, staring out at the relentless waves, lost in thought. She hadn't seen or heard Kent. "Sorry I missed you," she said noncommittally.

"You okay, babe?"

Taking a deep breath, Dani looked up at him and put on a bright smile. "Sure."

"You guys going to play, or what?" Larry yelled from across the net.

"I was trying to get Dani to go skinny-dipping, but she wants to finish the game," Kent told him, moving back to his net position.

Dani stepped farther back, hoping not too many shots would come her way, since she had a tendency to drift into daydreams lately. So unusual for her—she usually had perfect control of her thoughts and actions. and she knew the exact reason for this change. Adam.

She hadn't seen him since the somewhat strained ride home from his mother's place last Sunday, nearly a week ago. She'd gathered some books for him to read, and some records of the type of music he wanted to start listening to. But he hadn't called, so she'd just stacked them.

She and Mutt had strolled down the beach several evenings, as they often did, but each time she'd come close to Adam's house, it had looked dark and empty. Had he really been gone every evening, or had he been sitting in the dark, staring out to sea, as she'd done all too often lately? A self-confessed workaholic, he probably hadn't been home. Men didn't sit around mulling over their thoughts the way women did, she supposed. Not *that* man, anyway, because Adam had no reason to think long and hard about her. He was interested in Sabrina and chums, not Danielle Ames.

Luckily she saw the ball coming this time, and leaped to meet it, slamming it easily over the net and catching Robin by surprise.

"Atta way, Dani," Chris yelled, pleased that their side had scored.

Chris was one of the more serious of the Saturday group, a short, wiry fellow who worked for the library by day and tried to write the great American novel by night. Dani liked talking with him, because his ideas, though sometimes a little dark and deep, were clever and interesting. Kent, on the other hand, fell just short of being a beach bum; he supported himself with an assortment of odd jobs and a generous monthly check from an understanding family.

Nice guys, Dani thought, but like several others she knew, they were "searching for themselves," and she wasn't interested in joining in the quest. The rest of the men she knew were like Howard, upwardly mobile, devoted and unfortunately quite dull. She was much more drawn to a man who knew who he was, where he was going, what he wanted out of life. Someone like her father. Someone like Adam.

Squinting into the sun, Dani applauded a good return with the others, trying desperately to keep her wandering mind in check. Yet her gaze kept straying down the beach in the direction of Adam's house. She'd mentioned their Saturday games to him the night they'd met, and now she admitted to herself that she'd been hoping all morning that he'd come join them.

Adam's resemblance to Carter had not escaped her. They were both men of power, so used to running the show that being in charge had become a subconscious part of each of them. They were self-made men, used to having authority, comfortable with it, unabashedly manipulative, slightly arrogant, often domineering. The kind of men thinking women should turn and run from. The kind she'd always wanted in her life. With a sigh, Dani dragged her attention back to the game.

Her own fault. This turmoil she was in was all her own fault. She could have, *should have,* said no to Adam's unorthodox request. Maybe she'd already been deeply attracted to him. Hard to say, since she'd never felt anything quite like this before. She could still walk away, tell him, if and when he finally came around again, that she'd changed her mind. No explanations necessary. Her decision. But as sure as the sun would rise tomorrow she knew she wouldn't.

Suddenly, as if she'd conjured him up, she saw him walking barefoot toward them on the hard-packed sand, blond hair blowing in a strong summer breeze, bare chested and wearing faded jeans that rode low on his slim hips. He wasn't smiling, and his dark eyes were trained directly on her as Kent handed her the ball for her serve.

She came alive. Squaring her shoulders, she held the ball in her left hand, took aim and whacked a powerful serve that flew past the heads of two opponents, landed at the feet of the third and scored neatly. Acknowledging the cheers with a delighted grin, she went on to score still another point, before having her third shot grounded. As she stepped back, she sought out Adam on the sidelines. He tipped two fingers to his forehead in salute and smiled at her. Dani felt better than she had all day.

She played like a demon, Adam was thinking, volleyball, tennis, whatever. And played to win. She was beautiful to watch, strong and healthy, a worthy opponent. He hadn't planned to come out this morning, thinking to sleep in after a bear of a week during which one thing or another had gone wrong on several of his projects. But he'd awakened, tugged on his jeans and found himself strolling down the beach, wondering if she'd be there.

He hadn't even had time to call her all week, and he hoped she hadn't decided to back out of helping him. He hadn't meant to touch her like that Sunday night. He'd been seconds away from kissing her. *That* would have really messed things up between them. Dani Ames wasn't interested in his kind of man, not the man he was now or the man he was trying to become. She would most likely one day wind up with someone like Carter—educated, urbane, rich, oozing class from every pore yet every inch his own man. She'd deny it, but that's the kind of man who would ultimately win her.

Jamming his hands into his pockets, Adam watched the game finish. He knew he wasn't like these guys, either, many of whom were drifting aimlessly along, chasing a flyaway dream, living off a generous father. So he wasn't like Carter, or Dani's friends, or Howard, the stockbroker who wore red bow ties. And though he was enjoying his makeover, he knew that his new life-style would be a temporary one for him. He would live it until his sister had all that was necessary to ensure her future happiness, including a husband, then he'd return to the life he led now, which basically pleased him.

In either case, his world wasn't Dani's. Too bad, since there seemed to be some powerful sexual chemistry between them. Which he would have to keep a lid on if he wanted her to continue helping him.

He heard a victory yell as the game ended, and waited as the exuberant winners congratulated one another, while the other side demanded a rematch. He noticed Brock, one of his closer neighbors, who occasionally stopped in for a beer, walk toward him. Adam put on a welcoming smile. Brock clapped him on the shoulder in greeting, implored him to join the next game and quickly introduced him to the players he didn't know.

Adam stood head and shoulders above all of them, even Kent, Dani noticed as he shook hands with several of the group and flashed that quick smile. Her heart pounded when he joined her side since her team had one player fewer. On his way to guard the back of the court, he passed very near her.

"Looks like you're this team's ace in the hole," he commented, winking at her as the others lined up.

"Oh, I don't know. We just lost the second game. Maybe you'll make the difference." She knew she didn't need to tell him she was glad he'd joined them; he could see it on her face. And so could Kent, who gave her a long look before turning to face the net.

Adam did make the difference, as their team easily won the next two games, amid much shouting and laughter. The other side vowed to get even, and they began the tie-breaker. About halfway through, a fast ball came hurtling toward Dani and she took several steps backward to get better leverage. Her eye on the ball, she didn't see or hear Adam coming up behind her. She jumped up to slam the ball just as he did. His superior height enabled him to smash the serve back, but not fast enough to keep from colliding with Dani. She went down with a grunt.

Adam's forward momentum caused him to lose his balance, too. Jerking his body quickly, he managed to avoid landing completely on top of her. Laughing, she shook the sand from her short curls while he caught his breath. He lay sprawled half atop her, his legs entangled with hers.

"Didn't you see me backing up, you big oaf?"

"Didn't you hear me yell that I had it?"

Smiling into her eyes, he saw sea and sky reflected in their blue depths. Her face was morning fresh, free of makeup, cheeks rosy from exertion. She smelled of sunshine and some wildflower he couldn't name. His gaze drifted to her full lower lip and saw it tremble ever so slightly. Was it a nervous reaction, or was it that chemistry at work again?

Just like last weekend, Dani thought. His touch made her wary, apprehensive, yet suddenly excited. Her hand, trapped between them, pressed against the soft, golden hair of his chest. His eyes were full of questions, a vague reluctance and an unmistakable awareness. She wanted him up and off her so she wouldn't have to wrestle with those feelings, new and restive. She wanted him off her beach, out of her life, finished with his schemes. She wanted to stop wanting him.

In the background Dani heard shouts as someone scored again. Evidently the game had gone on without them. With some effort, she tore her gaze away from Adam and saw someone come nearer. She recognized Tina, a short blonde who'd been openly appreciating Adam's assets since his arrival. Hands on her hips, head cocked, she regarded them as Adam turned toward her.

"Hey, you two, you want time out, or are you rejoining us?" she asked in her high-pitched voice.

With seeming reluctance, Adam scrambled up and offered a helping hand to Dani, who took it and pulled herself up. He grinned at Tina. "Just taking a little rest," he explained. He glanced toward Dani, who was brushing herself off. "You okay?"

"Fine," she answered, not looking up as she walked back to her position. Tina was the biggest mouth on the block. How much had she noticed in that measuring look she'd given Adam? Dani wondered as she brought her attention back to volleyball.

The last game seemed to take hours to finish, but at last they won it, and Dani heaved a sigh of relief as Kent came over and gave her a sweaty hug in celebration.

"Nice playing, lady," he told her, "even if you're a little distracted today."

Over his shoulder she saw Adam watching, and gently disengaged herself from Kent. "Thanks. You scored quite a few yourself."

"Is he the reason you suddenly woke up?" Kent asked, nodding toward Adam, who had turned to talk to Brock, while Tina hovered nearby.

Frowning, Dani shoved her hands into the pockets of her shorts. How had she suddenly become so transparent, she who had always guarded her privacy and her relationships so carefully? "I scarcely know him," she answered.

"Be careful, babe. I hear he's got a string of broken hearts stretched up and down the state."

She looked up at Kent. "Thanks for the warning, but it isn't necessary. I'm working with him on a project. That's all we've got going."

Kent's smile was skeptical. "Right. See you later, Dani." He turned and jogged off down the beach.

Sighing, Dani trudged up a small sand dune and sat down, gazing up at the dark clouds that had moved in. Rain by late afternoon, she predicted as Mutt came bounding over to wiggle down next to her. Deliberately she ran a hand through his fur and talked quietly to him until she could stand the suspense no longer. Lifting her eyes, she saw Brock start to walk away and Adam turn toward her. Tina was nowhere in sight.

When he reached her, he eased his tall frame down beside her and crossed his feet, leaning his elbows on his knees as he faced her. "Where'd you learn to play so well? College Volleyball 101, freshman year?"

"How'd you guess? And backyard volleyball in the sand, starting last summer. Where'd you learn?"

He shrugged, looking out at the choppy sea. "We played in the street, tying a rope between two trees for a net. Traffic was light, but the few drivers who had to stop while we unstrung the barrier got quite annoyed. Clancy used to tell them to go to hell." Smiling at the memory, Adam lay back on the warm sand.

Dani shifted to her side and propped her head against her hand. "Who's Clancy?"

"Michael John Clancy. We grew up together, only he had it much rougher than I. His father drank and left his mother, who died when Clancy was twelve. He went through half a dozen foster homes, winding up with us in between them, constantly running away, getting in trouble all the time."

She could hear the affection in his voice, and the love. Much the same as she felt for Nora. "And where's Michael now?"

"'Clancy.' No one calls him 'Michael.' He's a sergeant on the Boston Police force. Would you believe it? He works in homicide, and he's tough as nails. On the outside. But he sends my mother flowers on her birthday, came over with a kitten for Bonnie the day after her dog got hit by a car, and when no one else would, he loaned me the rest of the money I needed to buy my first company. He's more than a friend. He's..."

"The brother you never had."

Turning his head, Adam stared at her. Damned if she wasn't looking into his mind. Spooky. He sat up. "Yeah." He rubbed his unshaven chin. "I was so busy all week I didn't have time to call you about our next lesson. Are we still on?''

Here's your chance, Dani told herself. Say no, break away, end it. "Sure. I gathered some books for you. And the records we talked about."

Mutt jumped up and raced out to chase a low-flying sea gull that had swept inland. Adam watched the dog and wished he were as carefree. When would he find the time to read the books, listen to the music? Yet he'd have to. Hearing Bonnie defend that Jeff character last weekend had only reinforced what he'd already known. He had to get her interested in the right kind of man, and soon. He'd have to allocate more responsibility at work and free himself until he learned all he needed to know.

"Great," he said. He swung his attention to Dani, and studied her as she lay on her side, sifting sand through her long fingers. Why couldn't she be different? he asked himself for not the first time. Why did she have to reject her family's life-style when it would be so much easier for him if she could be the one to take him in? He was getting used to her, comfortable with her; he even liked her. It would be no hardship for him to spend weeks, maybe months, with her as she introduced Bonnie and him to the right society people. But, no, she was stubborn and unbending when it came to this subject. So he'd have to be content with their present arrangement.

A stray cat of a nondescript color wandered over, thin and meowing. Adam watched as Dani petted his scruffy head. "Yours?" he asked.

"No one's, poor thing. He's a loner. I feed him now and then."

"He looks old and sick. Someone should put him out of his misery."

"Adam! Shall we do that to you when you're old and sick?"

"Animals are different."

"Yes, they're kinder than people."

He could see he would get nowhere with her on this topic. "Are you busy tonight?" he asked, and watched her raise her eyes from the cat to him.

She wished she could honestly say yes. Yet how would postponing things help? Her fluctuating emotions were maddening, Dani decided. "What do you have in mind?" she inquired cautiously.

"Dinner at my house. You could bring the books and records. Also, I have something I want to show you."

"What's that?"

Slowly Adam got up, running his hand through his windblown hair. "I got a couple of copies of *GQ*, *Gentleman's Quarterly*, the men's magazine."

Her lips started to curve into a smile, but she managed to hide it as she sat up. "Yes, I've heard of it."

He shuffled his feet self-consciously. "I need to have my hair styled, I think. We could glance through the magazines, and maybe you could advise me on the right cut."

Dani stood and looked up at him. "Sure. I used to stay with my college roommate and her family frequently, the ones in Connecticut. One summer her mother taught both Nora and me to cut hair, and we practiced on her four younger brothers." She smiled, remembering. "We went from awful to better to passable. Great fun."

There was that note of nostalgia in her voice again, Adam noticed. Great fun learning to cut hair on four young and undoubtedly wiggly boys? Dani Ames found fun, it seemed, where most people wouldn't think to look. "That's even better. I'll take my chances on your rusty memory. Bring your scissors. Seven all right?"

"Fine." She ran her eyes over his hair. Blond, thick and soft, with a tendency to curl. "What's wrong with your haircut?"

He gave her an exasperated look. "Would Sabrina approve?"

That again. "Right. See you at seven." Dani started down the beach to her house as Mutt ran up to join her. *GQ* hairstyles and Sabrina. Why did the thought of that unlikely combination leave a sudden sour taste in her mouth?

The rain was at the sprinkle stage when Dani arrived at Adam's beach-side house promptly at seven. She had four current best-sellers in the crook of one arm and half a dozen record albums in the other. The house was dark and very quiet. Surely he hadn't forgotten.

With her elbow, she pressed the bell. When, after several seconds had elapsed, she heard no one moving about, she pressed again, longer, harder. Finally a scuffling sound grew louder and Adam appeared, wearing only a pair of brown terry-cloth shorts.

"I fell asleep," he murmured apologetically as he held open the screen door for her. Taking the books and records, he set them down on a table and switched on a lamp.

"This is quite a house," Dani commented, looking around. "And Clancy helped you build it?"

Adam nodded, yawning.

Dani inhaled the musky scent of him and abruptly turned away, walking toward the kitchen. He was so very large and male, and wearing so few clothes. She found it a shade overwhelming. Switching on the kitchen light, she glanced around.

Neat. Good heavens, but he was neat. Not a little bit neat, but with a fanatical orderliness that had her mouth dropping open at the kitchen counter, which boasted one spotless toaster and four shiny canisters all in a row. The refrigerator was free of fingerprints, and even the chrome faucet was clean of water marks. Place mats were lined up just so on a spanking-clean butcher block table, and a fake fern dangled from a chain near the window. How could someone live like this? Dani was honestly perplexed. Hearing Adam come up behind her, she turned to him, a question in her eyes.

"I have a housekeeper," he explained, used to people's amazement over such perfection. "She was here this afternoon. I'm not home much."

"Much? My house wouldn't be this neat if I dropped in only at Easter and Christmas."

He thought of the comfortable clutter of her house and a feeling of warmth drifted through him. He also thought of the cramped, crowded, dingy rooms he'd grown up in as a boy. "I like things orderly."

"I guess you do." Through the archway, Dani glanced into the living room, considering going in there but unwilling to wrinkle a fluffed-up pillow or leave an indentation in a smooth chair. "We may have to postpone your haircut. We can't do it in the house, and it's starting to rain outside."

Adam stifled a yawn and stretched lazily. "We can use the kitchen."

"Your housekeeper will be upset," she warned him, gazing about again. She realized she couldn't smell anything cooking. "Did you take a nap in lieu of making dinner?" Her voice was teasing.

"I took a nap trying to catch up for all the late nights I worked last week."

So he had been working and not out with others. She wished the knowledge didn't please her.

"Dinner's being delivered later. Pizza with everything." He grinned.

The first smile of the evening, she thought.

She relaxed. "Junk food. I love it." She watched Adam run his hand through the curly blond hair on his chest, and again her nerves were set on edge. "Why don't you put on a shirt while I wait for you in the living room?" she suggested pointedly, turning to walk over and gaze out at the stormy sea.

So his somewhat undressed state bothered her, did it? Adam thought, smiling. He strolled to his bedroom and pulled on a blue knit shirt. It would seem that the poor little rich girl wasn't as immune to him as she'd like to believe. Since her scent and her nearness had been playing havoc with his control, he was pleased to see the tables turned for a change. Whistling, he joined her in the living room.

Legs crossed primly, she was seated on the sofa, thumbing through a *GQ*. Peach was definitely her color, and the lightweight jumpsuit hugged her in all the right places. He turned to his bar. "How do you feel about Châteauneuf-du-Pape, 1959?" he asked, reaching for a corkscrew.

Brows raising in surprise, she smiled at him. "My, my, you do catch on quickly."

Adam uncorked the bottle, as if he'd been doing it for years and poured the burgundy liquid into two glasses. He walked over and handed her a glass, then set the bottle on the coffee table, before seating himself alongside her on the couch. "I didn't want you to think I drank only cheap Italian wine." He saw no reason to tell her he'd enlisted Clancy's aid this afternoon in selecting a wine that would impress her, buying the corkscrew and wineglasses, as well.

Playing along, Dani sniffed, swirled and swallowed, then gave him an appreciative smile. "Wonderful."

"Here's to you, coach," he said, clinking his glass to hers.

They drank, eyes locked. Dani was the first to look away. "So show me what kind of haircuts appeal to you," she prompted him.

Adam moved closer, then leaned back and spread the magazine on his lap. For several minutes he leafed through it, then he pointed out a couple of possibilities.

Dani leaned in to look. "This cut's for really straight hair, and yours has curl. And this one is pretty formal. You'd have to blow-dry it daily, use hair spray. I don't know how it would hold up on your outdoor job." She looked up from the page. "You sure you want to do this?" His bare thigh pressed warmly against her leg. She took another sip of wine, though she certainly didn't need any more.

"You don't see *anything* here that appeals to you?"

As a matter of fact she did, and it wasn't on the pages of the magazine. "Not in that issue." She picked up another. They riffled through several back copies and current ones, and still she didn't see anything she could label an improvement. Besides, she was feeling warm and restless. She stood.

"Look, let's just go into the kitchen, find a towel, and I'll start trimming. You hold the mirror and check out the cut as I go," she suggested.

Undaunted, Adam continued to flip through the magazine. When he came across a photo of a male model wearing a close-cropped look, with longish sideburns, that he recognized as familiar, he folded back the issue and handed it to her. "What about this?"

Dani looked incredulous. "You like that?"

"No. I thought you might. That is, Sabrina might."

"I hope not. Howard wears his hair like that, and I hate it. Come on into the kitchen."

He'd gotten the answer he'd been fishing for, Adam told himself. But why had he wanted to hear it from her? He'd known all along that Dani couldn't be interested in that jogging stockbroker. And why should it matter to him if she had been? Shaking his head, he picked up their wine-glasses and followed her in.

In moments Dani had a shirtless Adam sitting on a wooden chair in the center of his spotless kitchen, a large towel around his shoulders. Standing behind him, she regarded his thick head of hair.

"I just washed it before my nap," he told her.

She could tell. It smelled of baby shampoo, and the thought made her smile. She ran her fingers through the fullness, then pulled the comb through. It'd been years since she'd cut the Mason boys' hair, and they'd been restless teenagers for the most part. She wondered how Adam would handle a mistake that might take a week to grow out. Gently she pushed his head forward and began snipping.

Head bowed, Adam sat holding the hand mirror in his lap. The rain was falling steadily now, and the damp spring air wafted through the open window. The sound of the surf breaking mingled with the steady snip of Dani's scissors. He fervently hoped she knew what she was doing. Some of those haircuts in the magazine had been too odd for words. He'd have to wear a cap at work if she got carried away, or he'd be laughed off the high beams.

"So you hate Howard's haircut?" he asked, making conversation to keep from thinking about his hair.

"Mmm."

"How about Kent's haircut?" He felt the slightest pause, then she resumed, comb in one hand, scissors clipping in the other.

"I have no opinion about Kent's hair." Bait her, would he? Not on her life was she going to get into a discussion of the men who lived along the beach. Time to turn the tables. "How do you like Tina's hair?"

He thought of the bleached blonde with the suggestive sway to her hips. "Too flashy," he answered, and heard Dani's throaty chuckle. "But we're discussing men's haircuts here. Give me an example of a man you think has a really nice haircut."

Carefully she trimmed along his left ear. "Mmm, let's see. Robert Redford in *The Way We Were*. Mel Gibson in *The River*. Donald Duck in *The Disney Special*." She waited for his laugh. "Natural, soft, casual—that's what I like. But we're not trying to please me. You should be asking what Sabrina would find attractive."

"All right. What would she?"

"I haven't the foggiest notion. We've never discussed men's hair." Silently she went on with her work.

Adam knew she was being evasive about Sabrina, and he wondered why, after she'd been the one to bring her up. Dani's hands weren't large, yet they were strong, and her touch gentle. Closing his eyes, Adam decided to enjoy the sensuous feeling.

"There," Dani said several minutes later. "Take a look and see what you think."

He held up the mirror. She was shaping it nicely, sort of layering it without removing much. Leaning toward the Robert Redford casualness. He hid a smile. "Looks good to me. How do you think Sabrina will view the new me?"

"We'll just have to wait and see, won't we?" Dani told him, going back to her clipping.

"Ow! My ear doesn't bend that way."

"Sorry." Served him right. She was getting a little tired of having to worry about Sabrina. Combing his hair again, Dani sighed. What was the matter with her? That's what this whole thing was about, wasn't it? She decided to try to stop being so touchy.

Finally she was satisfied. She hadn't a clue whether Sabrina or any of her buddies would like Adam's new hairstyle, but she did. "That's about it," she said, standing back as he examined his new cut. The cut had the wind-blown effect she loved, the untamed look she thought suited him perfectly. She watched him study his image.

At last his dark eyes met hers, and he smiled. "I like it."

Nodding, she returned his smile. "I'm glad." Carefully she removed the hair-sprinkled towel and with her hand brushed some feathery strays from his shoulders and back.

Mistake! her mind clanged. Strong muscles, smooth skin, so warm under her fingers. She wanted to go on touching, to slide her hands down over his shoulders and into the curly hair on his chest. Flushing, Dani swiveled, looking around, "If you'll tell me where you keep your broom..."

"I'll take care of it," Adam said, rising. He handed her her wineglass. "Here, you've earned it." He clinked her glass with his. "To my barber, who has hidden talents."

She sipped, not meeting his eyes.

Adam realized that he was making her nervous again. Evidently he hadn't spent enough time around women like Dani to know how to act. Why else would she have these funny little mood shifts? Quickly he shrugged into his shirt and started cleaning up.

Dani stood by the sink, gazing out at the gentle rain. She liked rainy nights, liked the coziness of being in a dry cocoonlike atmosphere while listening to the rain on the roof.

It was oddly comforting, somehow intimate, often—
  "How do you feel about manicures?" Adam asked.

Turning, she saw him seated at the table, examining his nails. She walked over and picked up the hand he held out. "Oh, my!" Nails were broken or chewed off, cuticles a mess. "This is a disaster."

He managed to look appealing while admitting to years of neglect. "I know. Think you can do anything with them?"

Setting down her wineglass, Dani reached for her purse, which she'd dropped on a chair. "I don't have much with me." She fished around in her bag and came up with an emery board. "When you said makeover, you weren't kidding, were you?" she commented, sitting down next to him. This was better, this almost brother-sister teasing.

"I have nail clippers in the bathroom."

Dani placed his hand in her left palm and regarded his thumb first. "There's not much left to clip. Do you bite your nails?"

"No, I work in construction. Hard on the hands."

She liked the feel of his roughened skin, finding even the callused ridges oddly pleasing. She began to file. "I thought you worked mostly in the office now."

"I do early mornings and evenings. I like the outdoor part, working on the buildings. I need to spend more time in the office and less in the field, but the field is my first love."

Dani nodded and moved on to the second finger. "I understand that. I'd hate a desk job, but there's some paperwork to all positions, I suppose. My friend Nora spends hours bent over her drawing table and loves it. Different strokes, as they say."

"Nora's your old college roommate, the one studying architecture whose brothers you practiced barbering on?"

She glanced up at him. She'd mentioned Nora only a couple of times, yet he'd remembered. So many people only half listened. Adam was more sensitive than she'd given him credit for. "Yes. She is to me what Clancy is to you, I think. Close as a sister." Closer than Sabrina, she thought.

"Tell me about her," Adam said. It was an odd feeling for him, he realized, to sit and talk with a woman, wanting to know more about her, *really* wanting to know. He felt comfortable with Dani, relaxed, at ease. She wasn't a date, or someone he needed to impress. Surprisingly she was turning into a friend, and he'd never experienced real friendship with a woman. He found he liked it.

And so, because the cozy, rainy evening atmosphere lent itself to confidences and because Adam listened well and seemed genuinely interested and maybe because she'd finished her glass of wine on an almost empty stomach, Dani did tell him. She told him about the depth of her friendship with Nora, about the family who'd accepted her like another daughter, Nora's loving parents, the brothers who, even after they had married, treated her like a sister. She described holiday visits and summer vacations at the wooden two-story Mason farmhouse, which always seemed to have room for one more. She finished her story at about the time she finished filing Adam's last fingernail.

"And you still keep in touch even though Nora's away at school?" Adam asked, pouring them each another glass of wine.

"Oh, yes. We write and talk on the phone frequently. Nora has to work this summer, but I'll find time to go visit her. And you can bet that when she graduates next year, I'll be there."

That hint of nostalgia in her voice again, Adam noticed. From the sound of it, he got the impression Dani wasn't as close to Sabrina as she was to her friend Nora. Was it because she disdained Sabrina's life-style, or had the rift come earlier in their lives? He remembered how tenderly she'd spoken of their housekeeper, Sarah, yet she usually mentioned Arlene somewhat coolly. Dani was much more complex than she appeared on the surface. He wondered if she knew how much she'd revealed about herself in the way she spoke of the Masons.

"Well, what do you think?" she asked.

"About what?" Adam asked, coming out of his thoughts.

"Your minimanicure, that's what."

"Oh." He examined his nails. "A big improvement."

"If you'd mentioned it earlier, I'd have brought my nail scissors, some lotion. Those cuticles need work."

"Next time." He ran his nicely rounded thumbnail along the soft skin of her wrist. "Will you finish the job next time?" He felt her pulse leap under his touch as her eyes met his. Before she could answer, the doorbell rang. "I think that's dinner." Adam got to his feet and went to the front.

Dani took another sip of wine she didn't need. Quite an evening, she thought. Unexpected confidences and unusual responses. It would be best if she ate and ran along, she decided as Adam returned with a large cardboard box....

They drank more red wine and ate steaming pizza off blue plates. They talked about the neighborhood and living on the ocean and the things Boston had to offer. And their eyes watched and studied and admired, revealing more about their thoughts than their lips did. Dani insisted on loading the few things into his empty dishwasher.

"You like that fake plant?" she asked, eyeing the false fern.

"My housekeeper brought it over because I kept forgetting to water the real ones and they died." He looked up at it. "Pretty awful, isn't it?" he asked, remembering her many healthy plants.

"Well, it doesn't invite conversation the way real ones do."

"Maybe you could include a side course in plant care."

"At this rate, the way you keep thinking up new lesson plans, we'll be at this when we're both using canes."

"Are you hinting that I'm taking advantage of you, lady? Didn't I just feed you the best pizza in town? Of course, it can't compare to that gourmet meal you served me."

"I know you won't believe this, but I liked this better. And I do thank you. It's getting late, though, and I'd better be going."

Adam had enjoyed the pizza more, too, but he didn't believe Dani. She was just being polite. He glanced out the window. "You could wait till the rain stops." He nodded toward the living room. "I could build a fire and pour us another glass of wine."

The picture he'd painted was far too appealing. She had to leave, because she wanted too badly to remain. "It's only drizzling. I won't melt." She moved to the door. "Let me know how you like the books and what you think of the records."

He glanced at the top one. Chopin? He frowned first, then shot her a quizzical look.

She said, "You're going to have to switch from country-western to the BBC—Bach, Beethoven and Chopin."

He made a face and she laughed.

She had a nice laugh, Adam thought. With a start, he realized he really didn't want her to go. But that was stupid. He opened the screen door. "Thanks again."

"Good night, Adam." Hunching her shoulders, she skipped down the porch steps, where Mutt joined her. Adam stood for a few moments watching them both run down the beach towards her house, then he turned and walked back into the kitchen, realizing how suddenly quiet, suddenly empty, the room seemed now that Dani and her bright laugh had left.

Chapter Five

We could be finished by the end of June, Mr. Kinkaid, provided the rest of the insurance money comes through."

Adam nodded, his eyes on the workmen cementing in the cinder-block wall that faced the high school parking lot. "I'll make a couple of calls, Stan. We'll get those bureaucrats to send the check." Hands on his hips, he slowly walked along, inspecting the progress of his pet project, his alma mater, as was his Sunday morning habit.

He turned to Stan Jackson, the short, balding job supervisor he'd personally put in charge, and smiled. "The men are doing a hell of a job." Stan was one of his best men, reliable, honest, firm with the men, yet highly respected.

Wiping his broad forehead with a red checkered handkerchief, Stan acknowledged the praise. "Working weekends these guys can make a bundle, so I don't have no trouble getting men to sign up. Those spring rains held us up, but now we're moving along."

Glancing over his shoulder, Adam saw the stack of charred boards from the fire still piled at the far end of the lot. "Let's get that stuff hauled away, Stan. It's an ugly reminder. These kids have enough to put up with, doubling up in the few classrooms that weren't damaged or finishing out the remaining couple of weeks of school in the gymnasium."

"Right, Mr. Kinkaid. I'll get on it tomorrow."

Moving outside, Adam strolled along the outer perimeter, checking the finished work on the section that housed the school offices, cafeteria and auditorium. He'd helped expand the original blueprints, making the new facilities larger, better, brighter, modernizing the lighting and adding more windows, improving classroom accessibility. Maybe, just maybe, if the place of learning was cheery and appealing, those kids who had a struggle at home would be encouraged to stay in school and not drop out. Sighing, Adam hoped it would work.

As they neared the gymnasium he heard shouts and a rousing cheer coming through the propped-open doors. Sunday mornings the gym was used for basketball games in a city-funded program for local boys. Adam had met Al Donaldson, the lanky, dedicated coach who was deeply involved in the program city-wide, and he admired the caring way the man handled the young mavericks, who tested him frequently yet seldom got his goat. It took a special sort to handle these street-smart kids, and he thought Al was that and more.

Adam clapped Stan on the shoulder. "Keep up the good work, Stan." He didn't need to remind his super that he'd promised him a nice bonus when this job was completed. All Adam's men knew that his word was money in the bank. "Call me if that check doesn't come in by the end of the week."

"Right. See you next Sunday, Mr. Kinkaid."

With a wave Adam started toward his truck, but he stopped suddenly, puzzled. In the first row of cars by the gymnasium door, he spotted something familiar. Moving nearer, he took a closer look. A red Mercedes convertible, its black top neatly folded down. First he wondered how many of these cars there could be in this neighborhood. Then he wondered what Danielle Winthrop Ames would be doing in an inner-city gymnasium on Sunday morning. His curiosity piqued, he walked through the gym doors.

Ten young boys, most skinny and awkward, who looked to be between eleven and fifteen, scrambled for the ball, dribbling and dashing between opposing baskets. A dozen more sat on the sidelines bench with Al Donaldson, who leaned forward, intently watching the game. And on the near side, hunched over, studying the action, a red whistle in her mouth, wearing a black-and-white referee's shirt and white shorts with her sneakers, was Dani Ames.

I'll be damned, Adam thought as he sat down in the first row of the bleachers. Just last Sunday he'd brought her to this neighborhood to show her the house he'd grown up in and the school he'd attended, sat in his truck with her right across the street. She'd vaguely hinted that she was familiar with the area, but he hadn't believed her. Teaching in a Boston school was one thing, but he never would have guessed she refereed inner-city boys in a neighborhood that had passed its prime many years ago. Dani, with her blue blood, her bulging bank account and fancy degree from an Ivy League school, had surprised him again.

A scuffle on the floor caught his attention. A tall boy had elbowed a scrappy curly-haired kid of about thirteen, causing him to lose the ball and almost lose his footing.

Acting on reflex, the shorter kid made as if to go after his offender, but a sharp blast from Dani's whistle stopped him in midstride. His eyes, dark and angry, shot to her, but she stood her ground, her gaze never wavering from his. Oddly, the boy relaxed, and she gave him a quick, approving nod.

"Foul. Two shots," Dani called against the tall kid with the sharp elbows.

Hanging his head, the offender lined up with the others as the shorter boy broke out in a grin.

"Atta boy, Duffy," another boy shouted, slapping the curly-haired kid on the back. "Go get 'em."

And Duffy did, scoring both times. When the second shot sank through the basket, Duffy turned triumphant eyes to Dani as one of the other boys threw the ball to her. Adam saw her give him a pleased smile and a quick wink as the coach called for time out and team changes.

Adam leaned against the bench. He knew as well as Dani that a referee was supposed to remain neutral, yet there was a certain rapport between her and Duffy that she tried, but didn't quite manage, to cover. As the game resumed, he saw that the wiry little kid responded by playing his heart out for her, showing off, sinking next-to-impossible shots, daring the opposition to stop him, glancing toward her regularly.

Déjà vu, Adam thought with a smile of remembrance. He'd been like Duffy once—cocky, irreverent . . . looking for approval and badly needing it from someone, anyone. His sister had been too young and his mother too tired to notice most of his minor achievements, and he'd felt frustrated much of the time. He wished now that he'd had someone like Dani to encourage him, to reward him with that terrific smile, to care enough to notice him, to make him feel special.

He could easily understand what drew Duffy and some of the other boys to these Sunday-morning basketball games, but what did Dani get out of them? She could be sitting on Arlene's plush patio being served a tasty brunch by a white-jacketed butler, with no more taxing decisions to make than whether to summer in South Hampton or jet to the Riviera next weekend. She didn't have to get up early, drive to a seedy section of Boston and run around a sweaty gymnasium with an assortment of youngsters most of her friends would label delinquents. Why did she do it? He was honestly perplexed.

Adam knew his own motivations and what drove him. He never wanted to be poor again, never wanted to lose control of his destiny, his life. He was helping rebuild his school because he felt he owed a debt, but there his charitable feelings ended. He'd had to work hard all his life. He'd made something of himself, and he had little compassion for those who didn't at least try to do the same. He greatly admired men like Carter Ames, who, though born with the proverbial silver spoon, worked as hard if not harder than any subordinate.

But women were different. Women shouldn't have to kill themselves with work, grow old before their time, as his mother had. Women should have choices. And men should help them make the right choices whenever possible, as he was doing with Bonnie. Yet Dani had had that kind of life and rejected it. It didn't make sense. Leaning forward, watching as she ruled on a close call, he wondered if perhaps by talking to her he might make her see that she belonged in that other world, not here, in a hot, dingy gymnasium.

It was ten full minutes before the game ended, to the whoops and hollers of Duffy's team, which won by a wide margin. And Duffy was clearly the high scorer of the day.

Like the cocky kid he was, he took his teammates' praise in stride, his eyes not really lighting up until Dani walked over and congratulated him. Adam watched as Duffy flushed and he all but stammered as her blue eyes smiled into his.

He's got a crush on her, Adam realized, remembering how easily that happened at thirteen. He didn't blame Duffy. Dani was a woman who could excite—both boy or man—with a look or a touch. And the most alluring part was that she was unaware of her effect on the male of the species.

The boys jostled and punched one another as they made their way to the locker room. Silently Adam stood as Al Donaldson walked over to Dani and placed a friendly arm across her slim shoulders. Enthusiastic and a skilled player himself, Al was a perfect basketball coach. As he talked with Dani, his eyes never left her face. Adam saw her ease out from under Al's arm, only to have him take her hand. Friendly? Or more than that? Adam thrust his hands into his jeans pockets, wondering how long it would take before Dani would turn and spot him.

"I'd offer to make breakfast for you, Dani," Al said, studying her fingers, "but I haven't had a chance to grocery shop. Why don't we go over to Denny's? They have eggs Benedict on Sundays."

"Mmm, thanks, Al, but I've got some paperwork to do. Only a couple more weeks of school left." She patted her flat middle, hoping she wasn't overstating the point. "Besides, if I don't cut down soon, I'm going to have to start buying bigger shirts."

"No danger of that. You're put together pretty nicely."

"Thanks," Dani said, gently pulling back her hand. "Can I have a raincheck?" She liked Al and had shared many an impromptu meal with him. She found him pleasant and fun to be around. Or had until recently. Until Adam had come into her life, three weeks ago. Suddenly Al had lost his appeal. It was unfortunate, because Al was a nice guy.

"Sure," Al said, bending to pick up his clipboard of notes. "See you in a couple of weeks." With a smile he walked toward the locker room, where the clanging of metal doors could be heard over shouts and laughter.

Dani picked up her shoulder bag from alongside the bench, slipped her sunglasses on and found her keys. She could have gone with Al and had a nice breakfast—he was a good, undemanding friend—but, there was no point in going with him when she really didn't feel like socializing. She turned and started for the door, thinking it was too bad, because Al was probably better for her than— He was standing about twenty feet from her in a splash of sunshine, hands deep in his pockets, the sleeves of his blue denim shirt rolled high on his muscular arms, his tawny hair untamed despite her careful cut of last weekend. He looked confident, slightly arrogant and sexy as hell. How had he found her? Why was he here? she wondered, suddenly uncertain in his presence.

She appeared as hesitant as he felt, Adam thought as he moved toward her. Yet she'd walked away from Al before she'd spotted him, though Al had obviously wanted her to remain. Well, why shouldn't men find her attractive? Why shouldn't she go out? She was free to date anyone she wanted. There was nothing between them now, nor would there ever be. He moved closer.

"Fancy meeting you here, in my old stomping grounds," he said when he reached her.

"I was about to say the same to you," Dani answered, wondering why her voice was so husky. Must be from all the shouting during the game.

"You're a friend of Al's?"

"Yes. You, too?"

"I know him." This was ridiculous, he thought. They were talking like wary strangers. He found a small smile and gave it to her. "I read one of the books—*Hunt for Red October*. I really enjoyed it." He wished she'd take off her sunglasses so he could see her eyes.

"I thought you'd like Tom Clancy's writing. He's written some others you might want to check into."

"Right." He touched her elbow, guiding her out through the double doors into the sunshine. "You're full of surprises, Dani. Surely this isn't the school where you normally teach."

She shook her head, adjusting the strap of her bag on her shoulder. "No. Al asked me to help out last year. Most of these city programs are low budget, so I do volunteer refereeing twice a month. I enjoy the change, and the challenge."

He remembered her father had said she loved challenges. "Some of these boys are real challenges, I'm sure. Looks like you've won that Duffy kid over. He's nuts about you."

Odd way to phrase it, she thought, wondering how long Adam had been in the gym watching them. She'd taken to Duffy almost from the beginning, recognizing that the great big chip on his shoulder hid a lonely young man.

She squinted up at Adam. "Duffy's quick, bright and not nearly as tough as he pretends to be."

"And he has good taste in women. I saw your father midweek. He said you didn't show up at some board of education fund-raiser."

Dani nodded nonchalantly. "I hate those things. I told Dad I *might* attend. I got busy."

"Too busy to advance your career with some PR work?"

Dani frowned at him. "My career should and will advance based on my work, not on how many stuffy dinners I attend."

Exasperating woman. He reached up and pulled off her sunglasses, surprising her. "I need to see your eyes."

"Why?"

"I want to ask a favor of you."

Oh, no. Just when she'd been trying to think of an excuse to back away from this project, which had royally messed up her life the past few weeks. She supposed she at least owed it to him to hear him out. "Yes?"

Adam ran a hand through his hair, searching for the words that would convince her. "I want to speed up the lessons," he began, then hurried on when he saw her eyes widen. "There's a ballet coming to Boston soon, a new play opening, and the opera will be here in short order, to say nothing of several charity balls I read about. I'd like to learn a little about ballet and opera so I won't feel stupid when I attend. I also need to spruce up my wardrobe and brush up on my dancing." He risked a glance in her direction, knowing he was asking a lot and feeling uncomfortable about it. "I haven't danced in years." He let the words hang in the air.

Dani cleared her throat, studying the toes of her sneakers. "That's a tall order."

"I know." He glanced up at the sky as if for confirmation. "It's a beautiful day. I could take you to breakfast, then we could go to my house and start by looking through my clothes to see what I need. Maybe later we could put on some records and you could walk me through some dance steps." He knew he needed what he was asking, but after a week in which he'd consciously avoided her, he also acknowledged that he'd missed her. Was he asking just so he could spend more time with her? He saw her hesitation.

Dani was thinking, two offers for breakfast within twenty minutes. Quite a morning. And she wasn't even hungry. She wanted to be with Adam, yet she didn't. And this ambivalence was driving her crazy. "I'd like to, Adam, but I've got some school papers I need to work on," she said, falling back on the same excuse she'd given Al. "I'm a bit behind."

He nodded, trying to accept her rejection. "Sure, your job. I know it's important to you." That again. Her dedication to her work. Why had she walked away from a fortune so by day she could teach runny-nosed kids sports they probably had no interest in learning and by night sit in her little house by the sea with her dog? Was that such a wonderful life for a bright, attractive woman? Surely she got lonely. Didn't she want a husband, children, a better life?

"Is this how you want to spend the rest of your life, teaching children sports weekdays, playing volleyball on the beach Saturdays, refereeing for free on Sundays?" He didn't bother to hide the strong note of derision in his voice.

Dani caught the mocking tone and was immediately disappointed in Adam's shortsightedness. But she'd all too frequently handled similar reactions before. He, who built towering office buildings and sprawling shopping malls, couldn't see the parallel in her work.

"I really want to understand," he said, shoving his hands into his pockets again. "Are you aiming to be a principal or to teach at a university one day, or what?"

Now he sounded as if he considered teaching a stepping stone. He really was having trouble pigeonholing her. Why should she even bother to explain? Dani asked herself as she stared off into space. With the possible exception of her friend Nora Mason, no one had ever understood. She shifted her eyes to Adam's face. A stubborn profile if ever she'd seen one.

"Let me ask you a question, Adam. Don't you think it's just as important to mold a child into a worthwhile adult as it is to mold a pile of bricks and wood and mortar into an office building?"

He gave her a skeptical look. "You think you're molding little minds by teaching them basketball?"

"I don't *think* it; I *know* it. I've been doing it for five years now. I couldn't have the same input if I moved to administrative work or to the college level. The mold is set at any early age, and principals all too often become paper pushers. A teacher doesn't do it alone, but she certainly contributes."

Dani knew she sounded defensive, but he'd pushed her. How could she explain to Adam what her students meant to her? They were individuals, not just a group to be taught the basics of a few sports. She hadn't known what to expect when she'd come to Chadwicke Elementary fresh out of college. She'd known only that she wanted to work with children, and she'd hoped to gain their respect for her position and her knowledge. She'd received that and much more. Unexpectedly she found affection, incidents of caring and occasional true progress, as with Duffy. But the deepest satisfaction had come from seeing that she'd made a difference in many of their lives and they in hers.

How could she have known she'd be the one seventh-grader Tammy would seek out when her mother suddenly died? Or how much it would mean to her when an incorrigible fourth grader named Brian brought her a wilting bouquet of spring flowers on the last day of school, even though he'd probably swiped them from a neighbor's yard? Or the pleasure she'd derived from turning the gangly members of the eighth-grade boys' basketball team into athletic whizzes who'd gone on to win the city championship that year? Had she received more than she'd given? In spades.

"You see," Dani said, warming to her own defense, "a basketball game—or any team sport—is a minislice of life. The players have to learn the rules, what they can and can't do, the limitations of their bodies and minds. They have to learn pacing, discover their strengths and weaknesses— how to take advantage of one and compensate for the other. They must learn to play with honesty and fairness, how to lose with dignity and win with humility. They suffer defeats but also experience the joys of victory. As a child masters a game of sports, he also picks up a few hints on how to master the game of life."

"That's all well and good," Adam agreed. "But you don't have to do it. There're plenty of do-gooders in the world to accomplish all that." He saw her eyes flash in annoyance, but he bent closer, trying to make his point. "You have a family who can provide you with every good thing the world has to offer. Carter would give you anything—I can tell—take you into one of his companies if that's what you wanted, or support you in any other activity. You could work with your sister if Arlene's lunch-and-charity pastimes bored you. But you'd be among your own kind, contributing to society, not wandering around this near ghetto on a Sunday morning, running around some smelly gym with a group of boys who'd likely steal your car if you turned your back. You're one of the lucky ones, the chosen ones. Why do you put yourself through all this?"

Adam watched her blue eyes turn as cold as the sea on a turbulent day, while her cheeks became an angry pink.

"Haven't you heard a word I've said? I don't want to work in my father's business, or with Sabrina, or attend luncheons with my mother, no matter how worthy those endeavors are."

Damn stubborn woman, he thought. "Why? What's wrong with what they do?"

"Nothing. But it's not for me. Why can't you accept me for what I am? Why do you want to persuade me to go back to a life I'm not comfortable with?"

"I'm trying to understand why you're not comfortable with it."

Dani whirled away from him, crossing her arms over her chest. "Oh, damn! Why am I bothering with this conversation?"

Adam walked around to her, forcing her to look at him. "Tell me. I need to know."

"Why? So you can justify this ridiculous makeover, justify manipulating your sister into a world she may not like?"

"Maybe."

Damn, but the man was stubborn. She took a deep, calming breath. "I'm not comfortable with that life-style because it smacks of making money for its own sake, to stockpile, to beat others at the same game. I hate the phoniness of endless luncheons and dinners and parties where you smile at people you don't know and eat with people you don't care a fig about and spend the evening talking to people you have nothing in common with. It's an utter waste of time. I don't care if Mrs. Jones has a new diamond necklace or that Edith's dress is the latest thing or that Jonathan got a promotion on Wall Street. I don't care about making more money or designing clothes. I simply don't care. I'd rather read a good book or watch an old movie on television or play basketball with Duffy.

That's fun, educational, interesting, time well spent. It's not dull, boring, repetitious and superficial."

Dani found Adam studying her thoughtfully. "Oh, forget it." She moved toward her car.

"Wait," he said, following her. "Come with me. Let's go have breakfast and finish this."

Shaking her head, she got into her car. "It's finished." She inserted her key in the ignition, her fingers shaky. "I don't want to talk about this anymore, Adam. We're worlds apart on this subject. And maybe on much more."

Closing the door for her, he leaned close. "No, we're not, Dani. I was just trying to understand you."

"No, you were trying to change me."

"Please, come with me this afternoon. We're partners, remember?"

How could she forget? Dani sighed deeply. "Not today, Adam. I'm . . . I'm due at my mother's," she told him, deciding that very minute to take Arlene up on a standing invitation for Sunday brunch. She desperately wanted—needed—to clear her head and not think about this stupid partnership for a few hours. She started the motor.

"I'll call you later," he said, backing off. He'd irritated her, he knew, but he'd also made her feel, made her think.

"You do that." Shifting into drive, Dani shot forward and headed for the exit, not looking back.

"Mimosa is a delicious drink. Don't you agree, Dani?" Arlene asked, holding her crystal glass up to catch the morning sun's rays in the orange liquid, which was frothy with champagne.

"Mmm," Dani answered, staring out to sea over the rim of her coffee cup. The view from Arlene's terrace was beautiful, with the calm waters rolling in, then receding on the sandy shore. The same terrace where she'd first stood and talked with Adam in the still evening shadows just a few weeks ago. His little scheme had seemed like a lark then. Today Dani wasn't so sure she viewed it as such.

"You seem a little distracted, dear."

"I'm wondering why Sabrina's not here," Dani answered, turning to her mother. A little white lie seemed preferable to telling Arlene the real reason her mind was drifting. "I haven't had a chance to really talk with her since her trip. Is she all right?"

Arlene set down her glass and patted her lips with a cream-colored linen napkin. "I called to ask her to join us after you phoned that you were on your way, but she begged off. She hasn't been around much, and she seems sort of melancholy lately."

"I wonder if she didn't get involved with someone while she was in Paris, someone unattainable or someone who hurt her. Sabrina's never been terribly confiding, yet these avoidance tactics sound like man trouble to me."

"Why, Dani, have you had so much experience with men that you can spot man trouble on a woman at thirty paces?" Arlene teased with raised brows.

More than you know lately, Mother, Dani thought ruefully. "I don't have to have a love affair in order to see the unhappy signs of one on my sister."

"Sabrina involved in a love affair?" Arlene waved dismissively, the sleeves of her floral caftan lifting in a light breeze as she moved. "I seriously doubt it. I think she's just working too hard. I don't know why she puts so much of herself into her designing when she doesn't need to."

Not another one who felt this way, Dani thought, groaning inwardly. But then, she'd always known Arlene's feelings about women working. The only child of wealthy parents, her mother had coasted through Vassar and had never done anything more strenuous than hostess a cotillion or plan a fund-raiser. Which was fine if that's how she wanted to spend her life and could afford to do so. But not fine if one had other priorities. Perhaps Arlene and Adam ought to get together. They certainly thought alike.

"Sabrina *enjoys* her work, and she's good at it. Why on earth should she stay at home and vegetate if she can make a worthwhile contribution?"

"I do *not* vegetate, Danielle, if that's what you're implying," Arlene said, her wide green eyes narrowing at her youngest daughter. "I have helped raise a great deal of money for several charities, I'm on the board at my alma mater, and as you well know, I've been involved in the Foreign Student Exchange Program for years. Perhaps if you would deign to attend a few of these functions, you'd see that they don't consist simply of a few silly, bored and wealthy women thinking up ways to spend an afternoon."

Dani felt properly chastised, and her face softened. "I didn't mean to imply that what you choose to do is without value, Mother. But you shouldn't criticize Sabrina's choice, either." *Or mine,* she silently added, knowing Arlene disapproved of her vocation more heartily than of her sister's genteel occupation.

Arlene sighed audibly. "Yes, I suppose we're all different."

"Yes, and poor Dad can't understand any of us."

"Oh, he understands better than you think." Arlene pasted on a smile as the tall mustached butler set before them a steaming seafood quiche and warm croissants, then poured them each more coffee. "Smells delicious. Thank you, Joseph."

Nodding, he left them alone.

Dani put a forkful in her mouth and chewed thoughtfully. "What makes you think Dad understands us all so well?"

Arlene took several bites before answering. "That's why he left us, Dani, because he realized, first of all, that he and I were vastly different and if he remained, we would grow to dislike each other more and more. As it is, we live separate lives, but we're genuinely fond of each other. And he knows that you girls aren't like him—or me, either, for that matter. So he lets you alone to be whatever you want. He may not always approve of what each of us does, but he lets us do our own thing. I believe the young people today call it 'giving you your own space.'"

That was probably true. Carter had been extremely supportive when she'd desperately wanted a career in sports, when she'd won a skating championship at the state level, then heartbreakingly lost at the nationals, eliminating her shot at the Olympics. He'd never been with her, but he'd been there for her when she'd wanted to talk.

"Do you ever wish things were different, that Dad would come back and you could be together, really together, again?" Despite Arlene's constant frenzy of activities, there were times when Dani noticed a certain sad look in her mother's eyes.

Crossing her shapely legs, Arlene sat back. "Of course I do, but I know that things would be good only for a short time and then our differences would surface again. Carter and I never should have married. We were and still are totally wrong for each other." Her eyes were brighter than usual as she met Dani's thoughtful gaze. "Sometimes you can love a man and not be able to live with him in harmony, not want the same things from life. Two such opposites can only hurt each other if they stay together."

Dani set down her fork and leaned her elbows on the table. "And what happens if a woman finds herself falling in love with a man she knows doesn't want the same things from life that she does, a man totally wrong for her, one who might easily hurt her and walk away because she isn't anything like the kind of woman he needs or thinks he needs?"

Arlene was quiet a long moment. "We're no longer talking about Sabrina's possible affair or your father and me, are we, Dani?" She, too, leaned forward, gently touching her daughter's hand. "Tell me about this man."

But she couldn't, Dani realized as she closed her eyes and clenched her hands. She hadn't been able to discuss her first boyfriend, Billie Joe, with her mother, and she knew she couldn't bring herself to tell her about Adam. Her feelings were too new, too frightening, too uncertain, to share with Arlene, or anyone, for that matter. Slowly she opened her eyes, putting on a smile she knew didn't fool her mother.

"There's nothing to tell—honestly. I was just speaking in generalities." She knew Arlene didn't believe the lie. She also knew her mother wouldn't press. The Ames family was gifted with impeccable manners, and no one ever pried. The trait was both a blessing and a curse.

"All right, dear," Arlene said, picking up her coffee cup. "When you're ready I'm here, and I've been through it, too. But be careful, Dani. You can get hurt always reaching for the unobtainable."

Yes, Arlene had been through it, and the signs seemed to point that Sabrina had, too. Only Dani didn't want to go through it. The Ames women weren't terribly lucky in love, it would seem. The unobtainable—a good way to describe Adam Kinkaid.

As she looked out to sea, she wished she could turn the clock back to that Friday night several weeks earlier when she'd come to Arlene's party feeling carefree and foolishly invincible. Before a giant of a man with dark eyes and untamed hair had enticed her into a scheme that had entrapped her in its velvet folds.

Had she thought herself some modern-day female Svengali who could make over this man, then have him see her as the one woman he'd been seeking all along? Had she been that starry-eyed, that unrealistic, that plain dumb? Or had she joined him in his plans without a thought to the next day and the one after that, never realizing that so much time spent in the proximity of an attractive man was bound to affect her?

Vaguely Dani heard Arlene excuse herself a moment and go inside. Blinking back tears, she watched several gulls dip low in the frothy waves. How brave, how stupid, how foolish, she'd been, flying high without a thought to a possible fall. The lessons had backfired, for it seemed the teacher herself had a few things yet to learn. First and foremost was how to stop from falling in love with a man who didn't want her.

Chapter Six

The day wasn't going at all as she'd planned. Dani sat in her small office at the far end of the gymnasium and stretched her arms high, rolling her head loosely, trying to get the kinks out of her neck. She'd had to deal with a badly sprained finger right after lunch, awarding trophies at the assembly program with two names misspelled and a nervous eighth-grade girl who'd become ill on stage right after receiving her letter in gymnastics. I've definitely had better days, Dani thought, tossing her head back and popping several M & M's into her mouth.

Another couple of weeks and school would be out until fall. Usually she felt elated at spring semester's end, satisfied with her students' progress and pleased at her growth as a teacher. Her professional life was going well; the principal was very complimentary of her work. It was her personal life that was a shambles.

Glancing at the large clock over the far basketball hoop, she saw that it was already past four. She'd finished the day's paperwork, cleaned up last-minute things, and she could find no real reason to remain. Still she lingered, getting up to stroll about the gym, hands shoved in the pockets of her white cotton slacks. She felt lethargic yet restless.

The conversation she'd had with Arlene at last Sunday's brunch filtered back into her mind as it had several times over the past week. Perhaps she'd been wrong for her to have measured her mother over the years by her own harsh yardstick. Arlene was what she was, and not nearly as frivolous as Dani had all too often judged her to be. Her mother had had her share of pain married to a workaholic who'd never had time for her. Despite that, Arlene loved Carter, though she was wise enough to know they couldn't share the same address. Adjustments. Everyone had to make them.

Before Dani had been able to sneak away from Arlene's, Toni Fischer had swept in, trailing a Hermes scarf that hid the wrinkles in her neck. She'd sat down to join them amid a cloud of perfume. Dani had groaned inwardly when she'd recognized Howard's heavy footsteps only seconds behind his aunt's. They'd all insisted Dani stay for one more cup of coffee as Toni had launched into a litany of Howard's latest accomplishments, undoubtedly meant to weaken Dani's resistance to her nephew. Instead it had made her want to bolt.

When she'd finally excused herself, Howard had followed her to her car, despite her request that he stay seated with the two transparent matchmakers on the terrace. He'd asked her out for that evening, the next evening, *any* evening, and she'd politely declined each invitation. Then, much to her surprise, Howard had suddenly changed from nice to nasty and demanded to know why she wanted no part of a relationship he told her would be just short of breathtaking. Gripping her arms, he'd waxed poetic in his high-pitched voice, telling her that he cared about her, that he had even thought about marriage but would settle for living with her, if that's what she would prefer. Dani's mouth had dropped open on that one.

So she'd told him in no uncertain terms that she had no interest in him whatsoever, and to remove his sweaty hands from her. Sighing, Dani acknowledged now that it hadn't been very nice of her, yet it was kinder to let him know that she'd sooner be left all alone on an Alaskan ice floe than spend one night under the same roof with him. Not that she'd said it quite like that. Where had Howard gotten the notion that she'd even consider such an arrangement, when they'd dated only twice—at Toni's insistence—and shared one wet, sloppy kiss that had all but nauseated her?

Picking up a stray basketball she'd overlooked earlier, Dani decided every man probably thought he was irresistible and the world's greatest lover. She hadn't sampled many, and those hadn't even known how to kiss well, so intent were they on getting to the main event. Unbidden, she saw in her mind's eye a tall, rugged blond giant of a man, and she felt again the sweet, hot rush, the desire, that seemed to accompany all thoughts of Adam.

With trembling hands, Dani locked up the basketball, took another quick look about and walked outside to her car. She hadn't seen Adam since last Sunday when they'd quarreled in the parking lot and she'd scooted away, leaving him standing in the wake of her anger. Starting the motor, she admitted that her temper had cooled, while her need to see him had grown huge.

Dani let her mind drift as she drove, yet she was not surprised when, half an hour later, she found herself stopped at a light opposite the construction site where

Adam's company was working on Ames Plaza. Giving in to the impulse that had taken her this far, she swung into the parking lot next to the fenced-in work area. As she got out, she tipped back her head and stared up at the steel structure that would be the base of the main twelve-story building.

Bright orange horizontal girders supporting the vertical loads of the beams gleamed in the late-afternoon sunshine. Stacks of lumber lay in readiness at the far fence line alongside rows of cinder blocks and piles of bricks. A small wire-cage elevator sat at ground level, its housing stretching toward the blue sky above. Fascinating, Dani thought, wandering closer.

A helmeted workman carrying a black lunch pail came through just as she reached the gate. He boldly ran his eyes up and down her.

"Hi," Dani said. "Can you tell me if Adam Kinkaid's here?"

"I think he's around the other side."

"Thanks." Walking past him, Dani wondered what kind of a reception she'd get from Adam, since he'd been strangely unavailable all week after he'd mentioned wanting to step up the progress of his lessons. Carefully she made her way among the scattered pieces of board, the nails and debris on the ground.

Adam had just yanked off his hard hat and was rounding the bend, when he spotted her. There was that momentary flutter deep in his chest, the one he always seemed to experience on first sight of her. Why? he asked himself, when Dani Ames was nothing to him except a means to an end. Or was she?

Stepping forward, he saw her lift her chin and meet his gaze. Her look was measuring, unwavering, somewhat challenging. He didn't quite know what to make of it. "I thought you'd given up on me," he said quietly.

"Did you?" she asked, her voice soft and low.

Out of the corner of his eye he saw the last two men leave through the gate and wave to him, but his gaze never left Dani's. He had to try to set things right between them. "I want your help, but I'm not going to beg."

"I wouldn't expect you to. I do expect you to remember who wants to be changed here and who doesn't."

Adam took a deep breath. He'd been wrong, and he'd been stewing over it all week. He'd had no business all but demanding she live her life as he saw fit. She wasn't his sister, or daughter. She wasn't his concern. "I was out of line. I'm sorry if I pushed."

She could see apologies didn't come easily to him. She was also never one to hold a grudge after an apology had been offered. She noted that he looked wonderful, in his snug jeans and black T-shirt, though he needed a shave. Slowly she let her face break into a smile and watched as the expression in his eyes immediately warmed. Feeling as if a weight had been lifted from her shoulders, she tore her gaze from his and looked up at the top of the uppermost structure.

"I stopped by to collect on a promise you made the night we met," Dani said, thinking it was as good a reason as any to explain her sudden appearance.

"You really want to go up?"

"I really want to go up."

"You're on, lady," he said, his smile coming easily now. "I hope you aren't the fainting type. It's no picnic up there."

"I've never fainted in my life."

"Good."

He plunked his hard hat on her head and smiled broadly when she adjusted it to a more becoming angle. He pulled open the metal elevator door and held it for her, then followed her inside. He started the elevator and turned to watch her.

Dani gave herself fully to the experience, relishing the air as it whipped against her cheeks, glorying in the sun's rays on her face. Though one hand gripped the elevator cage and her stomach churned as the clanking elevator whirred upward, inside she was unbelievably thrilled. A curious bird swooped by, looking disturbed by their territorial invasion. They jolted to a stop, and she turned to see Adam's amused gaze on her face.

"You're laughing at me," Dani told him.

She looked a little the way she must have at age six on Christmas Day—astonished, delighted. A child with no fear and very little hesitation. "Never." He held the door wide and stepped out onto beams only fractionally wider than his heavy work shoes. He hoped no one from the insurance company saw him up here with an unauthorized female. "Now comes the tough part. Just to be on the safe side, put one arm around my waist and run the other along this girder I'm touching. Stay close behind me and step only where I step. And *don't look down!*"

Taking a deep breath, Dani followed, gauging her steps to match his. Her hand slid along just behind his. When she'd suggested this ride up, she hadn't thought she'd have to be all but glued to him, but common sense told her it was necessary.

The wind was stronger up here, with swift swirls and unexpected billows. The air seemed purer, though, and she inhaled deeply. Close up against Adam, she breathed in his scent as well, one she now easily recognized, and felt it tug at her senses.

Abruptly Adam stopped. "I'm going to turn around now, so hold still," he said, disengaging himself from her. Then, facing her, he slid his arms about her and maneuvered her free hand around his back. Immediately she grabbed a handful of shirt and allowed herself to be held.

"Well, what do you think?" he asked.

"The view is breathtaking," she answered, trying to concentrate on it rather than the way her blood raced at his nearness. "How do you get anything done up here, on these narrow ledges? I should think you'd spend most of your time watching the scenery or concentrating on not falling off." The wind took the words from her mouth, making her sound breathy.

"You get used to it, like anything else. The men develop a keener sense of balance and can walk around without holding on. And they often work sitting down, straddling the girders."

She looked around, busily taking it all in. "Have you ever—has anyone . . . ever fallen?"

"I've heard of a few. Uh-uh! Don't look down. That's when the dizziness starts. Look up." He angled his head upward to prove his point.

No, the dizziness starts when a man you find yourself wanting holds you tightly against himself, whether on the ground or twelve stories up, Dani decided. Desire she had no business feeling made her shiver. Looking up, she tried to ignore her hormones.

Adam thought he felt her tremble. Was she more frightened than she let on? His arms encircling her waist, he leaned back almost lazily from her, leaving only the lower part of their bodies in contact. "When you were a kid, did you ever lie in the grass in the summertime, watch the clouds roll by and see pictures in them?" he asked, hoping to distract her. He still wasn't convinced she wouldn't faint on him.

"Sure," Dani answered. He thought she sounded grateful for the diversion. She twisted her neck. "Over there's an elephant. See his trunk in the up position? And alongside is an oak tree with a huge, gnarled trunk."

"How about on this side?" Adam asked, warming to the game. "I see Santa Claus just over there, with his puffy white beard and big, fat belly. And just right of your shoulder is an airplane."

Craning her neck but not losing her hold on him, Dani looked, then turned back to him. "That's a *real* airplane, goof."

"So it is," he said. The blue sky behind her made her eyes look bluer, and their beauty dazzled him. He'd wanted her to come back, and she had. He'd wanted to return to their earlier easy camaraderie, and it seemed she wanted that, too. Perversely, he'd wanted her to look upon him as a man, and now that he saw in her eyes that she did, he didn't know what in hell to do about it.

"Are you frightened of falling?" he asked.

Yes, frightened of falling, she thought. But not from the building. "I feel safe with you."

Safe. Is that all she felt with him? he wondered. Her eyes told a different story. A gust of wind shuddered by. Dani automatically leaned closer into him, her hand on his back moving restlessly. Then something startled her and she lifted her head suddenly, causing her hard hat to slip off.

"Oh!" she exclaimed, clutching his upper arms, her hands bunching the cotton of his shirt.

"Let it go. Don't look down." He watched her eyes grow wide as she heard the faint plink of the hat hitting the ground twelve floors below.

"I'm sorry."

"It's all right," Adam said, watching the wind toss her curls about her flushed face. He'd always liked long hair on women—long and full and thick. But that had been before he'd seen Dani's.

Tenderness was new to him. He'd had no time for it and not much need—his mother had always been self-sufficient and had tirelessly seen to his sister's emotional crises. Why, then, should this slender young woman, despite her superior education, breeding and wealth, seem so vulnerable to him, evoking a tenderness in him he thought himself incapable of feeling?

"Have you ever been kissed high atop the world, with the wind racing through your hair and the blood churning through your veins?" he asked, his voice suddenly throaty. The words were no sooner out of his mouth than he regretted them, for he felt her withdraw, and not just physically.

Mesmerizing, Dani thought. That's what he was, his strong, hard hands soothing her, his deep, soft voice lulling her, his dark, mysterious eyes challenging her. But she couldn't be so affected. There was no point, when he would lead her nowhere except to heartbreak.

"No, I haven't," Dani said in a voice that was suddenly firm. "And I don't plan on starting today." Grabbing hold of the girder, she steadied herself. "I think it best that you save your high-rise kisses for the woman we're grooming you for." Carefully she turned. "I'd like to go back down."

During the creaky ride back to the ground, Adam berated himself. Damn, but he couldn't seem to make a move without screwing up lately. At this rate he was going to have to cough up an apology every day or so. He opened the elevator door and let her out.

Clearing his throat noisily, Adam grasped at a straw. "Clancy's coming over tonight, and I was hoping you could join us."

Damn him for turning every touch into a caress, Dani thought, for twisting every small encounter into a mini-seduction, for reminding her that she was a woman yearning for a man. This man. And damn her self-control for deserting her every time she was in Adam's presence. Putting on a cool look that required no small effort, Dani stopped and looked up at him. "Join you for what?"

"Well, I've mentioned this...this project of ours to Clancy, and he knows a guy who owes him a favor. Clancy knows most of Boston, and half of it owes him favors. Emile's a tailor, owns a little shop near town. He's bringing some sample tuxedos. I'd sure appreciate your help in picking one out." For long minutes, Dani just stared into his eyes. Adam shifted his weight from one foot to the other. "For the opera we talked about attending, you know. Or maybe the ballet."

Nervous, she mused. He was nervous. And nervy, too, talking about kissing in one breath, then making a business request the next, as if they hadn't been pressed together, hearts beating seemingly in unison, just minutes earlier. Well, if it didn't bother him, she'd be damned before she'd let him see that it bothered her. There would be safety in numbers with Clancy and the tailor there. She'd go and tough it out, show Mr. Kinkaid a thing or two.

"All right. What time do you want me there?"

"You'll come?"

"I just said I would."

He'd been dead sure she'd turn him down, but again she'd surprised him. He glanced at his watch. "About eight, okay?"

Nodding, Dani turned on her heel. "See you then. Thanks for the ride to the top."

Watching her long-legged strides, Adam ran a hand through his hair. Moodiest damn woman he'd ever met, he thought, shaking his head.

"You look like a blond penguin, my friend," Clancy said with a grin. "A muscular, blond penguin."

"Thanks. I needed that," Adam replied with a frown, looking ill at ease in tuxedo pants, a tuxedo jacket unbuttoned over a white T-shirt, and his stocking feet.

"The formal wear, it takes some getting used to," Emile the tailor said in a silky French accent as he fussily danced around Adam, pulling at a sleeve, patting a shoulder. "Maybe if you put shoes on, we get the whole effect."

"He owns only sneakers and work boots," Clancy commented from his vantage point on Adam's couch.

"Oh, no," Emile moaned. "We need the patent-leather dancing pumps."

That nearly finished Clancy, who leaned forward in a fit of coughing.

"The coat seems a little snug," Dani interjected, trying for a serious note. "Don't you agree, Emile?"

The little tailor, balding and not quite five feet tall, squinted through thick glasses. "Perhaps. We go back to the bedroom. Try another one s'il vous plaît?"

"Right," Adam answered, leading the way.

Dani let out the giggle she'd been suppressing as Clancy, struggling for control, lost it. She'd liked Clancy at first sight. Not much taller than she, he was so muscular that he gave the impression of being far bigger. His shoulders were broader than Adam's, his strong facial features could only be described as craggy and he had a thick head of very black hair. His eyes were a startling blue, and his nose had been broken twice, giving it a slightly off-center look. And he had a deep cleft in his chin. Her father would have described Clancy as black Irish. He was, Dani decided in the hour she'd spent with him, amazingly genuine, extremely loyal and very likable.

Clancy reached for his beer mug, downed half the contents, then set the glass down. "So you're trying to turn that sow's ear into a silk purse, are you, Dani?" he asked, settling back and stretching an arm along the couch.

"I guess you could say that." In the opposite corner of the couch, Dani angled her body toward Clancy. "You don't approve?"

"I like him the way he is." He gave her a lazy smile. "What about you?"

The direct approach. Dani rather liked that. Fencing always made her nervous. And she wasn't fooled for a moment by Clancy's seemingly nonchalant look. A hard-boiled cop, a protective best friend and a shrewd interrogator lurked behind those deceptively innocent blue eyes. "I like him the way he is, too. Adam's the one who wants to change."

Clancy nodded. "So I've heard. So Bonnie can make a big splash at a coming-out party. Did you have a debutante ball given for you?"

"Yes."

"What was it like?"

She'd hated it. She'd been too thin for the dress Arlene had selected for her and too tall for all the boys her mother had invited. Dani shrugged. "Like all the others. A painful ordeal when you're shy. I think Bonnie's a little too old for all that, and she should be grateful."

Clancy reached for his mug and crossed his long legs. "You don't impress me as terribly shy."

"I was at sixteen." Maybe she could get a few answers from this man, who'd known the Kinkaids since childhood. "How do you think Bonnie will view all that Adam wants for her?"

His shrug was noncommittal. "Bonnie's more her own person than Adam realizes."

A careful answer. But then, behind that Irish charm lived a careful man. "I certainly hope so."

"And now we have another fine suit to consider," Emile announced, scurrying into the room ahead of Adam. "The morning coat, to go with pleated trousers."

As they studied the gray-striped cutaway, Adam stood frowning. Dani could tell he wished he were anywhere else but here, doing this.

"No, that won't do," she told Emile regretfully. "We're not attending a wedding but a formal evening affair."

Chuckling, Clancy rolled his eyes. "Looks like that should be *mourning*."

Adam's scowl deepened.

"Don't you have something like the Pierre Cardin tuxedo, styled with slim lapels and classic lines?" Dani asked, trying to get an image in Emile's mind before Adam got thoroughly discouraged.

"Ah, yes. Come, Mr. Kinkaid. We try again."

Adam followed the tailor out of the room as Dani shook her head. "This may take a while," she said, sipping the beer Adam had poured for her earlier. Putting the mug back on the glass-topped table, she saw several wet rings and hoped Adam's cleaning lady wouldn't scold him for allowing his guests to mess up his immaculate living room. "Adam certainly keeps a neat house, doesn't he?" she asked Clancy.

"Yeah, too neat," Clancy stated emphatically. "But when you spend the first twenty years of your life sleeping on a daybed, sharing three rooms with a mother and younger sister, having one drawer to stuff all your belongings into, clutter and confusion everywhere, you tend to lean toward neat and orderly when you get the chance.''

She had to agree. "I understand you helped Adam build this house."

"Sure did," Clancy said, gazing around the high-ceilinged room. "About seven years ago. Worked all summer long and halfway into fall, but we finished before the rains came."

"It's a great house."

He turned to her, his look bland. "It needs a woman's touch. Not this *House Beautiful* decorating, but the homey, warm look only a woman can give it. Like that plant you brought over tonight."

On an impulse, Dani had stopped on her way home from the construction site to purchase a huge potted philodendron, and brought it over for Adam, introducing the plant as Felix, brother to her Oscar. The gesture, more than the gift itself, had taken him aback, and his awkward acceptance had made her smile. She hadn't bothered to tell him she'd brought it more in an effort to deinstitutionalize his house than as a present per se. Felix now sat in the far corner, adding, as Clancy had pointed out, a certain warmth that had been lacking, though the room could use a few more changes.

"Madam, is this more what you had in mind?" Emile inquired, entering and standing aside as Adam walked in.

Dani's breath caught in her throat. She'd never seen Adam really dressed up, and she nearly reeled at the sight. *Handsome* seemed inadequate, *attractive* not strong enough. *Magnificent* was closer to the mark. The black tuxedo fell over his broad shoulders, narrow waist and lean thighs as if the suit had been designed for him and him alone. The pleated white shirtfront all but sparkled against his tanned skin, and the broad bow tie added an elegant touch. No frills, no fuss, just masculine perfection.

Swallowing, Dani nodded. "Yes, it's exactly what I had in mind."

That set her back on her ear, Adam thought, valiantly trying to hide a smile. Had him pegged as all blue jeans and work boots, did she? Nice to know he could surprise her, since she so often threw him a curve.

"Damn if you don't clean up pretty good," Clancy stated. "For a construction cowboy."

Cowboy, my elbow, Dani thought. At this moment, Adam Kinkaid looked every inch the city sophisticate, from the top of his blond head to the tips of the black shoes he'd found somewhere.

Adam smiled, enjoying Dani's gaze traveling over him again. He'd never been one to look forward to dressing up, but if doing so got this kind of reaction from women, maybe he'd do it more. "Do you think Sabrina would be embarrassed to be seen with me in this?" he asked.

She dropped her eyes. "Hardly."

Emile beamed. "Then this is the one, no?"

"This is the one, yes," Adam told him.

"Good, good," Emile said, nodding happily and hurrying Adam off to the bedroom before he could change his mind.

Clancy drained his mug and stood. "So you're going to drag my buddy off to the opera and give him a shot of culture, eh?" He swept a large hand through his hair and gave Dani a doubtful look. "I wonder if there's a woman in the world worth making myself over for. I'd be more inclined to say that if she doesn't want me the way I am, I don't want her. You've been in that world Adam wants to conquer, Dani. What's so special about it?"

She shrugged. "I suppose it has a certain appeal for some people."

"But no longer for you?"

Dani saw why Lieutenant Michael J. Clancy was good at his job. Who could lie looking into those bright blue eyes? "No, no longer for me."

Clancy glanced at his watch. "I've got to run." He reached to shake her hand. "Dani, I'm glad to meet you finally after hearing Adam talk about you for weeks."

He had? she thought. "It was my pleasure."

"I know you're not crazy about this scheme, but as long as Adam had to take on such a project, I'm glad he found someone like you to guide him. I think you're good for him."

Good for him. Like vitamins, fiber and moderation. Great. She gave Clancy a weak smile as he turned and went into Adam's bedroom to say goodbye. Moments later he left with a wave, but it was several minutes more before Emile emerged with his suitcase and wished her a goodnight.

Back in jeans and a T-shirt, Adam stood before her and heaved a deep sigh. "I'm glad that's over with."

Dani was, too. Inexplicably, she suddenly felt tired, as if she'd just run the hundred-yard dash several times on a hot, muggy day. Quickly she stood. "I'll be leaving, too."

"Wait one minute, can you?"

Now what? She shot him a questioning look.

"It's early, only a little after nine. Let's go outside, where it's cooler. I need to talk something over with you."

Why did she get the feeling she should have quietly crept away when Emile had been busily taking Adam's measurements? Warily, she followed him out onto the back patio, where he dropped down on a two-seater swing that hung from two sturdy chains. She sat beside him and waited.

"Did I thank you for the plant? It adds a lot to the room. What did you name it again?"

"Yes, you did thank me, and his name is Felix."

"Right." Adam stretched an arm along the back of the wooden swing but refrained from touching her. He looked up at a star-studded sky, wondering how to begin. The waves rolled in relentlessly, leaving behind a salty foam on the sandy shore. He let out a whoosh of air. "I'm not sure where to begin."

"Try the beginning."

"Okay. It's occurred to me that I've overlooked some important details in the past. About women, I mean. I've never bothered learning the niceties. You know, pretty words, hearts and flowers. Women like that sort of thing, right?"

"Most of them, yes."

"Do you?"

She felt a flash of temper. "Of course I do. What did you think, that I only care about basketball and field hockey?"

Testy, he thought. She'd been real testy since this afternoon up on the building. Now probably wasn't the best time to bring this up, but if he was to get anywhere with her kind of woman—that is, women like her sister and her who were well-bred—he had to know how to do certain things he hadn't considered important before. "I need to know how to romance a woman, Dani."

Her eyes flew to his. Was he mocking her? No, she saw only a sincere plea. Damn! How could this man be so—so insensitive in his sincerity? "That isn't as easy as it sounds, Adam."

"Could you try? Could you tell me how a woman like Sabrina might expect her date to behave, what would win her over?"

She'd never thought this would be part of the lesson plan. She crossed her bare legs and tucked her blouse more neatly into her shorts to give herself a little time to think. "Well, most women like flowers, especially when they're sent for no particular reason, just as a reminder that her special man is thinking of her. One rose sent unexpectedly can mean more than a dozen sent on a birthday. Women also like to be pampered a bit. You know, ordering a limousine for a special event. A sincere compliment is always nice to hear, especially an unexpected one at the end of a tiring day. Looking up, she saw he was listening intently.

"Go on."

"Let's see. Maybe a man could recognize a woman's favorite perfume and get her a small bottle. Or give her a basket of strawberries on the first day of summer. Or surprise her with tickets to a play she'd casually mentioned wanting to see. Crazy gifts, fun things that they can enjoy together, often mean more than an expensive pair of gloves or an imported handbag." Dani smiled at an old memory. "I remember once when someone gave me a cluster of balloons with a note that read 'Just because it's Thursday and I thought of you.' Now there's a romantic soul."

A twinge of jealousy caught him unawares. "Who was he?" Adam asked.

"Carlos, a sixteen-year-old exchange student who lived with us one summer. Even at that age he was romantic."

"How old were you?"

"Nineteen."

Yes, he could see why a young man would feel romantic toward Dani. There was a gentleness in her that would evoke tender thoughts in any man. "What other romantic gestures would please a woman?"

"Oh, surely you know some yourself. Some are almost clichés. A touch on her cheek or her hair as you pass. A look across a crowded room, as they say in old songs. A kiss that makes her feel cherished."

Adam raised his eyebrows as he angled his body toward hers. "What kind of kiss is that?"

"Now, Adam, I'm certain I don't have to explain kissing to you," she replied, thinking he probably could have written the book on that one.

"Ah, but we both know there are all kinds of kisses." With his voice he teased, lulled, as he moved fractionally closer. He trailed his fingers along her nape, then traced her jaw, turning her face toward him as the thought occurred to him that this was exactly what he'd been subconsciously leading up to since she'd moved out of his embrace this afternoon twelve stories up in the sky.

"There's the kiss a man gives his mother," Adam said, his voice whisper soft as he kissed her cheek.

"And the kiss a man gives his sister." He brushed her forehead with his lips. "And the kiss a young man gives on a first date." Adam chastely pressed his mouth to hers. He pretended not to notice as Dani stubbornly kept her lips tightly together. "I know all those kisses. Now you show *me* a kiss that would make a woman—or a man—feel cherished."

Show him! Oh, no. "Er, let me see if I can describe it. A soft kiss, a slow and tender kiss, a loving, involved kiss." Frustrated and feeling herself flush, she shook her head. "This is silly. You know what I mean."

"No, I really don't." He slid his arm around her shoulders, again gently turning her toward him. "One demonstration is worth a thousand words. Come on, Dani. It's just a simple kiss. What are you afraid of?''

"I'm *not* afraid." He was challenging her, and she knew it. Knew it and should be smart enough to ignore it, to walk away. But the male scent of him enveloped her; the taste of him was already on her tongue. Impatience to know him sprang to the surface. What harm could there be in one kiss?

"Then show me."

Swallowing, Dani shifted her eyes to his and found his gaze fastened to her. "All right," she said. This one time she would indulge him—and herself. Slowly she raised her arms and placed a hand on each side of his face, enjoying the slightly scratchy feeling of him. "If a woman were to give you a kiss to make you feel cherished, she'd probably begin by touching you lightly, like this, then perhaps linger to caress you for a long moment." And she followed her words with the action, feeling her heart pound like a trip-hammer.

Adam watched her silently without changing his expression. He'd started this game knowing full well where he wanted it to lead, and now that the moment was at hand, he wondered what had happened to the self-control he'd always been able to count on. She had him damn near trembling, and she'd scarcely touched him. The experience was as new to him as it was alarming.

Dani let her gaze drop to his mouth as her thumbs slowly traced his lower lip. Though he didn't move, she saw the pulse in his neck leap to life. Challenge her, would he? she thought.

She moved closer, sliding her hands to his shoulders. "Then she might run her lips along your cheeks, like this." Her mouth quivered as she touched his skin, once, twice, three times. "And perhaps kiss your eyelids." He closed his eyes, and she felt the shudder he couldn't control when she demonstrated. She was beginning to enjoy this.

"Then she'd taste your throat—" and she did "—feel your pulse beat with her tongue." Her breathing was shallow now as she moved on, tasting him, learning him. "Perhaps she'd kiss each corner of your mouth, like so...then place a soft kiss on your temples." As she did, he moved his hands to her back, pulling her nearer, and she wondered if he was aware he had.

Never had Adam had a woman draw out the prelude to a kiss to this extent; never had he thought there could be so much pleasure in anticipation. Her lips were incredibly soft. Where had she learned to torture a man so... deliciously? he wondered hazily.

Dani lifted her eyes and saw that Adam's had darkened to a charcoal brown. She felt a sizzling heat move down her spine. Too late to turn back now, she told herself. Slowly she buried her fingers in the thickness of his hair as she shifted and touched the tip of her tongue to his lips and trailed it along the bottom lip, then completed the circle. She closed the gap between them as she felt him open to her. Gentle still, savoring, she allowed her tongue to enter and touch his. At the contact, she felt his arms tighten about her.

Adam felt a need to take charge as the power of the kiss whirled through him, shocking his senses, all but destroying his control. He'd meant to nudge her into a kiss— strictly a male trick he'd employed often enough—and had instead wound up the trapped one. Trapped by sensations that demanded more than teased, trapped by the realization that what he'd been looking for, he'd found.

She hesitated only moments, then offered, unquestioningly, and gratefully he took from her. He could smell her—that elusive wildflower fragrance she seemed to exude from her pores, that exhilarating warmth that emanated from her. He could taste her—captivating, tantalizing, giving. He could feel her—tight up against him, slender and soft, not holding back.

Her hands in his hair, her mouth moving under his, Dani absorbed from him, drank him in, delighted in him. Her body fit so snugly into his—had it been fashioned for this? Her heart beat in time with his—had it been waiting for this? Her need churned inside her—had it been building toward this? Where had this passion come from, this almost painful yet glorious passion?

As she moved against him, Adam felt his mind and his good sense spin away. How had they come so far so quickly, when he'd merely wanted to sample her? Even as he formed the thought he recognized the lie. Who was he kidding? He'd been wanting to hold her from the beginning. Wanting to hold her, to touch her, not just her face but everywhere.

This was madness; this was going to ruin a growing friendship, ruin everything. And it was this thought that had him pulling back, when he wanted so badly to take her inside to his bedroom and let the pupil become the teacher.

Dani opened her eyes slowly, blinked to clear them, then quickly pulled back from him. Stunned, she dropped her gaze and clenched her hands to still them. "Adam, this isn't..."

He stood, causing the swing to glide into motion. "I know. This isn't what you want. It isn't what I want, either." He raised a shaky hand and touched the top of her head. "I'm sorry, Dani. I got carried away. I shouldn't have pushed."

Not what he wanted, not what she wanted, Dani thought. They wanted altogether different things from life, and an involvement, even a brief, merely physical one, would only complicate things. As Adam said, he'd gotten carried away, and so had she. It would have to be up to her to see that it didn't happen again. Or she'd simply have to walk away from their little project.

Mutt came leaping out of the shadows, surprising them both. Somewhat unsteadily, Dani got to her feet and stepped off the porch, avoiding his eyes. "Good night, Adam."

"I'll call you next week," he said, watching her walk away, questioning even as he said it if that was such a good idea. Damn! Why her? She was everything he seemed to need in a woman, yet she rejected everything he needed for his plan. He'd plotted too long, worked too hard, to abandon it all now. As he opened the door and went inside, Adam wondered how something that had seemed so simple had become so complicated.

Chapter Seven

He's probably killed him by now, Oscar," Dani mumbled as she gently pruned a few leaves from the philodendron. "Killed your adopted brother right in his pot in the corner of the living room. I shouldn't have given him a nice plant like Felix. Five will get you ten he's neglected him."

Rising from her kneeling position, she stood back to admire her handiwork. "There, that's better. Let's concentrate on staying green, shall we?" A warm night breeze from the open window ruffled the top leaves, and she took that as Oscar's nod of agreement. Sighing, Dani put away her clippers.

"Or maybe that fastidious cleaning lady of his has spray-waxed him. I wouldn't be surprised." Throwing out her half-eaten peanut-butter-and-jelly sandwich, she popped a couple of M & M's into her mouth. As she chewed thoughtfully, she wondered why she was dwelling on the fate of the plant she'd given Adam. Because, she had to admit, it was easier than thinking about the man himself.

If Adam was troubled about their odd relationship, he was handling his feelings admirably. He hadn't called or come by in seven days—and three hours and twelve minutes, but who was counting? She'd dropped off several librettos he'd asked for, but the house had been empty and silent, and she'd stuffed them inside the screen door. She hadn't had any contact with him since the night she'd helped him pick out his tux, the night they'd shared a stunning kiss that had tilted her world, maybe permanently. And she had no one to blame but herself.

At nineteen she'd fallen in love, but not since. His name had been Billie Joe, and they'd both been hoping for a spectacular career in ice skating. She'd thought him wildly handsome, bright, funny and terribly romantic. She'd almost given him her innocence, until she'd realized he wanted to change her, make her into someone she didn't want to be. It had been a heartbreaking lesson. Loving made you sometimes foolish, often the butt of jokes, always vulnerable, she'd discovered. Next time would be different, she'd vowed. She'd be careful, move slowly, use her head, and she'd kept that vow. But now...

Stop it! Dani chided herself, as she walked into the living room. She'd done enough soul-searching, enough agonizing, this past week to last a month of Sundays. Switching on a small lamp, she sat down at her piano and idly ran her fingers over the keys. Often she could lose herself in music, let her hands transport her to a place where troubles melted like lemon drops. Yes, she needed to go over the rainbow. Closing her eyes, Dani began the soothing chords of a Chopin nocturne....

Feeling oddly like a voyeur—or at the very least a trespasser—Adam stood in the shadows outside Dani's living room, watching and listening to her play. He'd been walking restlessly on the beach and had heard the music when he was several houses away. Curious, he'd walked closer, and now stood caught up in her spell.

She put all her energy into her playing, caressing the keys with the intimacy of a lover's touch, bringing out the intricate harmony. He wasn't a student of classical music, but he recognized an involved performance when he heard it.

She was playing with unbridled passion, revealing emotions he'd seen in her only once before—the night he'd kissed her. This was no quiet lamb. This was a woman with hidden depths and a wildness he was only beginning to discover. The pity of it was that she was not for him. With a hard knock on her door, he walked in, calling her name.

Startled, Dani stopped playing. She turned to see Adam walking through the archway into her living room.

"I knocked several times," he said.

"I didn't hear."

She was skittish, wary. Trying to put her at ease, he smiled as he removed a stack of magazines from a chair and sat down. "I'm here on official business, partner. I read the librettos you dropped off, and though I'm not sure I understand opera, I'm willing to take a chance. *Madama Butterfly* is on in Boston, and I got two tickets for us for Friday night."

Frowning, Dani swung her legs around on the piano bench and grabbed a handful of M & M's. Official business, she mused. What a charming invitation. "Were you so certain I'd jump at the chance to go with you?" Savagely she crunched on the candy.

Putting on a boyish smile, Adam looked her squarely in the eye. "I was hoping you would."

Presumptuous, arrogant, demanding. She'd wanted to see him and now that he was here, she wanted...she wanted... Just what did she want? "Why don't you ask Sabrina?" she challenged him, hating the perversity that fueled this unreasonable anger.

"I don't think I'm ready for her."

So Dani Ames was to be a practice model, she thought. Wonderful. How flattering. The sweet chocolate stuck in her throat, and she swallowed thickly. But she had agreed several weeks ago to attend the opera with him. Well, she'd follow through on her promise. And then he could damn well be on his own, sink or swim. She'd about had it with this dumb project.

"What time will you pick me up?" Dani asked as she stood, hoping he'd interpret her move as a dismissal.

Slowly Adam got to his feet. "It starts at eight. Seven all right?"

"Fine."

She'd get over this by Saturday, Adam reassured himself. Nodding, he turned to leave. "See you then."

Walking home, he was oddly hurt that she hadn't even said goodbye. Maybe she'd had a bad day. School teachers had it rough, kids being what they were today. Sure, that was probably it.

He saw the car pulled up close in front of his house and grinned. Clancy's beat-up black '72 Mustang. You'd have thought that one of Boston's finest would drive a more presentable car, but Clancy loved his disreputable hunk of junk. A talk with his best friend might be just what he needed, Adam decided.

He found Clancy in the kitchen, finishing the bucket of chicken Adam had only made a dent in for his dinner. Clancy had his own key, one of the privileges of friendship that went back more than twenty years.

"Thought you had to be out walking, since both your vehicles were in the drive," Clancy said, looking up from his plate, which was heaped with chicken bones.

"Yeah, I was," Adam said, getting them both a beer from the refrigerator. He sat down across from Clancy, popping the caps and placed a bottle in front of him. After taking a long swallow, he looked at his friend. "What's new?"

Clancy polished off the drumstick and peered into the shallow bucket. "Not much. Haven't heard from you lately, so I thought I'd come see how you're doing." He picked up the last piece of chicken and gazed at Adam. "How's the makeover coming?"

Adam shrugged. "Okay."

"Uh-huh." Clancy took a bite and chewed. "You don't look any different. Sounds like the program's run out of steam."

"We're going to the opera Friday evening. *Madama Butterfly.*"

"You in the monkey suit and Dani in a slinky gown?"

"Guess so."

Finishing, Clancy wiped his hands and took a big swig of beer. "What's she like, Adam?"

"Who?"

"Danielle Winthrop Ames. Your teacher. Your partner."

"She's okay." Shifting, Adam realized his comment was inadequate, but he wasn't quite sure how to describe Dani. "She plays classical piano, beats me at tennis and serves four-course meals, each course with its own wine."

Clancy raised his brows. "That's different. Doesn't sound like you have much in common."

No, not much in common. "Her house is a mess. Even her purse is a disaster." But she's squeaky clean and smells like wildflowers. "She talks to her plants like they were her friends, and she feeds this mangy old cat who should have been put to sleep two lives ago and refuses to listen to me when I tell her he'd be better off that way."

Clancy nodded, his eyes watchful. "Good thing you're not romancing her. She doesn't sound like your kind of woman."

"You got that right." Adam swallowed more beer he didn't want. "She'd rather teach school than get a good-paying job, she has this scruffy dog who follows her everywhere, and her favorite food is peanut butter." And Adam had never been drawn to anyone so much in his life.

"Well, maybe her sister or one of her friends will be more to your liking when you get to know them."

"Bound to be." Adam crossed his long legs. "You know how Dani spends her Sunday mornings?"

Clancy got up to throw away the paper container and rinse his hands. "No, how?"

"Hangs around Central High and referees basketball games for inner-city kids." Adam shook his head. "I told her that one day she'd walk out into the parking lot and find the hubcaps missing off her Mercedes, if not the whole damn car."

Sitting down again, Clancy ran his hand through his dark hair, which he wore regulation short. "I don't think so. She's got Duffy watching out for her, and most of those kids wouldn't want to mess with him."

Adam looked over, surprised. "You know Duffy?"

"Sure. Most of the cops know Duffy. He's been in and out of trouble for years. His dad took off years ago, and his mom cleans office buildings. And drinks a little. Sound familiar?"

Adam didn't miss the parallel with Clancy's troubled youth—and a bit of his own. For a moment he was re-

minded of the brash young hellion named Clancy, who'd
been born fighting.

Clancy continued, "But since he met Dani, he keeps his
nose clean."

"I saw he had a crush on her, but I didn't think she
could influence him all that much, seeing him only a couple of times a month."

Clancy drained his beer and leaned forward. "More
than that. I first met Duffy last summer when I used to go
back to the old neighborhood now and again, toss a few
baskets with Al Donaldson and his kids. Duffy was flunk-
ing out of school and running with a gang of petty thieves.
We all knew it was only a matter of time before Juvenile
hauled him in. I'd had several talks with him, but I wasn't
getting through. I found out later from his counselor that
Dani Ames had learned about Duffy's problems and
stepped in. She started tutoring him on the side, got him a
job, spent time with him. Even took his mother to an AA
meeting, but I haven't got high hopes of that lasting."

Adam nodded. That sounded like something Dani
would do.

"Anyhow, Duffy graduates from grade school next
week. Not at the top of his class, but he is graduating. And
Dani's finagled him a scholarship to a parochial high
school. Now you know why he's so crazy about her. She's
taught him a lot more than basketball."

*"As a kid masters a game like basketball, he also picks
up a few hints on how to master the game of life,"* Dani
had told him. And he'd been skeptical, thinking her na-
ive. Perhaps she had molded a few minds. "I've heard
she's a pretty good teacher."

"Sounds like it. Look, Adam, I don't want to come on
like a big brother here, but you sure you want to continue

with this project? Maybe you should just let Bonnie take her chances. A rich guy could hurt her, too.''

Stubbornly Adam shook his head. ''I'm going to be there, get to know those people, introduce her myself. I'm not leaving this to chance. She can just as easily fall in love with the right guy as the wrong one—but first she's got to meet him.''

Looking weary, Clancy stood and shoved both hands into his pockets. ''Look, Cupid, I don't think it's all that easy to find two people, push them together and say, 'Here, live happily ever after!' You're overlooking feelings and personal taste and maybe the most important thing.''

''What's that?''

''Chemistry.''

Adam stood firm. ''I say *any* two people can fall in love, given the right set of circumstances.''

''Really? Why haven't you?''

''I haven't been looking.''

Clancy clapped his friend on the shoulder as Adam got to his feet, and they walked to the door together. ''Sometimes it hits hardest when you're not looking, old buddy. Thanks for dinner. See you later.''

Standing in the darkened doorway, Adam watched Clancy leave, wondering what he'd meant by that last remark.

Jasmine for tonight, Dani thought, reaching for the bottle and spraying on her favorite scent. Her bedroom clock chimed seven as she checked herself in the mirror, remembering how sophisticated Adam had looked in formal clothes. Yes, she would be a good counterpoint to him tonight.

It had been a long time since she'd dressed up, and though she didn't choose to do so often, occasionally it was fun and made her feel feminine. She'd chosen a backless silk halter-style gown, that was softly clinging and settled around her ankles like a cloud of white smoke. Her shoes, high heeled and consisting mostly of straps, wouldn't be a problem with a man as tall as Adam. As usual, she'd chosen subtle makeup, using a bit more eyeliner, which gave her eyes a large, luminous look. The doorbell sounded, and, taking a deep breath, Dani picked up her evening bag and went to answer.

Adam had his eyes on his shoes when the door opened. As he raised them and settled his gaze on Dani, she felt the heat of his response. Beautiful. She was absolutely beautiful. The anger was gone from her wide blue eyes, replaced by a sultriness he'd never seen there before. He'd felt a lot more comfortable with her in blue jeans and cotton shirts. Swallowing, he stepped inside.

"The tux fits you beautifully," Dani told him, finding her voice before he found his. Evidently she'd jarred him a little. Good.

"Thanks." He suddenly seemed to remember what he was holding. "This is for you."

One long-stemmed perfect red rose. He'd taken her romance lessons to heart, she marveled. "It's lovely," she whispered, bringing it to her nose.

"Not nearly as lovely as you."

Dani dropped her gaze, amused at his reaction. "Thank you." Had he thought she owned only sportswear and gym shoes? He seemed uncomfortable, yet he'd been preparing for this evening for over a month. His hair was nicely shaped and behaving; his clothes were just right. Even his hands were well groomed. Only his eyes hadn't changed much. They were still dark, probing, intense.

Giving him a smile, she laid a hand on his arm to put him at ease. "Are we ready to go?" She watched as he seemed to give himself a mental shake.

"Yes, we'd better. It's half an hour's drive."

Walking carefully in her long dress, Dani didn't look up until they were almost at the curb. When she did, she stopped short. A round-faced uniformed chauffeur held open the door to a long white limousine. Turning, she smiled up at Adam, who wore a self-satisfied look. "You learn your lessons well," she told him.

"I like to think so," he answered, helping her inside. Dani checked out the plush white interior, the soft music, the impressive bar, as Adam and the chauffeur got in. A woman would consider it romantic if a man surprised her with a limo for a special occasion, she'd told him. Was that what he was doing, romancing her? But she was only the stand-in, Dani reminded herself. Holding her rose, she leaned back as Adam reached for a chilled bottle of champagne.

The limo started out as he held the label up for her to read. "Was that a good year?"

Mumm's, '72, Brut. First class. The man was catching on. "Hard to find a bad year for champagnes." She watched him drape the cloth over the bottle and pop the cork, his movements smooth and unhurried. The little ceremony convinced her he'd been rehearsing on the side, the rascal. Out to impress her, was he? He'd find she wasn't an easy sell.

Adam poured the first glass for her, then filled his own. Setting down the bottle, he turned to catch Dani studying him. Never would he tell her how many bottles now sat open in his refrigerator because he'd labored so hard to perfect that little ritual. "What shall we drink to?"

"Graduation, I think," she answered, remembering the awkward man she'd had over to dinner weeks before who'd tossed back his first glass of wine like a shot of whiskey. "As they say, you've come a long way, baby."

"No, I won't drink to that. I'm not ready to fly on my own yet." He leaned closer, his glass almost touching hers. "To us."

"There is no 'us,' Adam," Dani said, her voice steady.

"Sure there is. We're partners, remember?" He clinked her glass. "To us."

Lowering her eyes, Dani took a sip, not repeating the silly toast. *Us. What foolishness.* Tonight was her swan song, whether Adam knew it or not.

As he leaned back, his shoulder touching hers, she caught a trace of an expensive after-shave she immediately recognized. She'd never much cared for artificial scents on men, preferring a clean, soapy, masculine smell. She wondered what Adam would think if she told him she'd thought him infinitely sexier high atop his building, needing a shave after a day's work, than all duded up in his snazzy tux and high-priced cologne. Probably he wouldn't believe her.

She let her mind drift to Sabrina. Which Adam would she prefer? Dani had to admit she couldn't call that one. Sabrina was more secretive than she used to be, and more elusive. Twice Dani had called her sister lately, and each time their schedules hadn't worked out for a get-together. Something was troubling Sabrina; Dani was sure of it. Next week she'd— "Penny for your thoughts," Adam interjected.

Guiltily Dani yanked her attention back to him. He'd gone to so much trouble that the least she could do was be attentive. "I was thinking I'm probably going to have to beat off with a stick any of my single women friends we meet by chance tonight," she improvised. "They'll all want to meet you and get to know you." She realized she'd inadvertently spoken the truth.

"You think I'm ready to meet them?"

"Sure. Shall I give you a Dunn & Bradstreet rundown on each one before or after introductions?" She saw him frown. Perhaps that had been a bit unkind, she thought.

"I think not. I'm not after their money."

"All right, how about a Social Registry readout, listing lineage, whether the woman has eligible younger brothers?" She was being downright mean tonight, after she'd promised herself she'd see this one last evening through. Whatever was the matter with her?

Slowly Adam turned her chin toward him so that she had no choice but to look at him. "Have I done something to offend you? When I came to ask you to the opera the other night, you seemed angry. Yet tonight you seemed happy to see me. Now you're chipping away at me with cheap shots. What is it?"

Dani's eyes filled with tears. Lowering her gaze, she blinked rapidly. He was right; she was wrong. "I'm sorry. Chalk it up to the letdown of the school year ending. And maybe the full moon. Forgive me, please."

Reaching over, he squeezed her hand. "I want things to be right between us, Dani. I like you—a great deal." His fingers moved over hers, caressing, reassuring.

"I like you, too, Adam." In control again, Dani looked up and raised her glass. "Let's just have fun tonight." *Only don't touch me. Please, don't touch me, or I'll fall apart.*

Adam looked unconvinced. She was relieved when they pulled up in front of Symphony Hall. Maybe with others around she would shake off this strange emotional mood. The chauffeur opened his door, and Adam helped her out.

Dani strolled through the crowd with Adam, plastering in place the social smile that had served her well throughout her teen years. She found it impossible to be invisible. The Durants, old friends of Arlene's, caught Dani and Adam in the lobby and gave him a once-over that would have cowed a lesser man. He seemed only to be amused. Toni's widowed sister sailed up and demanded to know who Dani's new young man was. The woman's shrill voice carried a city block, embarrassing Dani, but again Adam took it in stride graciously. And Steve Elkhart, whose family owned the compound in Hyannis next to Arlene's, literally bumped into them at the top of the wide staircase, anxious for Dani and her friend to meet his new fiancée. When Steve, someone she thought of as a neighborly kid brother, leaned close and asked her in a stage whisper if things between her and Adam were serious, she almost lost it and popped him. Adam just smiled pleasantly. By the time they found their seats, Dani fervently wished she were sitting on her beach, watching the sunset.

"You seem to know half this town," Adam said, settling into his seat.

"Hardly. They're my family's friends, not mine."

"None of your friends are here?" he asked, stretching his neck. The tight collar took some getting used to.

"I seriously doubt it."

"Where would they be, then, at the Red Sox game?" he teased her.

"More likely than here."

He caught her chin again, forcing her to face him. He'd had to do this a lot lately, since she seemed intent on avoiding his eyes. "You know you're a reverse snob? A very beautiful one, but a snob nevertheless."

Adam saw her eyes widen, but she didn't comment. Leaning over, he lightly kissed the end of her nose, surprising them both. He smiled as he watched her blush and glance to the right then the left. "Wild behavior for this staid and proper place?" he asked, enjoying her discomfort.

"Mmm," she responded.

As the first act opened, Dani sat back and let herself absorb the musical drama. Though not a real connoisseur of opera, she'd attended quite a few, and the poignancy of *Butterfly* never failed to move her. Glancing at Adam, she saw he was watching and listening intently, and knew he was probably trying to compare the action onstage with what he could remember of the libretto he'd read. At least he didn't seem bored.

They didn't stretch their legs during the first intermission but remained seated, taking in the elaborate old music hall, with its heavy red curtains and ornate gold-leaf design. As the second act began, Adam reached over for her hand, twining her fingers through his, as if they'd sat like that often. Though it unnerved her for a moment, Dani made herself concentrate on the performance.

It was during Madama Butterfly's impassioned aria, "Un bel di," where she sings of one fine day when her absent lover will return to her, that the light pressure of Adam's fingers on hers became more insistent. Though Dani kept her eyes on the stage, she was intensely aware of his touch and found herself squeezing his hand in return.

Warm and comfortable and right—that's how his touch felt. What on earth was she doing? This was exactly the life she'd turned away from, and here she was, dressed to the nines in the company of a man who wanted just this, while she wished they were sharing a hot dog under the stars. Why did this man, with his impossible dream, have to be the one who made her blood race? she wondered, wishing Act Two would end soon.

As the lights went on for intermission, Dani stood. "Let's take a walk before Act Three," she suggested, moving out into the aisle with an edge of restless impatience.

She felt a bit calmer as they shared a drink near the bar. Wanting to end the uncomfortable silence between them, Dani asked Adam how the shopping mall project was going, and he'd just begun to tell her, when she heard her name spoken. Turning, she saw Sabrina making her way through the crowd toward them, dragging along Josh Logan, a frequent date.

"Dani, I thought you'd given up the opera," Sabrina said, smiling at her sister's surprise at this accidental meeting.

"I thought so, too. Sabrina, this is Adam Kinkaid. Adam, my sister, Sabrina Ames."

Sabrina smiled as Adam took her hand, then she introduced Josh to Adam. "Kinkaid . . ." she said with a puzzled frown. "I've heard that name somewhere."

"Yes, you have," Dani interjected. "Adam's company is building Ames Plaza."

"Right," Josh added. "Did the Commerce Bank Building recently, too, didn't you?"

"Yes," Adam said, nodding. "Are you a banker?" He really didn't need to ask, since the conservative look of the man gave him away. Nor did he really want to know, but he supposed this small talk was part and parcel of all this sociability.

"Right. Commonwealth Bank," Josh said with pride.

"How do you like working with Carter?" Sabrina asked, looking up at Adam.

"I admire him greatly," Adam answered, watching Sabrina's green eyes study him. A beautiful woman, artfully dressed in black again, just as when he'd last seen her at Arlene's. As different from Dani as opera was from baseball.

"We all admire Daddy," Dani inserted. Adam thought she seemed amused by something. Turning to Sabrina, she touched her arm. "Are we ever going to get together?"

Sabrina looked at her sister. "Is something wrong? Do you *need* to talk?"

Exasperated, Dani shook her head. "Not need—want. Do I call your secretary for an appointment?" She studied her sister's face, noting that although she was smiling, there was a sadness in her eyes that hadn't been there a while ago.

Evidently Sabrina caught the look and sobered. "Next week. I promise." As they heard the warning bell for the third act, Sabrina put on her bright smile again. "It's been lovely meeting you, Adam. You're both going over to Arlene's after, aren't you? She and Toni are throwing a big bash."

"No, I don't think—" Dani began to say.

"We'd love to, thank you," Adam said.

Sabrina raised a brow and winked at Dani as the two men shook hands. "See you later," she said, walking away with Josh.

Adam swung his gaze to Dani's face and saw her questioning look. "Don't be angry. Please," he said, giving her his best smile. "I thought it'd be a good place to...you know, start feeling my way." And a good place to loosen Dani up a bit, since she certainly seemed uptight tonight. "Is it okay?"

Fitting, Dani decided, that she should leave Adam where she'd found him. A couple of hours more and she could walk away from this project. She gave him the smile she knew he was waiting for. "Why not, partner?"

A quick study, that's what Adam Kinkaid was, Dani thought as she stood on the sidelines of the party two hours later and watched Adam work the crowd.

Sipping her white wine, she saw him charm Toni, even bowing at one point and unabashedly kissing the woman's jeweled hand. Dani hadn't thought Toni capable of blushing, but then, it seemed the night was full of surprises. Arlene, who just a few short weeks ago said Adam had some "rough edges," now smiled up at him as if his arrival had changed a dull party to a delight. And perhaps it had for some. Frankly, Dani thought, stifling a yawn, she'd rather be in bed with a good book.

Yet she couldn't fault Adam too much, for he hadn't left her side until she'd urged him to mingle and even then he'd been attentive, fetching her drinks and canapés, asking her to dance. Every inch the gentleman. She'd done a good job on him. Maybe too good.

Why should that thought depress her so? she wondered, finishing her wine. Because he was getting caught up in a world he'd said he wanted to enter only for Bonnie's sake. Yet, watching his strong profile as he talked with her father and a Wall Street broker, Dani could see he would fit in well. Fit in and feel a part of things as she'd never been able to do. When the makeover was completed and the woman he sought to please was a reality he'd change even more. And then he'd be gone from Dani's life.

She reached for another glass of wine, realizing in her present mood that she shouldn't but feeling reckless enough to ignore the warning. She'd known all along that Adam wouldn't stay, that he wasn't for her. Known in her head. Her heart was another matter.

She wanted him; that much was a given. But more than just physically, although she wouldn't discount that part, either. She wanted to know more of him, to experience him . . . the pleasures and pains, the yesterdays and tomorrows. She wanted to walk on the beach with him, listen to his concerns and share hers, to laugh with him, to lie with him and wake up next to him. She wanted what she'd known from the start he didn't want—a life together. Hadn't Arlene warned her that she could get hurt always reaching for the unobtainable? This time, perhaps, she should have listened to her mother.

Adam wiped his forehead with a white handkerchief, feeling hot, constricted by too many too tight clothes and slightly bored. Make that mostly bored. The polite small talk he'd been engaged in for the past hour or so was exhausting him. He felt as though the smile he wore were plastered on. Arlene was fluttery, Sabrina deliberately vague and most of the others just plain dull. Was it because he'd only recently entered their world that he felt out of place?

He had to keep in mind that Bonnie, having been educated much as they had, would fit in better. Soon he'd see to it that she'd be exposed to even more—drama, art, music. Perhaps it was too late for him even to try to shift his tastes. He'd endure it awhile longer—for her.

He noticed Dani on the edge of the crowd, and a smile formed without his bidding. She was easily the most beautiful woman in the room, though she'd argue the point. He'd felt so close to her as he'd held her hand in the darkened theater during Butterfly's passionate love song. And Dani had returned the pressure of his fingers. Yet as soon as the lights had come on, she had withdrawn. Well, he couldn't blame her. He'd definitely been sending her mixed signals.

Although he tried to maintain a distance, almost an aloofness, with her, he slipped easily and often. His desire for her had become a problem he didn't know how to solve. She was responsive to him, but she was so sensible that she pulled back always, knowing he wasn't right for her. And he had to admit that he couldn't afford the luxury of pursuing an interest in Dani right now. Not until he'd accomplished what he'd set out to do for Bonnie. But afterward, Adam thought, watching her chatting with Sabrina's banker friend, he and Dani had some unfinished business to discuss. Maybe in time...

Finishing a somewhat dry conversation with Josh, Dani turned, seeking and finding Adam's tall form again. She watched as a friend of Sabrina's, dressed in a shimmering gown of gold, approached him and engaged him in conversation. His expression was polite, interested, but certainly not flirtatious. Despite that, Dani fought down a quick pang of jealousy.

He was, as Sabrina had pointed out the first night, awfully good-looking. Even in formal clothes, he had a rugged, nonconformist look. What would it be like, Dani wondered, to let him make love to her? He was big, strong, undisciplined. He made his own rules and would be an uncommon lover. He would not walk softly in the night and offer a gentle coupling. Nor did she want that. He would take her to heights she'd only dreamed about. He would meet her needs and go one step beyond. She took another heady swallow of wine.

Now it was Sabrina who came up to Adam and coaxed him out on the dance floor. Adam had said his dancing was rusty, but it didn't appear so from where Dani stood watching. She noticed that Sabrina did most of the talking, her shrewd eyes measuring his every word and action. If she and Sabrina got together next week, Adam was sure to be part of their conversation.

As he swung Sabrina about, over her head he mouthed "How am I doing?" She sent him an approving nod. Adam Kinkaid, social climber, was officially launched. She rubbed the back of her neck tiredly.

Moments later, as she stood chatting with Arlene and Toni, evading their probing questions as best she could, Adam came for her. He simply took her hand, nodded to the two women and led her onto the dance floor. As she moved close up against him, her fatigue suddenly melted and her senses came alive.

"You've been holding out on me, Kinkaid," she said, tilting her head back to capture his dark eyes. "Have you been renting Fred Astaire movies in your spare time?"

"No. It's my partner. You make me look good." Adam took a deep breath, his face in her soft hair. Jasmine. She smelled of jasmine, rich and ripe.

The right thing to say, Dani mused. Yes, sir, the man really knew the right thing to say. His large hand on her bare back was warm, pulling her nearer. Her grip on the here and now wavered as her blood hummed with a barely suppressed need for him. Closing her eyes, she embraced the magic. There was little enough of it in life, she decided.

The music picked up in tempo, and so did Adam as he talked of some of the people he'd met that evening, as well as some lessons he had in mind. He wanted to learn more about plays, the symphony, and someone had mentioned antiques. Endless, Dani thought. This whole project as he outlined it was endless. As if from a great distance, she listened to him go on, all the while realizing she had to bow out.

The frankly admiring stares and impressive interest he'd received this evening told her his makeover was a fait accompli. He'd changed into exactly the kind of man Sabrina or one of her friends would be attracted to. Maybe one of them already was. Her job was done, Dani thought, and just in the nick of time. She could no longer spend so much time in Adam's company without revealing her true feelings. And she'd sooner die than let him know she was in love with him, when he saw her only as a teacher and friend.

It was nearly two in the morning, Dani noticed as she stepped out of the limousine at her house. She walked slowly to her door as Adam dismissed the car for the night, having decided to walk the short distance to his house. Reaching her side, he took her hand and pulled her along to the beach side of the house.

"Mmm, look at that moon. Let's walk for a minute, please."

She, too, was suddenly reluctant to end the evening. Slipping off her shoes and tossing them and her handbag on the patio, she walked with him arm in arm. "A million stars tonight, but no clouds and no pictures."

Silently they strolled on the sea-washed sand. The ocean air was gentle on her skin as Dani raised her face toward the night sky. The salt spray danced over her bare back and tickled her nose with its tangy aroma. As she and Adam turned to retrace their steps, she felt his arm slide around her.

Moonlight did wondrous things to her skin, Adam couldn't help thinking as he tried to ignore the thought. He felt strangely nostalgic, even a little melancholy. "I walked my first girl home along the beach like this," he murmured, smiling at the memory. "We'd been to a bonfire, and it had started to rain. I couldn't afford to take her to movies, so I had to keep coming up with free things to do, like marshmallow roasts and swimming and bicycling."

Dani smiled at the picture of a young Adam. She wondered if his dark eyes had been as serious then, his hair as untamed. "How old were you?"

"Fourteen, and she was a year younger."

"Didn't waste any time, did you?" They'd moved full circle and now stood in a patch of moonlight near her back door.

Adam turned her to face him, one hand tracing the satin smoothness of her bare shoulder as he reached with the other to brush a curl from her cheek. "She had short brown hair like yours." He caught a strand in his fingers. "Only yours is a richer color, softer, like silk. And it smells like..."

"Baby shampoo," she finished for him.

"Right. And when we got to her door, I leaned down to kiss her." Adam moved his head a fraction lower. "Only she turned her head, so I landed a noisy kiss on the corner of her mouth." He smiled gently, then moved his hands up to cup her face as he bent to her. "Please, Dani, don't you move away."

She couldn't if she'd wanted to, and she most decidedly did not. She felt rooted to the spot, waiting for his mouth to claim hers, as if she'd been waiting all evening for this moment. Urges she couldn't put a name to had her restless. As his mouth touched hers, her eyes fluttered closed and she moaned softly. She reached to bring him closer as a hunger that had been steadily building made itself known deep inside her.

His roughened hands were gentle on her cheeks, his lips soft yet hard and demanding. She opened her mouth to him, surprising herself with the sudden fierce need his touch had awakened, just like the last time.

Intellect and emotion battled inside her as his arms wrapped around her, tighter and tighter still. The Irish had a song about thunder and lightning. It was exactly how she felt as the kiss deepened. Feeling the night breezes dance around them as she stood crushed against him, she knew nothing was important to her but this moment and this man. No matter the consequences, she wanted his kiss, his taste, his passion.

The surf pounded in Adam's ears, or was it his blood rushing through his veins? Her mouth was wine sweet, soft, urgent. He plunged his tongue into her, taking from her, more, then still more. She met his demand with her own, his heat with a fire he'd only suspected. Desire rose in him so quickly he was already weak with it. Her hands moved up his back, over his shoulders, then into his hair, roaming, restless. The way she touched him, suddenly confident, suddenly sure, had him groaning with needs unanswered.

Shifting breathlessly, he trailed kisses along her face, over the delicate skin of her eyelids, down to the throbbing pulse in her throat. But she reached up and drew his mouth back to hers, needing more. Through the thin material of her dress, he felt her flesh warm to his touch, and the ache inside him grew. Her jasmine scent teased him as the taste of her drove him half-mad.

"I want you," he whispered in a ragged breath, wishing he could take her right there on the shore with the surf sliding softly onto the smooth sand. "Do you know how much I want you?"

"Yes," Dani said. Her voice sounded strained. "As much as I want you." But suddenly she pushed him away.

Eyes dark and anguished rose to meet his. "And it's not enough for either of us."

Dani turned and ran to her house, needing to get away, away from Adam, away from her problems—before she gave herself away.

Chapter Eight

How the hell had she gotten under his skin so quickly, so powerfully, so thoroughly? Adam asked himself. *Damn!*

Downshifting, he moved his silver Porsche into the passing lane and zoomed around a camper that was chugging slowly north along Highway 95. He'd opted for his car rather than his truck because of its speed. Brock had told him it would take about two hours to drive from Grand Haven to the Ames cottage just across the Maine border in the seacoast city of Portsmouth. Adam intended to shave at least half an hour off that time.

He reached for the large paper cup, stuck the straw into his mouth and drew in a generous swallow of chocolate milk shake. There'd been no time to stop for lunch, so he'd pulled into a fast-food restaurant and ordered a milk shake, which he'd sipped on and off, hoping the milk would calm him. So far it hadn't.

He'd hated to ask one of the neighbors for information, but he'd had few options. After spending a restless night wrestling with his feelings and arriving at some conclusions, he knew he had to see Dani. Way too early for the usual Saturday-morning volleyball game in the sand, he'd hung around the beach, waiting for her to put in an appearance, needing to take her aside and convince her they should talk. But when the regulars had straggled out, she wasn't among them.

Disappointed, he'd begged off playing and strolled down to her house. He'd found it locked up and empty, windows closed, when they were usually open to catch the sea breezes; Mutt was nowhere to be seen. Peering in through the small garage window, Adam had discovered that her car wasn't there.

As he'd walked home, he'd realized it was too early for her to be shopping, and why would she take her dog? By ten he'd checked most of his sources. No, the school didn't have an athletic event that Dani Ames was involved in this holiday weekend. No, Al Donaldson hadn't asked her to referee for him Saturday or Sunday. A quick call to Sabrina had told Adam nothing about Dani's whereabouts but a great deal about Sabrina's curiosity regarding Dani's relationship with him. Frustrated, Adam had taken a shower.

It was after he'd made himself a big breakfast, only to find that he had no appetite, that he'd known something was happening to him. Shoveling the food down the garbage disposal, he'd walked back outside and called Brock away from the game.

Adam smiled. He must have sounded desperate, because Brock had given him a long, studying look, then told him that when Dani needed to sort things out, there was only one place she ever went: the family cottage in Portsmouth.

Before giving him directions, Brock, ever protective of Dani, had bluntly asked him why it was so imperative that Adam talk with her immediately. But it wasn't easy for him to give Brock—or himself, for that matter—an answer. He'd explained that he cared about Dani and that they had some things they needed to straighten out between them. Nodding, Brock had explained the route and wished him luck. And just before he'd gone back to his game, he'd given Adam something to think about. "Don't hurt her, Adam," he warned.

Having finished his milk shake, Adam set the empty container on the seat beside him. Hurting Dani was the last thing he wanted to do. He wanted to . . . to . . . to what? He wasn't quite sure. He knew only that he had to see her, had to sort out the confusion, make her see.

His plan to make himself over in order to bring Bonnie into the world of the elite had seemed flawless in the beginning. If he could interest a woman like Sabrina, she would ensure his acceptance and ultimately Bonnie's. But it wasn't Sabrina he wanted, or anyone else he'd met. He wanted Dani.

After holding her in his arms last night, kissing her, not wanting to let her go, he'd known he'd pushed them both to decision time. But what was the right decision? During the long night, he'd faced some facts but hadn't found too many answers. Dani wanted to disassociate herself from the life he wanted for Bonnie. Which left Adam caught between his desire to help his sister and his desire for Dani.

Letting out a deep breath, he shook his head. What the hell was he going to do? He had no set plan for what he'd do when he found her, but he had to see her. His eyes on the clear highway ahead, Adam stepped down harder on the gas pedal.

Mutt ran ahead on the blacktop, then scooted back to see what was keeping his mistress. Carrying a brown bag of groceries, Dani scarcely noticed her dog's playful antics. Tall elms and leafy maples bordered the country road, filtering the sun and casting rippling shadows that danced across her bare arms. In sneakers, jeans and a sleeveless top, Dani strolled along, lost in troubled thoughts.

She'd been too damn inexperienced to know how to handle him, to be strong enough to refuse him. Too late, Dani thought. She now realized she never should have gotten involved with Adam Kinkaid.

She had always loved the wrong people. People she couldn't really relate to—like Arlene. People who didn't stay around long enough to get to know—like Carter. People who scarcely spoke the same language as she—like Sabrina. People who wanted to change her—like Billie Joe. And people who wanted someone or something else—like Adam.

He'd made quite an impression at the party last night with people who usually weren't easily impressed by outsiders. Odd, how he'd been almost invisible at her mother's gatherings before and yet now he hadn't been able to escape notice. Was it his new aura of confidence that had come through, his sense of purpose, or perhaps his concentrated efforts to charm the right people?

Wearily Dani ran a hand through her windblown hair. She hadn't slept more than an hour or two, and even then she'd tossed and turned. Why hadn't she had the good sense to back away from the kiss she'd seen coming?

Memories of him kept dancing across her mind: a bouquet of limp daisies, cloud sketches, a perfect rose and champagne in a white limo, a stunning kiss on the beach and an elevator ride to the sky. And the man didn't think he was romantic.

It had still been dark when she'd forsaken her tangled sheets and showered away the night's frustration and tears. She'd hated to call Luke so early, though she'd known the balding caretaker was not a late sleeper. He'd assured her he'd open up the cottage, air it out, lay in a supply of firewood, and he had.

A haven, that's what the cottage had always been to Dani. In her youth, whenever she'd felt misunderstood and miserable, she and Sarah had spent long weekends there, to regroup, to rethink, to renew. When she'd needed to be alone to get over the defeat of the national ice skating competitions and the disappointment of Billie Joe, she had gone there alone to lick her wounds. And now, here she was, to try to accept once more that she couldn't have what she desperately wanted.

Shifting the bag of groceries to her other arm, Dani turned down the winding driveway that led to the cottage nestled among the old trees. Sarah had always taught her that a wise person accepted life's little defeats, learned from them and grew stronger. A fool wallowed in her misfortune, crying out at the fates, and became weaker. Dani always tried to follow that sage counsel, but it wasn't easy. Today she felt every inch the fool. Maybe a few days or a week alone would shift that self-perception, maybe...

Once she'd rounded the last curve, Dani stopped short just as Mutt bounded onto the porch, barking. Gleaming in the late-afternoon sunshine that dappled the driveway, sat a silver Porsche she immediately recognized. She blinked behind her sunglasses as her heart began to pound. What was Adam doing here?

Dani opened the screen door, and stepped into the large main room of the rustic house. He was crouched in front of the fireplace, where he'd evidently been laying a fire. His back was to her as he stopped to rub Mutt's shaggy head. Slowly he turned to look up at her.

"You really should lock your doors," he said, standing. "You never know who'll walk right in."

"No one does up here," Dani answered, wishing he didn't look so damn good to her. No tuxedo now. He wore faded jeans and a blue shirt, and he had the same commanding edge she'd noticed when they'd first met. Tearing her eyes from his, she moved through the archway into the small kitchen. "Why are you here?" she asked, her voice even.

He ignored her question and walked over to join her at the counter. "Let me help with those," he said, taking items from the sack she'd set down. Looking over her groceries—eggs, cheese, milk, bread, peanut butter—he said, "Real gourmet fare here."

Dani took a step back and crossed her arms over her chest. "You're the one who prefers gourmet food, not me." She narrowed her eyes, trying to look cool and disdainful. "How did you find me?"

"Brock told me where you were," he said, bending to put the food in the refrigerator.

"You called Brock?"

"I pulled him away from the volleyball game to ask him where you might be. Ah, I see there's chilled wine in here. Could we have a glass?"

Enough! "Adam, would you stop fussing with the food and tell me why you're here?"

"Where do you keep the wineglasses?"

"In that cupboard. I—will you answer me?" The man was deliberately being maddening, and she was beginning to lose her cool.

Moving slowly, Adam took down the glasses and poured. Irritation was better than indifference, he thought. Or that vulnerable look she had when she'd first walked in. As though she half expected him to hurt her. He turned and offered her a glass. "You owe me," he said.

Impatience danced across her features, followed by annoyance. "Owe you?"

"Dance lessons, remember? You promised." He took her hand and curled it around the glass, then picked up his own. "Here's to the tango, the merengue and other fancy footwork numbers."

Dani set down the glass he'd forced on her. "Are you telling me you tracked me down and drove two hours in holiday traffic so you could learn the tango?" Shaking her head, she moved past him and opened the refrigerator. "You're crazy. And you've wasted a day. I have no intention of teaching you another thing. As far as I'm concerned, you've graduated. With honors." Savagely she slammed the loaf of bread and peanut butter onto the counter and reached for a knife.

She sounded bitter, and he wondered why. "What are you doing?"

"I'm hungry," she lied. "Do you mind?" With shaky hands she lathered peanut butter on the bread. Why didn't he leave her alone? Dance lessons. That's all she needed in her present state—to be held up close against him with seductive music swirling around them. Angrily she plopped the top slice of bread on, picked up her sandwich and took a big bite. As she chewed, she prayed the food wouldn't stick in her throat.

Adam regarded her as he took a deep sip of the dry wine. "I...uh...haven't eaten much since yesterday," he said.

She noticed him eyeing the meager makings. "Help yourself," she mumbled.

Mutt came eagerly over to make sure he wasn't left out of the dinner plans. Sitting back on his haunches, begging with his large front paws, he gave a short bark and cocked his head at Dani.

"Okay, boy," she reassured him. "Make Mutt a sandwich, too, will you?"

"He eats peanut butter sandwiches? Are they good for him? I would think he'd be better off with dog food."

Nervy, Dani thought, washing down her last bite with wine. "He gets dog food all week. On weekends he eats what I do. Everybody has to have something to look forward to, something that's not just good for you, even dogs." She swallowed more wine, deciding the tart coolness went well with peanut butter.

"Interesting philosophy," Adam admitted, gazing into the refrigerator again. "No jelly?"

"Sorry. Up here we rough it."

"Right." Finishing his preparations, he placed one sandwich on a napkin on the brick kitchen floor and watched Mutt sniff appreciatively before tackling his weekend treat. Adam took a bite of his own sandwich. "You may have stumbled onto something here."

"A convert? How nice." She'd begun to relax. Was it the wine? No, not on half a glass. Being around Adam had always been easy. Too easy. And too pleasurable. Her initial anger was dissolving. Another weakness: she couldn't stay angry with him. She didn't for a minute believe he'd sought her out for dance lessons, which he really didn't need. *What, then?*

Adam drained his glass and poured them each a refill. "Yes, you could say I'm a convert. Over the past weeks you've changed many things about me, Dani."

And not necessarily for the better, Dani thought. Wiping her mouth, she picked up her glass and walked into the living room, where she flipped on the stereo.

Thoughtfully Adam put the food away and wiped the counter. There was that contrast again—his neatness and Dani's casualness. Did it really matter? Why should it? he asked himself as he rinsed his hands. He didn't have permanency in mind here. He wasn't thinking marriage and forever, giving up all his well-thought-out plans. He cared for her, really cared. Their differences were many and they had conflicting philosophies, but that shouldn't keep them from having a meaningful relationship—at least for a while. He wiped his hands and hung up the towel. Only how would he convince Dani? Adam followed her into the living room.

He approved of the Ames retreat. A nice, solid house with rough-plank flooring, a huge window that looked out onto the grassy bank that sloped to the sea, a stone fireplace and big, comfortable furniture. Comfortable, welcoming. Only Dani didn't look too welcoming as she sat in the corner of the couch with her legs drawn up, as she gazed out at the darkening sky. Maybe coming here hadn't been such a good idea. Maybe she really didn't want him in her life.

"Night falls pretty early up here even in summer," Adam commented as he stood looking out at the choppy sea.

"Mmm."

Angling his head, he concentrated on the music coming from the stereo. "Beethoven, eh?" he said, pleased that he could recognize it.

"Mmm."

His good ear didn't seem to thrill her. Next he'd be reduced to discussing the weather. Up to last night they'd never seemed to run out of conversation, had even enjoyed the occasional shared silences. He looked around the room, searching for an opening. Spotting a multihued earthenware bowl on the fireplace ledge, he walked over. A saguaro cactus sat next to a squat prickly pear. "Do these two have names?"

"Abbott and Costello," Dani answered without shifting her gaze from the window.

He should have known. He swung back to look at her. She was a tall woman, but small boned, fragile in many ways. She sat huddled with her back to him, hugging herself, avoiding his eyes.

"Maybe I should go," he suggested lamely. They were getting nowhere. She'd shut him out. The visions he'd entertained on his madcap ride here dissolved in the face of her obvious rejection. They were from two different worlds, and it seemed she wanted those worlds to remain separate and distinct.

And then he saw it. Her shoulders were shaking, quietly, rhythmically. Was she weeping?

Instantly he was beside her on the couch. Her face was pale in the dim light of the lamp she'd turned on, her cheeks tear streaked, her eyes anguished. Wordlessly she moved into his open arms.

"Hold me. Please, just hold me." Her voice was a hoarse whisper as she burrowed into his solid chest. She searched for reasons for her uncharacteristic behavior even as the sobs shook her. It wasn't the wine—she hadn't had enough. Maybe it was the sleepless night, the helpless hunger, the unrelenting frustration. She'd struggled so long against this overpowering attraction. Too long.

Choking back the strangling fear that she would never know him, never have him, she felt utterly defenseless against him and his comforting warmth chased away the chill that had invaded her. Dani closed her eyes against her fears. She didn't want him to know the power he had over her, the passion he aroused in her, the love he evoked in her. She was certain that if he discovered it, he would run.

Adam kissed the top of her head, stroking her fragrant hair. He felt helpless against her tears, yet glad that she'd allowed him to offer some measure of comfort. Since arriving, he'd seen distrust in her, then a short, angry outburst, and now this emotional upheaval. He felt her tremble under his hand as he stroked her back, felt her fighting the spasms that shook her. He wanted to make her forget whatever had caused her unhappiness. He wanted to take the pain from her eyes. He wanted her to smile again, to laugh. He wanted her.

At last Dani was spent. "I'm sorry," she said, feeling slightly ashamed and moving away from him. She pulled a tissue from her pocket and blew her nose, then wiped her face.

"You needn't be," Adam told her. He reached for her wine and handed it to her. "Are you all right now?"

"I think so." She took a sip, then set the glass on the table. Taking a deep breath, she looked at him. In his eyes she saw confusion mingled with caring. Could it be that he felt as mixed up as she? Did he really want to leave? She wanted to remember that he would walk away and she'd be left to hurt alone, that he needed a woman as unlike her as night and day. She wanted to remember but couldn't, for her mind was filled with only one thought: Adam.

"Don't go," Dani whispered as she touched a hand to his damp shirt and brushed away the tears. "I need you," she added so softly that Adam had to strain to hear.

"Oh, Dani," he said, easing her back into the circle of his arms, feeling inadequate, shaken. He closed his eyes and buried his face in the wildflower scent of her hair.

She needed him, he thought. For weeks now, he'd wanted her to realize that, wanted her to admit it to herself and to him. And now that she was so close, how could he make love to her when she was emotionally vulnerable? That's not how he'd pictured their first time, not how he wanted it to be for her.

Tilting back her head, Dani sought his eyes. "I'm tired of fighting this, Adam, so very tired. I've never felt anything so strongly before. Don't walk away. Love me, please."

How could he walk away? He bent and touched his mouth to hers in a sweet kiss.

Her hands moved up over his chest to his shoulders and neck, drawing him closer. Slowly the kiss changed from sweet to sensual as Adam shifted and gathered her to him. She tasted of wine and peanut butter and unbridled need. It was impossible to believe she was as anxious as he. Impossible that she was here in his arms, so pliant and giving, surrendering to a desire he hadn't been sure she shared. Impossible, yet she was wrapped about him, warm and real.

She was a woman to savor, to linger over, to worship. She brought him her innocence and offered him fulfillment, and he felt an aching gratitude. Unanswered questions muddled his mind, yet he banished them, along with all thoughts of tomorrow. For tonight there was only Dani and these powerful feelings, Dani and her sweetness, Dani and the loving she offered him at last.

His mouth explored her with an expertise that had Dani gasping one moment, shuddering the next. Hadn't she guessed it would be like this, dark rich tastes, fire and ice, a slow journey into the sensual unknown?

As Adam buried his face in her throat, she heard her own sigh of surrender. Surrender? Not tough, independent, ever-cautious Dani Ames. His lips moved lower, warming her skin, making her blood race. Yes, surrender, she thought, arching as his hands touched the fullness of her aching breasts. Willingly, gladly, eagerly.

Slowly Adam slipped her shirt from her with hands that were none too steady. Fighting the urge to rush, to devour, he brought her hand to his lips, kissing the soft skin of her palm. Struggling with his control, he tried to remember the lessons she'd taught him on romancing. Go slowly, he warned himself, wanting to make their first time one she would long remember with a racing heart.

Lowering his head, he let his lips wander over the satin smoothness of her bare shoulders as he unfastened, then discarded her lacy bra. He leaned back and looked first into her eyes, which were dark and watchful. Then he let his gaze caress her and felt his body's own quick responses. "You're so lovely," he whispered just before he touched his mouth to hers.

Dani gasped as his tongue probed deeper. Her body, which had always obeyed her directives, was now straining to his commands. Her hands in his thick hair pressed him closer to her yearning flesh. Though she'd dreamed, never had her dreams come close to this.

With effort, Adam pulled back. "The couch isn't very big, and the floor looks hard."

Dani nodded toward the bedroom door. Then, losing her will to move, she kissed the scratchy skin of his cheek.

Standing, he easily picked her up in his arms and heard her soft chuckle.

"No man has ever carried me," she said, laying her head on his shoulder.

"No man has ever touched you the way I'm going to touch you," he told her, his eyes on her. Pausing in front of the door, he waited till she met his gaze.

"This is where the pupil turns teacher. No man has ever touched me at all, Adam." Heart thudding, she waited.

A gift, he thought. She was handing him a rare gift that he'd suspected was hers to give, although he'd never been sure. He only hoped he had the self-control to hold back, to make the loving as special as possible for her. "You don't have to be experienced to be good at making love. Sometimes the less experienced you are, the more spontaneous, the better."

He saw a flash of humor dance in her eyes. "I should be outstanding, then."

Adam pushed open the door and entered with her held close in his arms. Twilight slanted in through the mini-blinds on the high window above the four-poster. As they reached the bed, Dani stretched to turn on the bedside lamp. Carefully he lowered her onto the mattress and eased himself down beside her.

The golden lamplight shone in her eyes as he smiled into them, wanting to reassure her, needing to regain his pacing. He'd almost lost control when he'd touched his mouth to her breasts and felt the heat of her response. "Just go with your feelings, Dani."

"I want to please you."

He removed a strand of hair from her cheek, his hand lingering on the soft skin. "There's no right or wrong way. If I do something you don't like, let me know and I'll stop."

Dani couldn't imagine what he'd do that she wouldn't like, and the last thing she wanted was for him to stop.

Perhaps she couldn't have him forever. Perhaps forever was a dream for fools, anyway. She could have time tonight, and for now that was enough. With a smile she reached for him.

She felt him nuzzle her neck, drawing out the pleasure. With her hands she explored his back as she'd longed to do, feeling the ripple of powerful muscles under his shirt. "You have too many clothes on," she said into his ear.

She felt as much as heard his deep chuckle as he straightened. "You're right," he said, pulling off and tossing aside his shirt. "Fair is fair."

As she watched him remove the rest of his clothes, Dani felt the insistent thrumming of her blood as it rushed through her veins. Anticipation was a forerunner of passion, impatience a new fire within her, setting her aflame.

And then he was back, with a kiss that had her reeling to catch her breath. She'd known he could bring her to this, known that first night she'd gaze across Arlene's living room and caught his hot, dark eyes studying her so intently.

Adam unfastened her jeans and felt her stomach muscles quiver at his touch. As he slid them down over her slim hips, he decided he wanted her to quiver again, only quiver with need for him, unable to catch her breath, wild and sweet and out of control. Then and only then would he join with her.

"You're beautiful," he whispered, and she became a believer, she who'd never believed the compliment before. "Exquisite." Listening, steeped in pleasure, she sighed.

He moved his mouth back to hers, his tongue invading, conquering, captivating. His hands removed the silk panties riding low on her hips, then returned to stun her with their intimate explorations. When he touched deep inside her, she arched to meet him, moaned softly, then shuddered with her first peak, which she was helpless to stop.

Adam left her mouth and buried his face in her throat. Fighting for breath, chest heaving, she lay beneath him. She opened her eyes wide with delight, then sought his mouth. No man had ever touched her like that, Adam was certain. No man had watched the rosy blush steal over her face as she lay drenched in passion, damp with desire. No man had ever loved her before, and he was humbled at the thought.

Loving a woman had never been difficult for him. He'd shared with them affection and friendship and a satisfaction of mutual needs. But loving this woman was somehow different. There was a depth, an intensity, that had been absent before.

Their scents mingled and meshed and became unbearably sweet to him. Taut with need and fighting for control, Adam let his lips roam over her skin, making her shiver, making her mindless with pleasure. Her body moved sinuously beneath his, craving completion, driving him to the brink. She tasted his flesh, skimmed her hands over him without hesitation, and he trembled with want.

He could wait no longer. As he shifted, she became suddenly still, watching and waiting, letting him lead. His eyes on hers, he entered her slowly, completely, deeply. She smiled then, a soft woman's smile, taking him into her. Lowering himself to her, he put his mouth to hers....

And then Dani was drowning in feeling, devoid of reason or coherent thought. She was overtaken by sensations so sharp, so strong, so real, she could no longer fight them but gave herself up to them gladly. Clinging to her love, Dani let go of the world as she had known it until now.

Chapter Nine

Running. Running easily with the grace of a natural athlete, Dani heard the slip-slap of her bare feet on the wet sand, felt the coolness creep between her toes and the summer breeze ruffle her short hair. Wearing a gray sweatshirt and sweatpants, she jogged along, her gaze skimming the familiar shoreline.

An old stone seawall bordered the edge of the beach farther up, and nearby a few anchored sailboats swayed at their weathered docks. It had rained earlier, and the sky was still cloudy and gray. The morning air was ripe with the smell of fish, a not altogether unpleasant scent as it mixed with the salt spray. She couldn't see another living soul, even in the far distance.

Running was something she'd used to do as part of her training. Then, when she was no longer in training, she'd continued on a less rigorous schedule for the exhilaration and the pleasure. Today she was doing it to give herself a little distance, a little alone time, so she could think.

Slowing, she bent to take the gnarled stick from Mutt's jaws and tossed it as far as she could, then smiled as he turned and chased it again, never tiring of the game. Stretching her arms and shaking the kinks from her legs, Dani resumed her pace.

Nothing was really different. Dawn had broken, the leafy trees still stood around the cottage and the ocean waves rolled in as they had for centuries. Same as yesterday. And as tomorrow. Yet everything was different.

How foolish and romantic and unlike her to feel this way, Dani thought. To think that because a man had made love to her again and again through the long, velvet hours of night, the day was different, *she* was different. Yet she was.

There was this thing about being loved—thoroughly, deeply and well—that gave her an inner edge, a confidence, a feeling of well-being. Forevermore it changed her perception of herself. Dani felt that edge today—for all the good it would do her.

She hadn't consciously sought out love, thinking she was not really good at picking out a recipient for her deeper feelings. Magic, she knew, was a myth, and fairy tales were just that. She'd supposed that one day someone would come along who would want to share her life, someone compatible, someone loving. What she hadn't suspected was the *power* of love—until Adam, that is—and now she badly wanted to be a believer. But she was too much of a realist to let herself.

Stopping, she took the stick from Mutt and threw it again. Her energy spent, she strolled along the water's edge and felt the cool water swirl around her feet. Her thoughts weren't as placid as the foam left by the waves but more like the sea during a turbulent storm—churning, chaotic, confusing.

Making love with Adam had been everything she'd dreamed, and so much more. But that final intimacy had left her with more problems than she'd faced before she'd set out for the cottage. After only just one night of love with him, where would she find the strength to let him go? Picking up a small, round pebble, Dani tossed it into the air and followed its descent with troubled eyes.

She'd made a terrible mistake. She'd fallen in love with Adam Kinkaid, and now she would have to watch him walk away. Just because a man made love with a woman didn't mean that he loved her. Men, she supposed, felt quite different about lovemaking than women. Most women, at least. Adam had been very careful to see that she'd achieved maximum pleasure. He'd been equally careful to avoid any and all words that would give her the impression he cared more than just casually for her.

Dani found herself at the secluded rocky cove at the far end of the beach, a favorite spot she'd often visited. She climbed atop a jutting rock and sat down gingerly. There was a quick flash of lightning, then a low rumble of thunder. More rain coming, Dani thought with a restless sigh.

She'd eased out from under Adam's arm and left him sleeping. His large, lean body had left her little room on the double bed, but she hadn't minded. Though she'd never spent a night wrapped in a man's arms, she'd adapted easily, and Adam's presence had comforted her. But it wasn't a need for comfort that had lured her to his bed, kept her there. It was his passion, which had awakened and fueled her own, leaving her slightly stunned. Under his tutelage and with his encouragement, she'd responded with abandon, becoming experimental, even bold. And now what? Dani wondered, studying the rising waves of the sea.

He'd go back, of course. Had she ever doubted it? Back to helping Bonnie, back to trying to interest women like Sabrina and her friends, back to social climbing. Having lived the life-style of the rich again during the past few weeks with Adam, she knew now more than ever that it wasn't for her. Yet Adam was becoming a convert.

So what would Dani Ames do? She'd pull back into herself, as she'd done after other disappointments, and she'd slowly forget. Forget the longing, forget the look in his eyes as he lay above her and moved within her, forget the way he made her feel, forget the love. She took a deep, steadying breath. Sure she would.

A movement up the beach caught her attention, and she turned to look. Mutt had found a new playmate. Halfway between the house and the cove where she sat, walking purposefully toward her, was the subject of her musings. And Dani felt her heart soar.

Huddled again, Adam thought as his gaze remained on Dani. Huddled up on a high rock, her slim arms hugging her bent knees, she quietly watched his approach. What was she feeling? he wondered as he picked up his pace. Regret? He hoped not.

In the beginning he'd thought her easy to read, though not simple. Surely not terribly complex. Now he knew different. She was not what she seemed. At social affairs she was poised, charming and interesting, though inside she might not want to be present. As a lover she'd first appeared shy, hesitant and inexperienced, but she'd quickly become the passionate woman she really was, instinctively giving, unabashedly sensual—a side of her nature very few would suspect, he imagined. Many might feel they knew her well, but Adam thought Dani like the proverbial iceberg, which had only ten percent showing above the waterline and ninety percent hidden.

Once again he threw the stick for Mutt to chase. As he neared her he could see her eyes, dark blue against her pale skin, with that edge of wariness he'd seen in them so often. Emotions washed over Adam that he was ill prepared for.

Only his mother and sister had ever moved inside his heart. He'd erected his own barriers for his own reasons; he was a man on the move who would take for himself when he felt the time was right. And it had never seemed right. Only now there was Dani, who'd moved the barriers aside without his permission. And that hadn't been part of the game plan.

Suddenly he wanted no one else to taste the sweetness of her bare skin. He wanted no other man to inhale the heated scent of her. He wanted no other lover to hear the soft sounds she made when she was almost there. And these new feelings scared the hell out of him.

A light rain was falling as Dani watched Adam stop in front of her. Hands on his hips, he cocked his damp head, his dark eyes probing hers as if wanting to see deep inside her. He was barefoot, wearing a zippered cotton shirt and gray sweatpants. She took her time looking him over, then let a hint of humor slide into her greeting.

"Looks like we have the same tailor," she said.

He reached out to trail his hand down her cheek, cupping her chin, taking in her fresh face, her wind-tossed hair. "You look about seventeen," he told her.

Just what she'd wanted to hear, that she looked like a teenager. The man was a knockout with compliments.

Abruptly Adam put his hands on her upper arms and pulled her into a bone-crushing embrace, his mouth taking hers. Dani tasted impatience and desperation and confusion as his tongue plunged into her, his movements almost savage, almost hurting.

But Dani, who'd faced the anger herself, wouldn't let it take him over. She didn't pull away but held him closer. She didn't shrink from him but kissed him back with equal fervor. Yet she didn't let him bruise, gentling him with sweet murmurs that lulled, soft hands that caressed, a hungry body that pressed into him, clearly showing her need. Resistance to Adam was only a token thing with her, a fleeting thought. She opened herself to him and let him drink his fill.

Lifting his head, Adam waited until she opened her eyes. "But you don't kiss like you're seventeen."

She saw the shadows leave his face and wondered what had caused them. Was Adam wrestling with some new emotions, too? "I'll bet there are plenty of seventeen-year-olds out there more experienced than I who could kiss you senseless."

"You kissed me senseless last night—several times, as I recall."

"Are you complaining?"

"Never." The rain was falling steadily now. Taking her hand, he guided her around the jagged formations to the seaward side. He peered into the small nook formed by the jutting rocks. "We're going to get soaked if we don't duck in there until this passes."

Dani cast a suspicious glance at the darkening sky. "I don't know. This may not be over for a while. Could be an all-day rain."

"All the better," Adam said, stooping and pulling her under the protection of the overhang. Mutt dashed up and settled down as if to guard the entrance.

The space was just big enough for two of them to sit on the dry sand and look out on the spectacular view of the sea. Backing in as far as he could on his bottom, Adam situated Dani between his legs and draped his arms over hers, burying his face in the damp fragrance of her hair.

"Now what could be cozier than this?" he remarked.

As she leaned back against the solid wall of his chest, Dani couldn't think of too many things. She snuggled in, threading her fingers through his. "I have to admit, it's nice. I used to come here a lot as a kid, and even later."

"Ah, now it comes out. A teenage trysting spot. Is this where you came to neck with the local boys during summer vacations?"

"Oh, there were a few bonfires on the beach and a couple of strolls in the moonlight, maybe. But I've never burrowed in here quite like this."

He squeezed her tightly, and nuzzled her neck. "I'm surprised that at least one of those young fellows wasn't inventive enough to spot this little cave, coax you in and have his way with you."

Dani squirmed in his arms as his lips on her skin began to send small tremors through her. The scent of soap lingered on his skin, mingling with the fragrance of the sea and his naturally musky smell. Intoxicating. "I don't coax very well when I don't want to do something." Yet when she wanted something, she mused, it wasn't that difficult. Just a few weeks since they'd met, and last night she'd practically begged him to come into her bed. It was moving into his heart that was the difficult part. But she wasn't going to think about that. For this weekend she had him here with her, hers to love.

Dani angled her head back. "What were we discussing outside, something about kissing till you're senseless?" She watched his slow smile form.

"If you don't think you've had enough practice in that department, I'll be glad to oblige with more."

"Practice does make perfect, I understand." Her eyes darkened as she opened her mouth, inviting his kiss.

The kiss was as gentle as the ocean on a calm day, softly sensual, deliberately drawn out. But not enough for Dani, as she reached out with a small moan and encircled his neck, bringing him nearer.

"Mmm, wait. This is awkward," Adam muttered. Deftly he shifted her until she was facing him, straddling his lap. He eased his hands under her sweatshirt and slid them up her back. "This is much better." His grip tightened as he captured her mouth, sliding his tongue inside. His breathing came faster as Dani responded instantly, avidly. Adam felt himself floating.

With a sureness of purpose, he eased himself back a bit as he moved his hands to the front of her to close them over her warm, aroused flesh. She moved against him in a rhythmic message he had no willpower to ignore, for he wanted her just as badly. He lifted his head and sought her eyes, but she kept them downcast.

"What is it?" he asked softly.

His hands, his hands. Those wonderful hands were making her pliant, melting her bones, her flesh. Heat spread through her, a slow heat that seeped through every pore. She leaned her forehead against his and let out a ragged sigh. "I can't get over how you can make me feel so much so quickly."

He took her hand and placed it on himself so she could feel how he was straining for control. "I'd say the feeling's mutual." Leaving her hand exactly where he wanted it, he raised his own to frame her face, forcing her to look at him.

"I love the way your body feels against mine," he murmured. His fingers, none too steady as desire licked at him, reached to stroke her hair. "Like silk." He buried his nose in it for a long moment. "Like wet silk sliding through my fingers."

The light was dim, both outside the cave and in, and thunder rumbled nearby. Dani felt as if she'd been waiting for this time with this man all her life. Her skin felt damp, chilled, except where he touched, where he looked. Lightning flashed behind her, illuminating the rocky cave walls momentarily, yet she never took her gaze from his.

"I suppose this weekend was inevitable," she said. "But I don't think it was very wise—for either of us. We don't want the same things."

"No, we don't," he said, sounding almost sad. "It's not too late. There are choices. You can get up and run."

Again she touched his unshaven face, ran her fingers along his rugged jaw, traced his strong mouth. "Can I? Can you?"

He saw that her eyes were turbulent, like the stormy sky. He said, "I tried."

"And?"

"I had to come after you." Desperately he pulled her closer, crushing his mouth to hers. He moved his hands down her flat stomach, inside the band of her sweatpants, seeking her. He found her, and she gasped with pleasure. He couldn't seem to touch enough, taste enough, he thought, watching her face flush with excitement.

When she'd come to him she'd been sexually untouched, but a long way from innocent. No innocent could have driven him to the brink so readily, destroyed his control so easily, brought him to his knees with need so badly. Other women had tried, but no one had succeeded. Until now. Until Dani. He moved his fingers inside her.

Nervously Dani lifted her head and glanced over her shoulder. "What if someone were to walk by?"

"In an early-morning storm along an empty beach? Unlikely." Almost roughly he pulled her back to him to kiss her again, letting her essence drug every cell of his body.

Dani drifted on a haze of feeling as his mouth moved over her skin, his teeth nibbling, his hands making her vibrate with need. Since she'd met Adam, pleasure was an old friend he'd introduced her to, desire a constant companion, passion a sleeping giant waiting to be roused. The need for her to be flesh to flesh grew unbearable. Desperation made her clumsy as she unzipped his shirt and tugged it from his shoulders. At last her hands were free to linger on his smooth, hard skin.

Adam shifted and struggled in the cramped quarters until he'd pushed aside their clothing. Lovingly she touched him, moving slowly over his chest, around his shoulders and down his back. Though she knew need raged inside him, he let her set the pace, as she learned him at her leisure.

Never had she been free to explore a man so intimately, so thoroughly. He was beautiful, and she knew her eyes reflected the knowledge. She ran her hands down his arms as the rain beat on the rocky roof overhead and splashed on the nearby sand.

She felt Adam quiver under her touch and gloried in his response. Then tenderness became passion as she sensed he would wait no longer. She, too, was spinning in a new world, dizzy with sensations. There came to her the certain knowledge that no man save him could ever take her to that special place. With his strong hands he lifted her, and she took him inside, her mouth reaching for his.

The kiss was hard, urgent, their movements frenzied with a burst of passion neither could forestall. Adam pulled his mouth from hers and heard her sigh his name as he felt her explode almost immediately. Pulsating, she absorbed the aftershock for a long moment, then finally sagged against him. At the same time the storm broke, but Adam held himself in check with desperate control.

At last she eased herself back, still dazed, her gaze dark and questioning.

"What is it you want from me, Dani?" he asked, knowing what it was, knowing he couldn't give it to her, not now, not yet.

She shook her head quickly as if to shake away the thought. "Nothing."

"Liar." He plunged deeper, his eyes locked with hers, and saw hers change. "Beautiful liar," he said just before he captured her mouth and began to move, taking her spiraling to a second, a stronger peak.

The sun was still playing hide-and-seek with a few lingering gray clouds on Monday morning as Dani glanced out the kitchen window. After plugging in the coffeepot, she opened the sliding window and discovered that the air was still damp and chilly. Not a lovely summer weekend, she thought, slamming the window closed.

Wrapped in her long white terry-cloth robe, she stretched her arms high above her head with a luxurious yawn. Despite the gloomy weather, the weekend had been a pretty special one for her. Running a hand through her hair, which was still wet from the shower, she felt a smile tug at her mouth. Yes, pretty special.

Like two giddy teenagers, she and Adam had guiltily struggled back into their clothes in the cave yesterday morning and then run all the way back to the cabin. Laughing at everything and nothing, they'd shared a long, warm shower, eaten a hearty breakfast, then spent the day in front of the fire which Adam had kept stoking. They'd

talked, held, touched. They'd fully intended to drive
somewhere to dinner, since there wasn't much food in the
house, but appetites of another sort, stronger and more
profound, had distracted them. They'd made love in front
of the fire on the thick patchwork quilt, then later trans-
ferred to the big bed, where they'd spent another wondrous night. Perhaps *special* was too tame a word, Dani
thought as she finished her orange juice.

Hearing Adam turn off the shower, she opened the refrigerator to start breakfast. As she grated cheese to go into
the eggs she sipped her coffee. Liar, he'd called her. Beautiful liar. Perhaps not beautiful, Dani decided, but lately,
definitely a liar.

She filled a mug with black coffee and took it into the
bedroom, but Adam was still in the bathroom. She set it
on the dresser for him and returned to the kitchen.

They hadn't mentioned that particular conversation
again, though they'd talked about everything else under
the sun. Dani took down the plates to set the table. "What
is it you want from me, Dani?" he'd asked, and she'd told
him, "Nothing." She wished she could tell him all that she
wanted.

*I want you to stop trying to be something you're not. I
want you to let Bonnie lead her own life, while you concentrate on yours. I want you just to be yourself, to accept people as they are and not as you'd wish them to be.
I want you to love me as I love you.*

Dani drained her cup and looked out toward the choppy
waters. Arlene had always warned her to stop reaching for
the unobtainable for it could lead to heartbreak. From an
Olympic medal, to a change in life-style, to Adam Kinkaid, she'd reached and never quite managed to grasp any
of the three. Was it failure on her part, had she set impos-

sible goals, or hadn't she tried hard enough? Dani rubbed her forehead, not sure where the answer lay.

What was keeping Adam?

She found him sitting cross-legged on the bedroom floor in front of the bookcase, wearing only his jeans. His coffee cup was beside him, and a large album was spread out on his lap.

"What did you find?" she asked, sliding down to sit beside him as she craned her neck to see.

Adam looked up and saw she didn't recognize what he held. "I walked by and jostled the bookcase. When I leaned down to put back the two paperbacks that had fallen, I spotted this." Marking his place with one hand, he turned the cover back to show her. "The heading caught my eye. 'Danielle Winthrop Ames, Superstar.' Is it yours?"

"No," Dani answered, puzzled. She reached for the book. "May I?"

Adam slid the album onto her lap but stayed close enough to watch her as she slowly turned the pages. First there were photographs, from her toddler days on through the school years. Most of them were of Dani involved in some sports activity. Swimming, sledding, bicycling, basketball, tennis. And ice skating. So many ice skating. The costumes got shorter as she got older and prettier. As she went through the book, Adam couldn't read her expression but saw that she was totally absorbed.

Dani strolled down the wispy lanes of memory. Arlene's careful, cultured handwriting noted dates and places under the photos, some of which Dani was seeing for the first time. When had the album been left here? she wondered, for she'd never noticed it before. Next came the certificates of merit, the ribbons she'd won ice skating, the yellowed newspaper clippings. There were pictures of her with the other skaters and one with Billie Joe, arms twined around each other, taken at the state finals. Finally came photos of tryouts for nationals, snapshots of a tense Dani practicing hour after hour, her coach huddled nearby.

The last photo was of the scoreboard. Not quite enough. Thank goodness no one had taken a picture of the tears that had followed. Dani ran a trembling hand along the frayed binding. "I never knew," she whispered.

"Your mother put together that scrapbook over, what, eighteen years and you never knew?"

Hugging the book to her chest, Dani closed her eyes and shook her head. "No. This family isn't . . . good at talking about their feelings. Arlene's advice to me always was to stop reaching for things I probably couldn't have. She never discouraged me in my sports, but she never encouraged me, either. All those years of training, the hopes, the skating camps. When I started winning, I think Arlene thought it was a fluke. She went along with my dreams, but almost as if she expected me to grow out of another teenage phase. I always felt she was disappointed she'd had a daughter who aspired in that direction and not in hers."

"I'd say that album was put together with a great deal of love and pride. I had no idea you'd gotten as far as nationals in ice skating, that you'd considered the Olympics."

"It was a long time ago."

"That life takes so much self-control and sacrifice and dedication."

She tried to give him a smile, because he seemed to understand. She was getting too damn emotional. Arlene proud of her? It was such a new thought. "I always felt that my mother thought I didn't have what it took to be a winner."

Adam drew closer and touched her face so she'd look at him. Tear-filled blue eyes stared back at him in confusion. "You are a winner. It's people who don't try who are the losers." He brushed her lips in a light kiss.

"Thank you." Annoyed with herself, Dani swiped at her tears. "I *never* cry, and here, in two days, I've done nothing but sob on your shoulder." She shook her head. "I don't know what's happening to me."

Adam took the album and set it carefully back in the bookcase before enveloping Dani in a big hug, rocking with her until they fell back onto the oval braided rug. "You go ahead and laugh, cry—do what you like," he said, seeing her face slowly brighten. "Just don't move away from me."

Half sprawled across him, tangling her fingers in the soft hair of his chest, Dani smiled into Adam's eyes. "Fat chance, fella. You're stuck with me—at least for another few hours." Keep it light, Dani told herself. So many emotions to sort out, but she'd do it later, when she was home again and alone. For now no pressures, and only mild pretenses.

"I couldn't think of a nicer person to be stuck with." He kissed the tip of her nose. "Tell me, that boy you're holding and smiling at in that one snapshot—someone special?"

He didn't miss much, she thought. "Billie Joe McKamey, and yes, he was special, for a while. My first love." Until you.

"Yet you didn't . . . the two of you never . . ."

"Made love? No, we didn't." Dani sighed deeply. "I wanted to, heaven knows. But I'd seen so many casual affairs in the training camps end badly. We were young, away from home and lonely. Arlene flew in frequently, but mostly I was with my coach, and she watched me like a hawk.''

Adam looked doubtful. "Every minute?"

"Sounds pretty silly, doesn't it? I guess I didn't want to badly enough, or I'd have found a way."

"Did you just drift apart from Billie Joe?"

Dani watched her fingers curl the hair on his chest. "No, I deliberately walked away. Billie Joe was from the South and hated it because he loved winter sports. He was so happy to get as far as the nationals, so sure he'd be an Olympic contender. Then, when neither of us made it, he was crushed, worse than I. We both had offers from an ice show, and he saw a way to continue doing what he loved to do, so he signed right away. He pleaded with me to go with him, but I wanted to finish college. He got very upset, and we fought.''

"And so you left him, just like that?"

"Yes. I knew the life traveling with an ice show wasn't for me. He wanted to change me, wanted me to be something I wasn't interested in being. I'd already had more than enough of that on the home front. So I walked away."

"That took a lot of guts."

"Perhaps. It hurt for a long time. Some decisions do."

"Danielle, you're a much deeper person than most." Adam pulled at the thick material of her robe, parted it and slipped his hands inside, where her flesh was warm, eager for his touch. "And you're lovely and exciting, and I'm glad you walked away from Billie Joe."

She loved what she was hearing. Too much. "I should tell you that the bread is drying out, the cheese is melting and the eggs are dying on the counter. How about breakfast?" Though she'd felt her blood heat, she tried to ignore it. They couldn't spend all their time in bed, could they?

Adam's eyes were suddenly serious as his hands stilled. "You're very lucky your family cares so much for you, Dani. We all need our families, need to do all we can for them. If we neglect our families, where are we, *what* are we?"

Back to that again, she thought. Was he trying to justify his resolution to help Bonnie and the methods he was using? Was he subtly telling her that although they had this obvious and very powerful attraction, his family was his first priority? She had no intention of making him choose. Could she even make him see how she felt?

Dani searched for words. "It wasn't a question of neglect in my family. I felt different from them, and I was and still am. I always wanted to belong yet never seemed able to. When I attempted things, such as skating competitively, I never sensed their approval. It was as if I'd chosen wrong. When I didn't make it, that only compounded the problem, as though they'd been right all along."

She raised her eyes to his. "Why didn't my mother let me know she had some pride in me—enough to put together that book? It would have helped me so much then. Yes, we need our families, but members of a family need to make one another feel that they are loved and accepted for what they are, not what others wish they were."

"It's hard to keep from guiding someone younger in your family when you see things they're too inexperienced to see."

His voice had a stubborn edge, Dani realized, and she knew they were stalemated on this one. Knowing no good way to end it except one, she leaned over and took his mouth with hers. The kiss was slow, soft and sweet, burying the feelings for now. Tomorrow they could sort out their many differences.

Just as Adam had pulled her fully atop him, the phone rang, jarring both of them. Reluctantly Dani lifted her head. "Not too many people have this number," she said, scooting from him, standing and retying her robe.

"I called Information and gave it to my service," he told her, scrambling to sit up. "In case there's an emergency on one of the work sites."

Dani reached the bedside and answered the phone. "Well, hello, Mrs. Kinkaid. How are you?...I see. Yes, he is. Just a moment."

Frowning, Dani held the receiver toward Adam, who'd come to stand by her. "It's your mother, and she seems upset."

Doris Kinkaid wasted not a moment when Adam came on the phone. "Bonnie's college counselor called. She's packed her things and run away."

Chapter Ten

Adam was a pacer, Dani decided as she watched him march back and forth across the long main room of the cabin, trailing the telephone cord. He was frowning, his face as agitated as the sea during yesterday's storm. After getting only sketchy information from his mother, he'd put in a call to Bonnie's college counselor, but for some reason the college was having trouble locating the woman. Impatience danced across his tight features as he swiveled and retraced his steps. Curled up in a corner of the couch, sipping her coffee, Dani decided to stay out of his way.

"Where the hell did the counselor go?" Adam asked no one in particular. "She talked to Mom a short time ago."

"It's a holiday weekend, Adam," Dani told him in a reasonable voice, hoping her attitude would be contagious. "She may be off campus."

"It's her job to be *on* campus when things go wrong." He ran a hand through his already mussed hair. "I should have known when Mom told me Bonnie wasn't coming home for the long weekend that she was planning some stupid stunt.''

Dani set down her cup. "I thought Bonnie was through school for this year."

"They're on four semesters, not three."

"Did she ever do anything like this before, just disappear?" Adam shook his head. "Does she sometimes stay at school over holiday weekends?''

"She drives home most weekends, but this time she said she had to study for next week's exams. Made sense to me.''

Dani refilled his coffee cup and handed it to him. "Perhaps she finished studying and decided to visit a friend off campus.''

"And take a large suitcase of clothes?"

Dani sat down again. "You're jumping to conclusions. You've told me Bonnie's a sensible girl, not given to wild escapades. Can't you give her the benefit of the doubt and hear her side of this?''

Adam threw himself onto the couch, nearly tangling his feet in the cord, and swore colorfully. "I know who's behind this. I'll bet my last dollar."

"All right, tell me.''

"Jeff Hayden, that's who. That scruffy, long-haired, no-account—''

"Adam, really! You're overreacting and sounding like an outraged father.''

Dark, angry eyes swung on her. "She doesn't have a father, remember? Someone has to look out for her."

"And if she had a father, he couldn't have prevented this from happening, either.''

"If that hippie's laid a hand on her . . .''

Dani flopped back on the couch and sighed. "If he has, it was probably with her permission. Did you want her to remain a virgin all her life?"

"You waited quite a while," he reminded her.

"By choice. As we said earlier, if I'd wanted to make love sooner, I would have." He couldn't see it, she thought. Couldn't see that she'd waited until she'd cared a great deal. From what she knew of Bonnie, she also cared a great deal for this young man, despite Adam's negative feelings about him. "She's nearly twenty. Women today—"

Abruptly he stood. "Dani, I don't want a lecture on women. I probably know more about them than you do."

Angry, too, Dani jumped up. "Then again, perhaps you don't know diddly-squat about women, period!" She moved to the kitchen before she gave in to the urge to punch him a good one.

She was staring out the window, when she heard him talk into the phone, obviously to Bonnie's counselor. She felt a wave of empathy for poor Bonnie, wherever she was, for she would really be in for it when Adam did find her.

"The woman doesn't know a damn thing except that Bonnie's been gone since yesterday morning," Adam said testily as he stormed into the kitchen. "But Bonnie's roommate, Diane, stayed at the dorm over the weekend, and they're tracking her down now. She's supposed to call me as soon as they locate her. Maybe she knows something." He poured the last of the coffee into his cup. "I could strangle Bonnie."

Perhaps I should try again, Dani thought watching him drink, seeing the worry lines on his face. It was hard for her to put herself in his place, never having had to worry about someone younger, less experienced. She took a calming breath and softened her voice. "Would you like some breakfast? We might both feel better with some food.'' They hadn't eaten since early yesterday and now were operating on coffee nerves.

Adam turned to look at her as if seeing her for the first time since the phone had rung. He set down his cup, moved over to her and pulled her into his arms. ''Thanks for putting up with me. I tend to get overexcited now and then.''

''I noticed.''

''When I care about someone, I worry about them.''

''Adam, she's your sister, a woman, not a child. You have to start letting go a little.'' She could tell by his quick frown that he didn't want to hear that.

Dropping his arms, he walked over to the stove. ''I'll make breakfast.''

Dani let him, and though they talked while they ate, she could sense that Adam's mind was elsewhere, his ear listening for the phone. They were just finishing the dishes, when it rang. He dashed into the living room to answer. Shaking her head, Dani decided to wait things out in the kitchen.

Adam was pigheaded, and so damn sure he knew what was right for everyone. She hung up the towel and sat down at the table. He was obsessed with running Bonnie's life. She couldn't help wondering if he'd designed and built his mother's new house without so much as consulting her about color scheme, simply because he felt he knew best.

The woman who married Adam Kinkaid would have to have the negotiating skill of a union boss, the patience of a saint and the stamina of a professional athlete. Dani laughed to herself over the last one. Stamina to survive the marathon sessions in his bed, she thought, flushing at the memory. Which is where they'd be right now if his sister hadn't decided to spread her wings this weekend. Hearing him slam the phone down, she got up to see what Bonnie's roommate had told him.

"What did I tell you?" he asked through clenched teeth. "She's with Jeff. Damn!"

"Is her roommate sure?"

"Hell, yes. Diane covered up for her until someone who wasn't in on things went looking for Bonnie and, when she was nowhere to be found, got worried and went to the counselor. Diane's a flighty little airhead. Told me that Bonnie and Jeff have run off to be married, and didn't I think that was romantic."

Dani gave him a long look. "There are those who think elopements are romantic."

He glared at her. "I'm not one of them. They're in a motel about twenty miles off campus." He marched angrily into the bedroom.

"A motel?" she asked, following him. "Are they married?"

Adam reached for his shirt. "No, thank God. It seems they hadn't figured on everything being closed on a holiday weekend. Bonnie called Diane earlier and told her they'd be at this motel until Tuesday morning, when they plan to go to the courthouse to get married. Over my dead body!" Scowling, he went into the bathroom and closed the door with a heavy thud.

Dani sighed, realizing she couldn't dissuade Adam at this point. He was hell-bent on dragging Bonnie back, kicking and screaming. She removed her robe, and slipped into silk panties and a bra. What would he have done if he'd learned they'd already gotten married and—heaven forbid—consummated the marriage? Had the marriage annulled, tied Bonnie to her bedpost and shot Jeff at dawn?

She'd dressed in tan cotton slacks and a black cotton sweater, and was just stepping into black leather flats, when Adam emerged from the bathroom, buttoning his shirt.

"I'd like you to go with me," he said.

"To the motel? Are you sure we should do this?"

Adam sat down to put on his socks and shoes, ignoring her questions. "I just can't get over Bonnie, throwing her life away on a man so wrong for her. A greasy-haired punk who can't even keep up with her, much less help her get places."

Dani felt a flash of anger at his attitude. "Have you met Jeff Hayden?" she asked, brushing her hair.

"I don't have to meet him. I've seen his picture and heard about his background."

Frowning, she turned to face him. "Adam, do I have to remind you that *you* came from a similar background?"

His eyes cold, he stood. "And I made something of myself."

"What makes you think Jeff won't?"

"He's a loser, and he's not dragging my sister down with him. Are you coming with me or not?"

Yes, she would go. Bonnie would undoubtedly need someone on her side. Dani reached for her purse. "Let's go."

A light rain was falling as they pulled into the parking lot bordering a neat row of cabins with a small, brick office at the far end. Rainbow's End, the blinking sign declared. Dani fervently hoped it was.

She'd followed Adam's Porsche during the two-hour drive on slick pavements, relieved that he'd kept his speed within limits. Knowing he'd probably take Bonnie home— if she survived his tirade, that is—Dani had decided to pack her car and close up the cottage, not wanting to face going back there alone after having shared the past two nights with Adam. Besides, she had classes tomorrow morning.

Adam could be so formidable, Dani thought, walking alongside him as they made their way to Room 112, where Diane had said they'd find Bonnie and Jeff. So unyielding. His usually amiable features had visibly hardened as the day had progressed; his eyes had become dangerously dark.

"I don't understand, Dani," Adam said, sounding truly puzzled. "After all I've done for Bonnie, all I've planned for her, how can she turn her back and choose that—that skinny creep?"

Dani shoved her hands in her pockets. "Adam, have you ever been in love?"

"Love? For goodness' sake, Dani, she's nineteen!"

"Almost twenty, and I've heard that love can hit pretty hard much younger than that." And damn hard a bit older than that.

"Puppy love, the kind you outgrow." He stopped, turning to face her. "Bonnie has two more years of college, and then the whole world ahead of her. Do you know Dennis DeBries?"

The question surprised her. "Howard's brother? Yes, of course. What about him?"

"Hell of a nice guy. I met him at Arlene's that night after the opera. Toni introduced us. He's not as stuffy as Howard, only twenty-four, and he was just graduated from Harvard. Harvard, Dani!"

"Yes, I've heard of Harvard, Adam," she said dryly, but saw that the humor went right over his head. They were standing under a dripping maple tree, and Dani watched as small puddles formed on the sidewalk. She wondered where this conversation was going.

"And he's going into the family business. His future's assured. He's the kind of man Bonnie should get to know. Not some kid in leather pants who just started to shave last week." He shook his head disgustedly and glanced away, then swung his gaze back to Dani. "Why are you looking at me like that?"

"You continually amaze me, Adam." She knew she didn't sound amazed, or even angry. She was moving toward resigned, and she knew that wasn't good. Maybe Adam never would learn. "What makes you think you can meet someone, take him by the arm, introduce him to Bonnie and say, 'Here, folks, fall in love, get married, because *I* know you're right for each other'? Suppose Dennis isn't interested in your matchmaking, or suppose Bonnie hates Dennis on sight."

"Then there'll be someone else, but the *right* someone, not some guy who, if he had married her, would have to quit school and pump gas so they could eat."

Feeling her temper flare, Dani narrowed her eyes. "Frankly, if it were me, I'd marry someone in a minute who pumped gas by day and went to school nights, if he loved me, rather than tie myself to some bore of a stockbroker who didn't even know how to kiss well."

"What's kissing got to do with it?"

A lot, buddy. A whole lot. "Never mind. A personal prejudice."

Calming, Adam took her hand. "Don't you see, Dani? If I get Bonnie set with someone like Dennis, I can stop worrying about her, stop all this socializing and concentrate on us."

She was shocked. "Us?"

"Yes, us. Hasn't this weekend meant anything to you?" His voice, suddenly soft and seductive, drew her.

"Of course it has." Did she dare believe what she was hearing?

"Then let me get my sister settled. Afterward it'll be our turn. We're good together. I'll build you a house, you can quit work and I'll take care of you."

Take care of her? What happened to love? He hadn't heard a word she'd said today, maybe not since they'd first met. "I was right earlier," Dani said, turning her back to him. "You don't know a damn thing about women."

"What did I say?"

Dani sighed. "Never mind. Let's get this over with." She found the right cabin and knocked sharply. Adam came up behind her as the door slowly opened.

Bonnie Kinkaid, wearing a navy school sweatshirt and blue jeans, stood just inside, looking impossibly young. Jeff Hayden, tall and slight, his dark hair worn just below the collar of his shirt, was close behind her. Dropping her gaze, Bonnie turned and went to sit on a chair alongside the bed, wiping a tear from her pale cheek. Jeff, his dark eyes blazing with contained anger, sat down on the arm and picked up her hand.

Scarcely glancing at the two of them, Adam followed Dani inside and closed the door, trying to curb his anger and channel his thoughts.

Dani looked around, then went to sit on the bed. Standard country motel, she thought, with Early American decor in muted shades of tan and green. The bed was made and didn't look mussed—for which she was grateful, considering Adam's present mood. Bonnie wouldn't meet their eyes, and her free hand twisted a tissue in her lap.

Dani reached over and gently placed a hand on hers. "Don't worry. It's going to be all right," she told her, including Jeff in a smile she hoped was encouraging. The girl looked at Dani with tear-filled, worried eyes.

Adam pulled up the other chair and sat down, facing the three of them. Where to begin? he wondered wearily. They both looked so young. And Dani, as usual, looked slightly challenging. If only he could convince Bonnie he was acting in her best interest. "I'm not happy to find you both in a motel room," he began. Damn, but he sounded like a Victorian father even to his ears.

"We weren't *doing* anything," Bonnie said, her voice strained.

"Have you ever...?" He saw his sister bend her head with a guilty flush. Adam swallowed hard. Nineteen, he had to remind himself, was a woman, as Dani had pointed out. "Bonnie, are you pregnant?"

"No!"

Jeff's thin arm went around her reassuringly. "We only checked in here because we made a mistake, forgot it was a holiday weekend. We drove around, even stopped at a justice of the peace we found. But he was out of town. It started to rain, so we checked into this motel. We got some burgers, watched TV, and we were waiting for Tuesday morning, when the courthouse opens." He pulled Bonnie closer. "Not that it's any of your business."

"Now, wait a minute..." Adam was half off his chair, when he felt Dani's restraining hand on his arm. Grudgingly he sat back down.

"No, you wait a minute, Mr. Kinkaid," Jeff said, getting braver. "Bonnie and I haven't done anything wrong. All we want to do is get married."

"That's out of the question," Adam said with finality.

"Adam," Bonnie pleaded, "I love Jeff. Please."

"Bonnie," Adam began, trying to take a reasonable approach, now that he knew she wasn't pregnant, "we all go through teenage infatuations. I'm sure Jeff's a nice boy. But we made plans for you. Don't you remember? We talked about them. Big plans.''

"*You* talked about them. They're your plans, not mine." She held Jeff's hand tightly, as if clinging to a lifeline. "My plans revolve around Jeff. I love him, and we're going to be married. You can't stop us."

"We'll see about that," Adam said, clenching his teeth. If he had to move her to another school, he would. He wasn't going to let this pimply-faced youth ruin his sister's life. "After all I've done for you, Bonnie, I don't see how you can turn your back on Mother and me and choose him."

Dani had heard enough. "Adam, did it ever occur to you that Bonnie might not want the life you've decided she should have?"

"You stay out of this!" Angrily Adam stood and began pacing. That's all he needed—three of them against him! Why couldn't anyone see? "You don't know what you're talking about. You didn't grow up in a couple of tiny rooms where you had to sleep on a daybed. You didn't watch your poor, tired mother stretch a chicken for a whole week so three of you could eat. You didn't go to school all day, then work every evening and weekends. The two of us did, though Bonnie seems to have forgotten."

He cleared his throat noisily. "If I let these two marry, all they'll be able to afford will be those same two rooms. Then they'll have a baby or two, and maybe Jeff won't be able to handle things, and maybe he'll walk out on Bonnie and the kids, the way our father did. And it'll be history repeating itself."

"I wouldn't leave Bonnie," Jeff interjected, raising his voice.

So that's what was behind all this, Dani realized. She should have guessed. "It doesn't have to be like that, Adam. Not every young marriage falls apart. If these kids care enough, they'll work and help each other. They'll postpone a family until Jeff's earning better money." She leaned across Bonnie to catch the young man's eyes. "Architecture, isn't that what you're planning on?" She waited for his nod. "Good field. I have a friend who's graduating next year with a degree in architecture. She did it on scholarships, too, and on lots of odd jobs and a little help from home."

Turning toward Adam, who'd stopped his pacing near her, she touched his arm. "You've got to let Bonnie lead her own life, Adam. Instead of interfering every step of the way, why don't you offer them a little help?"

"I never interfered until recently. Until she lost her head."

"People in love often do."

"And when they get their heads out of the clouds, they find they've made some really stupid decisions."

Jeff was beginning to lose patience. "Mr. Kinkaid, I can take care of Bonnie. I'll get a summer job and we'll find an apartment. I'm on full scholarship next year and—"

"No! Bonnie, where's your suitcase? I'm taking you home."

"I'm not going!"

"Yes, you are. I—"

"Don't touch her," Jeff said, tightening his grip on Bonnie's arm.

"I think everybody needs to cool down," Dani said, rising. "You've stopped the wedding, Adam. Now, let's buy a little time here." She turned to Bonnie and Jeff. "If I take you back to your dorms, will you promise Adam you won't leave again until after your exams are over? It's not going to help your future plans any to blow this whole semester."

Bonnie looked at Jeff a long minute, then they both slowly nodded.

"Okay. Adam, you can talk with Bonnie later, when you've calmed down. Perhaps at home, where your mother can add her thoughts."

"I don't like your taking over, here, Dani," Adam said, his mouth a tight line. "Who asked you to interfere?"

"You asked me along, and I came because I thought Bonnie might need one sensible person who would listen without prejudice."

"This is my family business, and I'll handle it. You can take Jeff to his dorm. Bonnie, get your things. I'm taking you home."

Slowly Bonnie got to her feet, pulling Jeff with her. "No, Adam. We're both going with Dani."

Adam's face registered shock mixed with anger. "I'm telling you one last time to go outside and get in my car."

Bonnie didn't waver as she met his steady gaze. "I'm sorry if I'm hurting you, Adam, but I can't let you run my life any longer." Gripping Jeff's hand, she walked with him to the door.

Dani held the door open for them, watching Adam's face as they filed outside.

"You're going to regret this, Dani," he said, furious.

She studied his dark eyes, hoping for some sign of compromise. Seeing none, she nodded. "I already do."

Chapter Eleven

All right, Oscar, we have some decisions to make here,"
Dani said, circling the plant she'd pulled out into the center of the kitchen floor. The ocean air wafted in through
the open window, causing the philodendron's split leaves
to undulate in an impromptu dance. "I've got to trim some
of this overgrowth at the bottom. The question is which
leaves."

Grabbing her pruning shears, she squatted by the red-
wood tub that was Oscar's home. "Now, hold still. This
won't hurt." Dani worked quietly for several minutes, until a sound from the stereo caught her attention.

She'd put on a stack of records earlier, and as the unmistakable strains of Madama Butterfly's "Un bel di"
came floating to her, she nearly moaned aloud. "Damn,"
she said, sitting down hard, her gaze drifting to the blue
sky out the window. Yes, it was one fine day, but would
her lover ever come back to her? Lieutenant Pinkerton

hadn't really come back to Cio-Cio-San, and it was unlikely *her* lover would come back to her.

Here it was Saturday, nearly a week after she'd left
Adam standing, tight lipped and angry, in the college
counselor's waiting room. She hadn't seen nor heard from
him since.

Dani still thought he was wrong in the way stubborn
people often are, determined not to see any viewpoint but
his. She'd talked for some length with Bonnie and Jeff
outside the dorm, where she'd driven them Monday night.
In the tight confines of Dani's two-seater car, Bonnie had
sat on Jeff's lap and poured out her heart, while Jeff had
backed up her story.

They'd met the first week Bonnie had arrived at school
as a freshman; Jeff, two years older, had been a junior
then. Over the past two years, they'd gradually moved
from meeting in the library to actual dates to falling in
love. Bonnie had tried to bring Jeff home, but Adam had
opposed it from the start, unwilling even to meet him, and
Doris Kinkaid had gone along with Adam's wishes. They'd
both thought she was much too young to be serious about
anyone, and they were less than thrilled with Jeff's image.

Leaning forward to trim a browning leaf, Dani didn't
think Jeff looked all that "hippielike," as Adam had labeled him. Jeff had confessed that he played in a rock
band on weekends to earn spending money, and couldn't
look too conservative. The prospect of their being separated the whole long summer, with Jeff not even allowed
visitation, had prompted their elopement. All in all, both
had impressed Dani as levelheaded, bright and sincere.
Though she'd tried to sound encouraging, saying that time
would take care of everything, she didn't see an easy solution to their problems in the light of Adam's stubborn

stance. And who should know better than she how truly stubborn he could be.

Finished trimming, Dani reached for the spray bottle to wipe the dust from Oscar's leaves. Get his sister settled, Adam had said, then there'd be time for him and Dani. He'd build her a house, she'd quit work and he'd take care of her. Just like that, without consultation, or conversation about love and marriage and how they both felt about a future together. *He* would make all the decisions, and she would roll over and say "Thank you, kind sir." The man was living in the Dark Ages.

Hadn't she explained how important her work was to her? Had he ever asked if she even wanted marriage, or how she felt about children? Or where she might like to live?

"Thickheaded, Oscar," she said, standing up. "The man is definitely thickheaded. Who needs him anyhow?" Wiping her hands, she stood back to survey her handiwork. "There, now, don't you look nice?"

"Who looks nice?" asked a voice through the back-door screen.

"Sabrina! How good to see you. Come in."

Sabrina came in, looking beautiful in white linen slacks and a white silk blouse. "Who are you talking to in here?"

"Oscar, who else?" Dani told her, shoving the large plant back into his corner. "I like talking to plants. They never sass me back." Smiling at her sister, she waved her to a chair at the kitchen table. "Want some iced tea?"

"Mmm, I'd love some. I'm beat, and it's only four in the afternoon." She looked up at Dani. "Is school out for this year?"

Carrying two frosty glasses over, Dani nodded. "Last day was yesterday." She sat opposite her sister and took a long swallow of the refreshing drink.

"Are you glad?"

"I'm always glad at the end of the year and equally as glad to get going again in the fall." She studied Sabrina's face, noting the shadows under her large green eyes. And that indefinable sadness still lingered in her gaze. If Dani chose her words carefully, maybe she could find out what was bothering Sabrina. "And why are you so beat so early in the day? I thought you were used to putting in ten-hour days like Dad."

"I often do," Sabrina answered, rubbing the bridge of her nose. "Lately, for every step I manage to take forward I find myself backsliding two."

"The business not going well?"

Sabrina shrugged. "I suppose it is, just not as well as I'd hoped by now. If only I could get that French connection."

"The one you were working on when you were in Paris last. I remember. Gabrielle somebody, the woman you were hoping to connect with. Is that the one?"

"That's her. Gabrielle DuMochelle, the grande dame of haute couture, to be exact. She holds all the marbles, and she damn well knows it." Sabrina took a cooling sip of tea.

"Wouldn't it benefit her, also, to tie in with your Boston firm?"

"Some, but the real benefit would be to me. To represent her clothes line in the States exclusively would put my company in competition with the best."

"And she's not willing to negotiate?"

"Gabrielle's a shrewd one, biding her time, keeping several of us dangling. It's not necessarily money that will win her over. I've offered her plenty, but she's already got more than she could ever spend. I wish I knew what would do the trick."

"Isn't there anyone else, another designer you could connect with, someone not so difficult?"

"A few, but they're insignificant compared to Gabrielle. She's quite simply the best. Her work is fantastic, and I don't want to represent someone who's second best." Sabrina crossed her legs and leaned back.

"How about getting to know someone who's close to her, someone who could act as a liaison?" Dani suggested. She saw pain flicker across Sabrina's expressive eyes, then disappear quickly.

"I've already tried that. There aren't that many people she trusts. The person I chose to speak on my behalf is her favorite nephew, but ..., well, it didn't work out." Sabrina toyed with her glass, her eyes downcast.

She looked unhappy, yet her eyes hadn't filled with tears. Rather, she looked as though she'd resigned herself to a great sadness. Dani got up to get more ice and refill their glasses. Once seated again, she wondered how to begin. "Are you hungry? I could fix us something."

Sabrina shook her head. "No, thank you."

Taking a deep breath, Dani plunged in. "Sabrina," she began, "do you remember R. J. Keach?"

Sabrina raised her eyes, frowning thoughtfully. "R. J. Keach. The boy with the boat who wanted me to sail around the world with him?" She laughed lightly. "I haven't thought of him in years. What were we both, seventeen?"

"Yes, seventeen, and you were so crushed when Arlene wouldn't let you set sail with him."

"He was so handsome, remember? With coal-black hair and those blue eyes."

"His body wasn't half-bad, either. You cried for a week when he refused to ask you out again because you'd turned him down."

Sabrina nodded, smiling. "I sure did, and you listened to me moan and groan dramatically the whole miserable time. Whatever made you think of R.J.?"

"I think that was the last time you confided in me, really confided, about something that was bothering you. Are you going to tell me who or what has hurt you recently? And don't tell me that what I see in your eyes has to do with your frustration over Gabrielle. Something happened on your last trip to Paris, didn't it?"

"You're pretty astute, Dani," Sabrina commented softly, "and a bit crafty to soften me with memories of R.J." Leaning forward on her crossed arms, she nodded. "Yes, something happened in Paris. I fell in love—for the first time, I think."

Oh, no, not both of them. And both of them feeling so unhappy about it. "Go on."

"He's a Frenchman, very good-looking, very charming. And very engaged-to-be-married. End of story."

"Engagements can be broken, if you care enough."

"Not in Phillipe's book they can't. Or, I should say, in his mother's. The marriage involves two families of great wealth, and the arrangements were made when Phillipe and the girl were both toddlers. And that's that."

"But who does Phillipe love?"

"A good question. He said he loved me, but..." She couldn't seem to complete the thought.

Dani wanted to hit something, hard. "And he let you go to marry this other woman because his mother wants their families joined? Sabrina, that's positively archaic. I didn't know people still did that in these modern times."

"Evidently they do in certain areas of Europe."

"And you're not going to fight for him?"

Sabrina drew herself up straighter. "I do have a little pride. I think Phillipe should have done the fighting. Since he didn't choose to..."

"Oh, Sabrina." Dani put her hand over her sister's.

"Don't worry, Dani. I'm all right now. I'm not even going to cry again. You can only cry so much. I didn't know all this when I met him, of course. And when I found out, I thought I'd die. But I didn't. I just came home. Funny how your whole life can change in just a few weeks."

Yes, funny, Dani thought. Only not so funny. "I'm so sorry."

"So am I. It would seem that neither Arlene nor I am cut out for marriage." Needing to shift the focus, Sabrina looked up. "And just why is it you're home alone on a Saturday, talking to your plants? Is that blond giant coming to pick you up shortly?"

It was Dani's turn to drop her gaze. "No. We're no longer seeing each other."

Sabrina wrinkled her brow. "I'm surprised. When he danced with me a couple of weeks ago that night after the opera, all he talked about was you and how special you were."

"He did?"

"He sure did."

Dani waved dismissively. "He's just impressed with our family."

"Mmm, I don't think so. His eyes followed you even when he was talking with the men or dancing with the women. That lean, hard face of his softens when you're in his sight."

Dani wanted badly to believe her sister, but she couldn't let herself. "He was just feeling insecure among strangers and—"

"Oh, bull! If Adam Kinkaid is insecure, I'm a striped baboon. Dad doesn't impress easily, and he was really taken with him. Did you know that Adam's rebuilding his old school after a fire nearly destroyed it?"

"Well, I know his company is doing the work."

"Dad told me Adam's paying the construction crew out of his own pocket. And he got some old schoolmates to kick in donations for a PA system and a cafeteria, which their rebuilding loan didn't cover. Sounds like quite a guy to me."

Yes, quite a guy. Dani closed her eyes, feeling her heart swell with more love for Adam—or was that possible? Why couldn't she have discovered that he was a colossal bore, kicked dogs for recreation and was a heartless womanizer, instead of learning that he was doing something important for young people in a neighborhood where not too many people cared?

Sabrina narrowed her eyes thoughtfully. "You care a lot about him, don't you?"

Sabrina had been honest with her. Dani owed her no less. "Yes, but it doesn't matter in the long run. We want different things from life."

"What does that mean?" Impatiently Sabrina leaned forward, touching Dani's arm imploringly. "Don't be crazy. If you love him, don't let him get away. Pride's a lonely companion. Learn to compromise, Dani. Go after him."

Dani's laugh was low and mirthless. "Compromise. I'm willing to try. He's not. As you said, end of story."

Sabrina looked exasperated. "What does Adam want?"

Dani sighed heavily. "He wants to be accepted by what he considers high society, he wants his sister to marry well so he won't have to worry about her and he wants to run the lives of everyone he cares about, including me."

Sabrina shook her head. "Looks like all three of the Ames women had better find other interests. Are you all right?"

She gave a small smile. "Like you, I'll survive."

"Yes, we're both survivors. Why is it that that fact doesn't cheer me one damn bit?" Glancing at her watch, Sabrina stood. "I've got to run. Josh is picking me up soon. Want to come to dinner with us?"

"No, thanks," Dani said, walking to the door with her. "Is Josh helping you forget Phillipe?"

Sabrina looked at her sister with serious eyes, and once more Dani saw the melancholia. "Josh is good company, and we like to do some of the same things. He's kind without pressuring me. But there's no excitement, no magic, you know?"

Dani nodded. "Yes, I know."

"Unfortunately Josh isn't someone who could make me forget. I doubt there is a man like that, Dani. Some of us get bit by the love bug only once, and if things don't work, we decide we prefer work over marriage. It's not the best solution, but it's not the worst."

"Come now, Sabrina. Twenty-eight isn't exactly ancient. Perhaps you should hold off on forever decisions."

"Really? Who's going to make you forget Adam Kinkaid?" She leaned over and gave Dani a quick kiss on the cheek. "Call me."

Dani stood watching Sabrina through the screen as she got into her car. Who, indeed, was going to make her forget Adam Kinkaid?

She was going to have to think of a way to fill her days more fully, Dani thought as she ran along the beach early Monday morning with Mutt. In previous years summer vacations from teaching school had never been a problem. She usually loafed awhile, visited friends in nearby cities, worked on her house, did some charity work. And always she and Nora spent a few weeks together, driving south or up and down the New England coast. But Nora had had a wonderful offer from a prestigious architectural firm in New York and had called to say she started her new job the week after finals. So for Dani, her first idle week stretched before her, empty, aimless, lonely.

She'd had brunch yesterday with Sabrina and their father at Arlene's, and she'd felt restless and somewhat defensive, especially when Carter's sharp gaze had searched hers. His quiet questions had caused her to leave early. She'd never done that before, but then, she'd never been quite so introspective before, either. And it was getting tiresome even to her.

A gull dipped overhead, then flapped its wings at her and swooped back out to sea. The day was beautiful, already warm and sunny, the sky cloudless, the beach all but deserted this early. One lone figure maneuvered a small fishing boat out toward the open waters but otherwise she and Mutt were alone. Alone. Somehow that no longer held much appeal.

Turning in the hard-packed sand, Dani headed back home. She'd never minded being alone before, often preferring her own company to crowds. But there was a difference between being alone and contented and being alone and lonely. Adam had taught her that difference, and she wished she'd never learned the lesson.

All right, enough, Dani told herself, her bare feet raising sand in her wake as she ran. Self-pity was most unattractive and positively boring. She'd work on a tan, get some flowers and do some planting around her house, make some calls and see if there were some summer athletic programs she could get involved in. She would stop thinking about Adam and— He was sitting on a lawn chair in her terraced backyard, squinting into the morning sun, watching her approach. He was wearing loafers, tan slacks, a pale yellow shirt and a cocoa brown linen sport coat, but no tie. The only time she'd ever seen Adam in a tie was with his tux. His hair was unruly again, bleached by the sun into various shades of amber. His tan was deep, his dark eyes hooded, and he wasn't smiling. Mutt ran over to nuzzle him and Adam patted the dog's shaggy head, never taking his eyes from Dani.

Huffing a little—whether from her run or nerves, she wasn't sure—Dani dropped into the chair opposite him and tried for a casual, noncommittal approach. "Good morning."

How could she look so damn good so early in the morning? Adam asked himself. Fresh and wholesome, her skin rosy from her run. She was wearing a pink one-piece strapless terry-cloth thing that ended at midthigh, he noted, eyeing the soft swell of her breasts and her golden shoulders appreciatively. Her long legs stretched out near him, legs he remembered had wrapped around him possessively as she'd lain with him, letting him love her. Why was it that he and the one woman he'd found who seemed to be the other half of him had to have such different outlooks on a few important matters? Adam shoved both hands in his jacket pockets as the urge to reach out and touch her overwhelmed him.

"I've come to explain," he said, his voice husky. "I was hoping you'd listen."

Dani regarded him coolly while her heart thundered in her ears. "I'm always willing to listen."

"I'm sorry I lost my temper the last time we were together." He saw she was watching him, though she said nothing. "I don't usually overreact quite that badly."

Needing to move around, he got up and began to pace the small patio. "It's just that when I learned that Bonnie had run off and might actually have married that long-haired hippie, I saw red."

Dani sighed, wondering if she should even bother to try to convince this stubborn, unyielding man. "Did you know that Jeff's in a rock band to earn spending money to supplement his scholarship and that's why he wears his hair longish? And he chooses his clothes with that in mind. Adam, every job has its conformities. You wouldn't show up for work on a construction site in a three-piece suit and hair spray on a stylized cut, would you?"

He nodded, knowing she was right as far as that went. "I could accept the way he looks, but that's not all of it. They're both too young. He's the first boy Bonnie's ever shown much interest in. I want her to broaden her horizons, meet and date others so she'll have a basis of comparison. I'm sure she'd come around then and see that she'd be wasting her life, marrying a nobody like Jeff Hayden."

Dani knew she was getting angry. "Some nobody like you?"

"What's that supposed to mean?" Adam said, raising his voice and stopping in front of her, his stance belligerent.

"Just that, Adam," she answered as she got up, not backing down one iota. "You were a nobody once, too. We all start off as nobodies, even people born with money. It's how you play the hand you're dealt that counts, not how many winning cards you start with. I talked to both Bonnie and Jeff quite a while that evening. Jeff's bright, personable, and has high ambitions. Just as you had once, until you glimpsed the high-society scene and decided to make yourself over to fit in so you could buy Bonnie status, when she wants love instead."

His eyes dark and furious, Adam glared at her. "You don't know what you're talking about. Jeff Hayden is from the wrong side of the tracks, and he's never going to find a way to cross over."

"Oh, you are the most impossible man!" Dani shrieked, upsetting Mutt to the point where he came to stand by her side, growling, ready to show his fangs to her opponent in this battle he couldn't understand. Absently Dani patted him reassuringly, while her eyes blazed back at Adam.

"You're willing to play God with two lives—that's how sure you are that you're right. You're from the wrong side of the tracks, too. Not railroad tracks, Adam. Emotional tracks." She jabbed a hard finger into his chest. "Inside, where it matters. People can't be manipulated like business deals. You don't have the right—no one has—to dictate to another adult how to run her life. Not your sister, not your mother, not anyone. People need to be allowed to make their own decisions, to fall down and get hurt if they're wrong and to learn from that. To celebrate if they're right. To be their own person."

Adam was grim faced. "It's taken me too long to become somebody so Bonnie can be, too. I'm not giving in now."

Dani's voice was low, sad. "You always were somebody to me, from the first time I saw you. The somebody you became is the one I'm not crazy about."

She felt the hot tears begin and knew she had to get away from him, fast. "And to think I almost let myself fall in love with you." Turning, she ran toward the shore without seeing, blinded by the tears that now fell freely.

"Wait, dammit! Come back here, Dani." Frustrated, Adam stood at the edge of her patio, watching her retreating back. He had half a notion to remove his jacket and shoes and take off after her. Glancing at his watch, he realized that if he didn't hurry, he would be late for his appointment with Carter Ames and several other investors in the shopping plaza. For another moment he studied the woman in the pink outfit, running with her dog. Running away from him.

Dani was wrong. She had to be. He had an obligation to guide his sister onto the right path. In years to come, Bonnie would thank him.

What had Dani said, that she'd almost let herself fall in love with him? There was no "almost" on his part. He did love her and had for some time, though he'd fought the knowledge. But knowing it, even admitting it, didn't change anything. They were still poles apart in their thinking. Loving her only complicated things.

He'd come here this morning to explain, to make her see. And because he'd missed her terribly. How could you love someone so much, want her desperately, yet not be able to get through to her on an issue as vital as this one? Damned if he knew, Adam thought as he ran a shaky hand through his hair.

He turned and hurried to his car. The last thing he needed this morning was a meeting with Carter Ames. The shrewd older man had eyes like a hawk and seemed to see right through people to the heart of a matter, which was probably why he was such a successful businessman. Adam would need all his professionalism to keep Carter's sensitive antennae from picking up that his daughter had gotten to him. Getting into his Porsche, Adam hoped it would work.

It did work—for about three hours. But when the meeting ended, with handshakes all around, and Carter asked for a private word with Adam in his office, he knew that Carter had discerned something.

"You're doing a fine job, Adam," Carter began as he seated himself behind his huge oak desk. "The committee members are as pleased as I am with your reports and your progress, as I'm sure you noticed. I'm recommending you for the Blair project, though we won't have final approval on that for another month."

Sitting back, trying to look relaxed, Adam put on a smile. "I'm glad you're pleased, Carter, and I appreciate the recommendation."

"It's based on several factors. Your past performance, my faith in your abilities and your integrity, the fact that I like you, and because someone once helped me and I like to do the same when I can and when it's justified."

"Thank you, Carter. I presume you mean your father when he brought you into the business?"

Carter Ames lit one of the long, thin cigars he rarely let himself enjoy, and sat back, regarding the young man in front of him as he blew smoke toward the ceiling. "My father died when I was six, my mother when I was ten. My brother and I lived with an aunt and uncle in Boston."

Adam frowned, confused. "But I'd heard that you had a monied background, that you went to Harvard. Your aunt and uncle were wealthy?"

Smiling, Carter shook his head. "Not by a long shot. My uncle was caretaker for a wealthy family, the Thurmonds, in Hyannis, and my aunt, the cook. Dwayne Thurmond was on the board at Harvard and head of the scholarship committee. He's the one who gave me a boost, took a liking to my brother, Troy, and me. We both went to Harvard on a scholarship." Carter turned his swivel chair to gaze out the window at the noontime traffic below. "Sometimes I wonder if old Thurmond did me a favor or a disservice."

"Why is that?" Adam asked.

"The Thurmonds didn't have children of their own, so they welcomed Troy and me into the household for family gatherings and occasional parties, especially as we got older. He introduced us to the good life, made us long for things, made us want to be superachievers, I think."

Adam crossed his legs. "Is that so bad?"

Carter carefully tapped the long ash from his cigar into a heavy brass ashtray. "Not if you can handle it. Troy was pushed into Harvard, but he didn't seem to have much of a head for studies or business. He flunked out of college after five years of trying, then started several small companies, all of which failed. He was crushed, realizing he could never be what others had expected him to be."

Troy Ames, the uncle Dani had said she enjoyed visiting because he and his family were so happy. Odd, Adam thought.

"Troy married a young niece of the Thurmonds, but that didn't work out, either. They were vastly different. Finally Troy left...knocked around the country for a while. Then he met a woman who changed his life. Lydia was a widow with two small children, who lived on a farm in Iowa. Troy went to work for her and, after a while, married her. They now have two more children, and Troy's a happy man. He stopped chasing the wrong dream."

"But you chased the right dream, created a financial empire, married a woman who could only help you, even now, after you're no longer living together. Things worked out well for you."

"Only partly." Carter laid the cigar in the ashtray and leaned forward, steepling his fingers. "I became that tireless superachiever, enamored of business and all its fine trappings. Perhaps you can understand this, Adam, since I feel we're very much alike. I no longer pursue a goal for the money, the acquisitions. Achieving can be its own reward, and very addictive. But it has a price tag, too."

Adam was beginning to get the uncomfortable feeling that there was more behind Carter's words than appeared on the surface. "If I'm not being too personal, I take it you mean that the price you paid was the failure of your marriage because you work so hard and Arlene resented your time away from her."

Carter's look became contemplative. "Partly. When a man grows up poor—a man like me, at least—he often overcompensates by working hard and sometimes neglecting his family. But Arlene and I probably wouldn't have remained together even if that hadn't been the case."

He picked up his cigar again and took several short puffs. "I'd worked night and day and had made my first million before I turned thirty. Then I was ready for step two, a beautiful wife who was socially connected, because I wasn't and felt the lack. I fell in love with Arlene almost immediately. She was so lovely—still is. She came from money, a lot of it, and I was determined to win her, to better her father. Well, I did both, but I lost her."

Adam watched as Carter's blue eyes, a shade lighter than Dani's, took on a sadness.

"Though we both care deeply for each other and will probably never remarry, Arlene and I can't live together. We make each other very unhappy when we do, because we're both very set in our ways, unwilling to compromise. While it's true, Adam, that opposites attract, people who are alike and who like the same things are more apt to *stay* married. Fortunate is the man who falls in love with a woman who is the other half of him, rather than the opposite. He's got a better than fighting chance. That's why I often envy my brother.''

Thoughtfully Adam gazed out the window. The other half of him. He'd thought about Dani that way just this morning.

"I had brunch with Arlene and both my daughters yesterday, sort of a Sunday tradition when we're all in town.'' Carter studied the smoke trailing from his cigar as if he could find answers in the wispy tendrils. "Something's bothering Dani. She's not her usual self, and when I tried to discuss it in a private moment, she brushed away my questions. When I mentioned your name, she found an excuse to leave early.'' His sharp gaze speared Adam. "Are you going to brush me off, too, Adam?''

Adam shifted restlessly in his chair. It had been years since he'd felt called on the carpet, as long ago as his school days. He'd persuaded Carter to ask Dani to help him that first night he'd seen her at Arlene's and now couldn't help wondering if Carter regretted that decision. "I'm not sure what it is you want to know,'' he said, well aware of what Carter was leading up to.

"I'm gone a lot and am very involved in my work, as you realize. But I love Dani more than I can tell you. Enough to let her go.''

"I'm not sure I understand.''

Carter shrugged. "Just that. Dani's not like her sister, or Arlene or even me. She marches to a different drummer, to use an overused phrase. She loves challenges, as I told you some time ago. Like her sports, the skating competitions. Like teaching—a truly challenging field. Like living away from us all in a small beach house, making her own friends, living her own life. Arlene—sometimes Sabrina, too—keep attempting to pull her back, draw her in, even make her feel guilty. But I've tried to support her decisions without trying to change her. If we change people against their will, we lose them. Troy tried to be someone he wasn't because of pressure from others, and finally woke up. Dani found out early where she didn't fit. The hardest thing I've ever done was letting Dani go, encouraging her to try her wings and being there for her and letting her know I care—win, lose or draw. Wait until you're a father, and you'll know what I mean."

Perhaps he already knew, had known for some time, but didn't want to let go. Not of Bonnie, not of Dani. Could Carter be right?

"Adam, I may be out of line here, but I'd like to know. Are you merely Dani's latest challenge, or do you really care about her?"

Adam needed to hear the answer to a question of his own first. "If I do care, and want some permanency to this relationship, could you accept me, a working stiff from the south end of Boston who has no Harvard degree? Could Arlene and Sabrina?" He saw a flash of temper in Carter's eyes, a reaction so much like his daughter's at times, before Carter answered in a level voice.

"If you honestly think the three of us judge people by that kind of yardstick, you don't know the Ames family very well. The man I want for Dani is the one who loves her unconditionally, as she is. There are no further requirements."

Adam nodded, satisfied. "I needed to hear that, sir, although I was fairly certain of your answer." They were two businessmen who worked well together, yet he'd slipped into the respectful term quite naturally. The serious tone of the occasion seemed to call for it. Standing, he smiled genuinely for the first time that day. "To answer your question, yes, I care about Dani—I love her very much. Now I've got to convince her of that." Taking a step closer to the desk, Adam held out his hand. "I want to thank you for your honesty and your concern. You've made me take a long, hard look at some things I hadn't considered. I want you to know that your faith in me is not misplaced."

Rising, Carter clasped his hand warmly. "I was certain it wasn't. Go get her, son."

Chapter Twelve

The shrill blast of the coach's whistle, calling for time out, grated on Dani's nerves. Straightening from having been hunched over, watching the last play on the court, she wiped her moist brow. The oppressive heat in the windowless gymnasium grated on her nerves, too. Dani glanced over at Al Donaldson, who was standing on the sidelines, and realized he was signaling for her to join him. She probably shouldn't have agreed to referee this morning, for everything irritated her, and that wasn't fair to the kids or to Al.

"You called that last one wrong, Dani," Al told her when she reached his side. "Joey was fouled and has two shots coming."

"Look, do you want to referee, or do you want to coach?" Dani asked defiantly.

Al looked at her a long moment, then put his hand on her shoulder. "Okay, simmer down," he said, steering her over to the bench. He turned back to the boys. "Take five, guys. Get some water and cool off." As the boys ran toward the lockers, he sat down next to Dani, who was rubbing the back of her neck. "Want to tell me about it?"

"There's nothing to tell," Dani lied, leaning back and propping her elbows on the bench behind them. "I'm sorry if I snapped at you. It's so damn hot in here." She blew a puff of air at her damp bangs.

"Are you feeling all right, Dani? And don't tell me it's the heat."

"I feel fine. Terrific. On top of the world."

"Sure you do. That's why you snarled at Duffy, who worships you, yelled at me and called three plays wrong so far, and we're not even through the first half."

Stubbornly Dani kept her eyes glued to the high ceiling and her mouth closed. For which Al should be grateful, she thought. If she told him what she was really thinking, he'd call the men in the white coats and have her carted away.

She wanted to get away, far away, from everything. She wanted to drive somewhere, or fly or sail somewhere, anywhere. She wanted to be with Adam, where they could start over, without his family or hers, without a thought to social status or their pasts. She wanted to float, to be free, to reach out and touch the impossible. She always had. And had never quite made it.

Wrong. Everything was wrong because Adam was no longer in her life. Nearly a week had gone by since she'd run away from their argument on her patio. What good did being right do her, when being without him made her so miserable? Learn to compromise, Sabrina had advised her. Dani at least had some options open to her, whereas Sabrina didn't. It was high time she examined a few, gave in a little, came up with a compromise.

Stretching her legs, she admitted to herself that she was being as stubborn in her way as Adam was in his. Both of them were so certain they were right. Adam's family, her family—they weren't what really mattered. Their feelings for each other were what counted. They'd both played games long enough. She'd go find Adam today, after this interminable game, lay her cards on the table and beg him to listen if she had to. Pride was a lonely companion, Sabrina had also told her. Yes, indeed it was.

Sighing, Dani looked over at Al, at the confusion on his face, and felt guilty. "I'm truly sorry, Al," she said with real sincerity this time. She stood. "Call the boys back in, and let's finish this game, then I'll leave. I admit I'm having trouble keeping my mind on basketball today. I've got some personal problems I need to work out."

Getting up, Al nodded. "You go ahead. I'll finish up with the guys. You're just having an off day."

An off day, she thought. Would that it were so. Dani stood on tiptoes and kissed his cheek. "Thanks, Al."

He started off for the lockers as she gathered her things. "I'll phone you later, okay?" he called out.

"I might not be home, but thanks anyway," she answered, then headed for the open double doors. The last thing she needed was Al hovering around her, trying to figure out what was wrong with her.

As soon as she walked out into the sunshine, she saw Duffy lounging against the wall, his eyes filled with hurt. Another fence to mend, Dani thought, taking a deep breath. Lately she was spending most of her days apologizing to people for her thoughtless actions and her short temper. Once she got things straightened out between Adam and her, that would end.

Dani walked up to within inches of the boy and put on her best smile. "I owe you an apology, Duffy. I was rude a while ago in there, and I'm sorry. It wasn't anything you did. It was ... Well, I think I'm getting a summer cold.'' She sniffed noisily to back up the lie. "I'm not feeling like myself." And that was the truth.

He regarded her for a long moment, then nodded and pushed off from the building. "I thought maybe I'd done something to hurt you," he said in that strange squeaky-deep voice of the pubescent male. He couldn't mask the lovesick look in his eyes.

She shook her head, placing an arm around his bony shoulders. "I know you wouldn't hurt me, Duff. I think I need to go home, take a couple aspirins and get some rest. I'll be fine by next week.... How's the job?" She'd spoken to a friend who ran a nursery and he'd hired Duffy for the summer.

His dark eyes lit up. "Great. You know, it works—that thing you told me about talking to the plants. I thought it was crazy at first, but we had this droopy split birch, young and real sick-looking. I started talking to him, gave him special attention. You should see him now."

Dani smiled at his earnest young face. That's what we all need, a little special attention, then we all blossom. "That's terrific, Duff. Keep up the good work. I—"

Dani felt more than saw someone approach. Turning, she drew in a quick breath. Adam Kinkaid stood glowering down at her, his hands on his hips. She was so surprised she said the first thing that came into her mind. "What are you doing here?"

"Why do you keep hanging up on me?" Adam asked through thin lips. "Why won't you talk with me? Why won't you agree to meet with me?"

She'd been foolishly stubborn, and now, just when she'd decided she wanted to talk things over with him, he'd arrived looking mad as a wet hen. She wasn't about to engage in a public shouting match with him in his present frame of mind. Stepping around him, Dani looped the strap of her bag over her shoulder and headed for her car. "Some other time, Adam."

He grabbed her arm and stopped her in midstride. "What happened to the woman who told me that she'd always be willing to listen?"

"Hey, mister," Duffy interjected, straightening to his five-feet-five-inch height, "get your hands off her."

"Stay out of this, young man," Adam told him with a warning look before he brought his hot gaze back to Dani. "Answer me!"

"All right, I will," Dani said, feeling oddly calm despite her hammering heart. She glanced quickly at Duffy to let him know it was all right, then narrowed her eyes at Adam. She'd been ready to crawl to get him back, but now he was making her mad again. "She got tired of hearing the same old arguments from a man too damn pigheaded to take seriously anyone's viewpoint but his own."

Adam's face was like a storm cloud. "I have an explanation, if you'll listen."

This wasn't the scenario she'd envisioned. She quickly decided she'd wait until he was reasonable to talk with him, and shook off his hand. "No, I'm through listening. We only go around in circles."

With one fast swoop, Adam gathered her up in his arms and flung her over his shoulder as if she were no more than a sack of flour, then started toward his truck.

"Put me down, you big oaf!" Dani squealed. Angry, embarrassed and frustrated, she pummeled his back with her free hand while holding on for dear life with the other. Then she yelled to Duffy, who looked as though he wished he were a foot taller and a hundred pounds heavier, "Go in and get Al and the boys. Get help!"

Adam stopped in his tracks, turned and walked over to Duffy, who eyed him warily. Holding on to his squirming bundle tightly with both hands, he bent over and whispered something into Duffy's ear.

Suddenly the boy grinned up at him. "Okay, man, I gotcha," Duffy said. He peeked around Adam and caught Dani's eye. "It's gonna be all right, Miss Ames."

Confidently Adam started back toward his truck.

"All right? What do you mean, all right?" She resumed her pounding, though she might have been a bothersome fly buzzing around his back for all the attention he paid her. "Put me down! This is outrageous. I won't allow it. I—"

Unceremoniously he dumped her onto the passenger seat of his Bronco. Landing with a thud, Dani glared up at him. "You told me you'd always be willing to listen, and I'm going to take you to a place where you have no other choice but to hear me out. You got that?" When she didn't answer, he nodded. "Good." Pushing down the lock, he slammed her door, climbed in behind the wheel and started the engine.

"Adam, wait. I—"

"No. Not another word until we get where we're going. Now we play by *my* rules, honey."

Crossing her arms over her chest, Dani stared out the side window. Duffy gave her the high sign. "Have fun," he yelled with a grin.

Fun! What had Adam told that kid to make him co-conspirator to a kidnapping? she wondered as he pulled the Bronco out into Sunday-morning traffic.

The metal elevator cage squeaked and groaned its way clear to the top, twelve stories above the city of Boston. They were climbing up the east wing of the structure, some distance from the section Dani had visited before, which was now nearly completed. Hands jammed in the pockets of her white shorts, she watched the ascent with pounding heart and nervous apprehension.

She wasn't fearful that Adam would harm her. Not at all. She was fearful that she'd give in too readily to his arguments, weak though they would be. A wise woman knew when her love for a man overruled her head. And she was well aware that Adam knew exactly the right buttons to push. Which was why she'd avoided his calls, thinking he'd tire of the game. But he hadn't. Dani admitted to a certain curiosity as to why. She'd been ready to go after him, but perhaps this way would be better. She'd play along and see what he had to say.

Adam was certain of only one thing: he didn't know how to begin; how to tell Dani all that he felt, all that he'd learned. Would she believe him? Had he overplayed his hand with her? Would she listen politely but still walk away from him? Was she already interested in someone else— that pudgy stockbroker or that skinny basketball coach? Unthinkable. Sometimes love hit hardest when you weren't looking, Clancy had told him. Truer words were never spoken, Adam realized. He hadn't been looking, but he'd surely been hit—hard. He had to make Dani listen. With a bit more force than necessary, Adam shoved open the elevator door.

Standing with his back to her, he pulled her arms around his waist. "Now, stay close behind me and don't look down," he instructed. He waited a long moment, expecting resistance, but she grabbed ahold of his belt and hung on. So far, so good. He stepped out onto the orange girder and inched along.

Once again Dani found the experience of being up so high thrilling. A little scary, but thrilling. Holding on to

Adam, she dogged his steps until they reached an L-shaped corner. Then Adam slowly turned within the circle of her arms and slid his own around her. He looked into her eyes searchingly.

"I love you, Dani. No matter what the outcome of this conversation, I want you to know that."

Dani let out a deep breath. "Well, you certainly know how to capture a woman's attention."

"I've made some mistakes...." He paused, waiting.

She didn't want to make this too easy for him. "I hope you're not looking for arguments on that."

"No. I readily admit to them." He stroked her hair, letting his gaze wander to the blue sky. "You know how your mother labeled your scrapbook 'Danielle Ames, Superstar'? Well, I think a long time ago I labeled myself Adam Kinkaid, Superson, Superbrother, and even Super Substitute-father-and-breadwinner. When my dad took off, I took over—if not literally, then figuratively. I put myself in charge, and soon my poor tired mother was going along with all my suggestions. Bonnie, who was so much younger, didn't have a chance." He brought his eyes back to hers. "I was wrong, not in all the things but in some."

Dani felt her heart turn over with hope. She stroked his back, soothing him, offering understanding. "Takes a big man to admit being wrong."

"And a foolish man to think he's got all the answers. I thought I was pretty invincible, that I didn't need anyone." He broke into a smile. "Until I met you. I think I knew that first evening that I wanted you in my life. What I couldn't know and wouldn't admit was how much I *needed* you in my life."

"Oh, Adam, you can't know how much I've wanted to hear you say those words." Dani tightened her arms around him as her heart soared. It was going to be all right.

Compromises. They had a few to make, but with love between them, they could.

"There are a few other words I think you might be interested in hearing," he said, burying his face for a long moment in the delicate wildflower fragrance of her hair. "I made an agreement with Bonnie and Jeff." He pulled back from her with a soft chuckle. "I know this isn't news to you, but Jeff's not such a bad sort. I've spent quite a bit of time talking to him, and you were right; he's a lot like I once was."

Dani just nodded and smiled, afraid to speak.

"Anyway, I've set Jeff up with a summer job at Kinkaid Construction. A future architect should know something about construction, right? He'll stay in the spare room. I told Bonnie and him that if by fall they still feel the same about each other and if they both promise to continue their schooling, I'll give them their wedding. Does that meet with your approval, madam?"

"More important, does it meet with Bonnie's approval, and Jeff's and your mother's? And yours? Don't do this for me, Adam." He had to do it for the right reasons, or he'd never be able to stick with his decision.

"I'm not. I was shortsighted. Your father made me see that."

"My father?"

Unable to resist any longer, he brushed her bangs aside with his lips and kissed her smooth forehead. "Mmm, yes, your father. Smart man. Told me to go get you."

Dani pulled back, astonished. "You went to my father and talked about us?"

"Not exactly. I was at his office for a meeting and we talked privately afterward. Your name did come up, as I recall."

She pounded a small fist into his back. "What did he say?"

"Ow! All right. He just pointed out a few things I hadn't seen. Why didn't you tell me that Carter Ames grew up dirt poor and made his own way?"

"I did tell you he was a self-made man, but you weren't listening."

Adam nodded, remembering. "I thought you meant he inherited a couple of million and turned it into more. I was pretty arrogant, wasn't I?"

She smiled up at him. "Yes, you were. And insufferable and single-minded and pigheaded and—"

"Hey, aren't there any pluses?"

Dani kissed his jutting chin. "A few. I like the feel of your scratchy face when you don't shave." She ran a hand through his unruly hair. "I'm crazy about your messy hair." Then she brushed her fingertips over his mouth. "And you learn your lessons well. You kiss like no one I've ever known." She saw his eyes darken as he pulled her close against the hard length of him. "When you kiss me, the world stops. I feel like I'm flying. You could make me believe in the tooth fairy when you kiss me—in anything." Wickedly she rubbed up against him. "And—not that I'm an expert, mind you—I think you're sensational in bed."

"You're an expert, as far as I'm concerned."

Just a breath apart from him now, Dani let her gaze stray to his lips. "Tell me, Mr. Kinkaid," she said, her voice suddenly husky, "have you ever been kissed high atop the world, with the wind racing through your hair and the blood churning through your veins?"

He remembered asking her the same question the first time he'd brought her up. "No," he whispered.

"Neither have I. Want to try it?" And with that she closed the gap between them, touching her lips to his.

His mouth was exactly as she'd remembered in her restless dreams, full, rich, magical. She'd been lost to him from their first kiss, drawn by his intensity, captivated by his surprising tenderness. Always, she could feel his boundless energy, the streak of wildness just under the surface, the innate sensitivity that was part of the enigma. The empty days and lonely nights without him melted away. She was his.

Adam strained to bring her closer and closer still, knowing he could never be quite close enough. Unhesitatingly she pressed her body to his, giving as she always had, and he felt the power of her flowering passion, aware it was a gift she gave only to him. With a groan, he deepened the kiss, drinking in her sweetness, drowning in her softness.

Her ardor matched his as her tongue entered his mouth. At last she, who had never felt as though she'd belonged, knew the true joy of belonging to one man, to this man, to her love. She, who had never truly loved before, loved now with a fervor she hadn't thought herself capable of. She, who had locked away her passion, waiting for the man who held the key, now let him inside, let him touch the core of her. Body pulsing with needs, she clung to him as the summer wind whipped around them.

The force of his feelings for this beautiful woman, who had stolen his heart, made Adam tremble, and he drew back from her and stared into her deep blue eyes, which were soft with arousal. "Nobody's ever been able to weaken me like this with just a kiss, Dani. Nobody." He trailed kisses over her face, her throat, as his hands caressed her back. He inhaled the lightly floral scent, the clean, soapy fragrance, the womanly essence of her.

Lifting his head, he took a deep, steadying breath, reaching for the control that seemed to elude him when he was with her. He had to stop, or in moments he'd have her beneath him on the bright orange girder.

"I'm sorry," he said, running a shaky hand through his windblown hair. "You . . . you make me a little crazy and—"

Dani touched two fingers to his lips. "Don't. Don't ever apologize to me again for wanting me. Knowing that you want me is the most exciting thing in the world."

Calmer now, Adam hugged her to him. "I do want you, Dani. Not for an hour or an afternoon, but forever. Your body does wondrous things to me. Yet making love with you is only a part of it. I want to go to sleep holding you and wake up with you beside me. I want to share all the laughs and the good times and know you're with me during the rough times—and there will be some. If you doubted it before, know it now. You are loved, Dani Ames, deeply, passionately. I want you to be mine and no one else's. I need to hear that you are."

She remembered what he'd told her of his youth, always sharing everything he owned, rarely having something new that no one had ever touched before him. She could give him this uncommon gift. In fact, she already had. "I'm yours, Adam. I have been from the start."

He crushed her to him, and his heart was so filled with feeling he couldn't speak for long minutes. Then he sought her eyes. "Life won't always be easy with me, Dani. I can't promise you perfection. You've seen glimpses of the worst of me and maybe the best. I do know that with you I'm better than I was without you. Talk to me. Tell me how you feel."

A tiny sparrow landed on the next beam and chirped at them curiously. A gust of wind playfully rearranged

Adam's hair as she studied him. Sunlight made his brown eyes appear lighter; he looked somehow vulnerable, still vaguely troubled. A strong man who struggled with his own insecurities. Dani chose her words carefully.

"How I feel..." she repeated, running her fingers over the stubble on his jaw. "I feel love, so much love for you that it overwhelms me—and frightens me, too. You're so strong, Adam, so assertive, that sometimes I feel I might get lost in your shadow."

Surprisingly, he nodded. "I know what you're referring to, the time I said I'd build you a house and take care of you. That came out wrong. What I meant was, we could design a house together, one that would be ours, not mine and not yours. I know what your work with the kids means to you, and I didn't mean that I wanted you to turn into someone who sat around waiting for my beck and call. I'm proud of what you do, of what you are. I wouldn't want you to give up teaching, unless... unless maybe one day you wanted to have a family. Do you?"

The thought made her smile. "Yes, I do. And then I would want to stay home. I was raised mostly by Sarah, and you didn't have both parents with you, either. I'd like to be there for our children—I'd like *both* of us to."

"You think I'll be like Carter, who loves his family but isn't around much?" He saw the truth in her eyes. "I won't be like that, Dani. I've worked hard all my life, poured myself into my business, and it's thriving. Now I want to enjoy what I've earned, to be with you, to be a real father one day. If I slip, you'll be there to remind me, won't you?"

"You can count on it." She toyed with the buttons on his shirt. No sense in not saying it all, she thought. "There's one more thing. This business of the social scene. I'll attend an occasional party to keep Arlene happy, but I want you to know that for the most part I want to live a simple life. Peanut butter, not caviar. The Red Sox, not the opera. A walk on the beach, not tennis at the country club. Can you handle that, Adam? Because I won't be coaxed back into the other, not even for you."

"You really thought I went for all that, did you?" he asked. Smiling, he shook his head. "I'll slip into that monkey suit, even put on a tie once or twice a year—for Arlene, as you said. The only reason I enjoyed the opera was that you were there, holding my hand. And the best part of the tennis lesson was when I put my arms around you to learn the grip. But basically, I don't care what we do, as long as we do it together. Danielle Winthrop Ames, will you marry me?"

She appeared to ponder a long moment, then nodded. "On one condition."

"Name it."

"You've got to get rid of that housekeeper. I can't live in such perfection."

Adam grinned. "Okay. I'll let you clutter up my house. I'll even learn to talk to your plants if it'll make you happy."

"Speaking of plants, how's Felix? You haven't killed that healthy philodendron, have you?"

"Not quite. He's a little droopy but still alive. I think you'd better move in with me soon and rescue him. The way you rescued me." His hands slid down low on her back, aligning her soft curves tightly against his hard frame. "If we don't get the hell off this girder soon and find a private place, I'm going to give the after-church strollers down below a show they'll long remember. And maybe get us both arrested."

"No control, eh, Kinkaid? All right, let's go."

Back in the elevator, Dani remembered something. "What did you say to Duffy to make him grin like that?"

Adam chuckled. "I'll never tell," he teased her. Then kissed her soundly.

Arlene had outdone herself. It was the weekend of her favorite charity affair, and the large ballroom of her Hyannis house had been transformed into a magical place, with shimmering chandeliers, dazzling floral displays, handsome men, beautiful women and a magnificent orchestra playing at the far end. Standing in the arched doorway, Dani took it all in with a small smile.

"Some things never change," she said.

Beside her, Adam ran a finger under the collar of his formal shirt and stretched his neck. "How long did you say we have to stay?" he asked.

She looked at him, again admiring the cut of the tux and the shape of the man in it. She lingered a moment on his tie, which he'd asked her to adjust for him earlier when they'd dressed together. Wearing only a pale peach teddy, she'd moved close to help him, but when she'd reached up, she'd lost herself in his eyes, and the tie had been forgotten as she and Adam had fallen onto the bed. The wonder of loving him filled her mind and heart now, and unconsciously she smiled softly.

Seeing her eyes change, Adam trailed two fingers down her soft cheek. "What brought about that smile?"

"I was remembering how much fun it was helping you dress," she answered lazily.

She wore a black dress tonight, high necked in front, dipping low in back, with a gold band at the neckline, and its soft flow accentuated her graceful curves. There was color in her cheeks, more from an inner warmth than from her makeup, Adam thought. Although she would deny it, Dani was stunning. And she was his.

He moved a step closer. "And after this is over, I'm going to show you how much fun it is getting me *un*-dressed. And you too."

"Mmm, I can hardly wait." Already Dani felt her blood heat. Never would she get enough of this man.

"Well, well, what have we here? Necking in the door-way?"

Dani turned and smiled at her sister. Sabrina had on green tonight, which was certainly her color. "You look fabulous, Sabrina," she said.

"You look all aglow yourself," Sabrina said, her eyes registering a quick twinge of envy. Quickly she shifted her gaze to Adam. "Does the look my sister's wearing mean what I think it does?"

Adam slid his arm possessively about Dani, drawing her nearer. "Dani seems to think I need looking after and has agreed to tackle the job."

Sabrina's eyes widened as they returned to Dani's. "Honestly?"

Dani nodded, unable to hide her pleasure. "No big an-nouncements, please. But yes, honestly. We're going to be married, quietly and soon."

Moving to hug her, Sabrina blinked happily. "I'm so glad for you." Then she reached for Adam. "For both of you. I'm glad you took my advice, Dani."

Adam raised a questioning brow. "Which was?"

Perhaps it was time to own up, Dani thought, a smile playing about her lips. "I believe it was 'If you love him, don't let him get away. Pride's a lonely companion. Learn to compromise. Go after him.'"

"But *I* came after *you*," Adam reminded her.

Squeezing his hand, Dani smiled up at him. "You only beat me by a matter of minutes. When I left the gymnasium, I was on my way to find you and tell you that our differences didn't matter anymore. I was so miserable without you that I was willing to compromise on each and every issue."

Adam put on a mock scowl. "Why, you little devil! You played hard to get to the very end, practically had me begging, and all along, if I'd waited another hour, you'd have been the one begging me?"

Dani's eyes filled with mischief. "I don't know about *begging*, but I *was* going to ask you to marry me."

He moved his face a scant inch from hers. "You're going to pay for that—tonight!"

Her smile widened. "I look forward to it."

"Ahem," Sabrina interjected, looking as if she felt superfluous, "it seems I let a cat out of the bag."

"And I thank you for that piece of ammunition, Sabrina," Adam said, placing an arm about her as well.

"What are sisters for?" she asked with a wink, kissing him lightly on the cheek. Quickly she hugged Dani again. "I'm so glad things worked out."

"Thanks," Dani whispered. "There's someone out there like Adam for you, Sabrina. You'll see."

"Perhaps. Now, you two had better get in there and mingle, or your names will be mud," Sabrina said, scooting them along.

And so they mingled and put up with Arlene's affectionate gushing and Carter's beaming approval and Toni's blatant curiosity. They chatted and smiled, sipped champagne and smiled some more. When Adam whirled her into a dance, Dani gratefully fell into his arms.

Here was the real magic, Dani thought, the magic she'd never found before at these functions. Here was what had been missing, the glamour, the glitter, all of it—in Adam's arms. The magic of true love.

As Adam waltzed her out onto the deserted terrace, Dani didn't object, for she, too, was ready to be alone with him. In another moment he took her hand and opened the gate guarding the stairs that led down to the sea far below.

"Come with me," Adam said, helping her down the first step. "There's something I want to show you."

Glancing hesitantly over her shoulder, Dani followed. "Adam, we can't just disappear like this. Where are you taking me?"

"Away from the madding crowd," Adam said in a singsong voice, "where I can ravish your gorgeous body." Carefully he led the way down the darkened stairs. "Watch your footing here." And then they were on the sand, which was still warm from the sun, strolling under the wide wooden terrace that ran along the back of Arlene's house. Dani slipped out of her shoes, trying to contain her curiosity.

From out of the shadows came a darting fur ball that all but hurled itself at Dani. "Mutt! What are you doing here?"

"I planted him here on guard duty," Adam explained, patting the dog's big, shaggy head.

"What's he guarding?"

"You'll see." Taking her hand, Adam led her to the secluded section at the far end of the overhang, where the relentless pounding of the ocean waves could be heard. Mutt ran over and sat down proudly at his post. "Good boy," Adam praised him. Bending, he picked up a wicker basket and held it up in a splash of moonlight.

"The lady said she prefers peanut butter to caviar, and I aim to please the lady," he said.

"A picnic basket! Aren't you clever? So that's what Mutt was guarding."

"Yes, and I was praying he wouldn't start before we got here!" Adam spread out a large plaid blanket on the sand, then pulled out a bottle of wine and two glasses.

"When did you do all this?" she asked, giggling at the thought of what her proper mother and her straitlaced father would say if they knew the two of them were picnicking on the beach in formal clothes, some fifty feet under their terrace.

Adam sat down cross-legged on the blanket. "I shouldn't tell you all my secrets," he said, uncorking the wine as Dani joined him on the blanket and began rummaging through the basket. "There are peanut butter and raspberry jelly sandwiches in there and potato chips, and for dessert, M & M's."

"The man knows all my weaknesses," Dani said, laughing. She unwrapped a sandwich and spread it out for Mutt, who attacked it hungrily.

Adam poured the wine and handed her a glass. "Ever since the cottage, I've gotten to like peanut butter and wine."

"I knew I could broaden your horizons."

"You certainly have." Smiling, he held his glass close to hers. "A toast. To the beautiful woman who changed my plans, and my life."

"Mmm. To the man who grabbed the brass ring and handed it to me, with love."

Clinking his glass to hers, Adam took a sip, watching her over the rim. "Yes, with love, Dani. With so much love."

Leaning toward him, her blue eyes shining, Dani smiled. "A lifetime of love to share, Adam."

"Will that be long enough?"

"It'll do, for starters."

As the party revelers danced and drank above them, Dani wrapped her free arm around Adam and lifted her face for his kiss, while Mutt howled in approval to the moon.

*   *   *   *   *

Silhouette Romance

LONG, TALL TEXANS

A Trilogy by Diana Palmer

Bestselling Diana Palmer has rustled up three rugged heroes in a trilogy sure to lasso your heart! The titles of the books are your introduction to these unforgettable men:

CALHOUN

In June, you met Calhoun Ballenger. He wanted to protect Abby Clark from the world, but could he protect her from himself?

JUSTIN

Calhoun's brother, Justin—the strong, silent type—had a second chance with the woman of his dreams, Shelby Jacobs, in August.

TYLER

October's long, tall Texan is Shelby's virile brother, Tyler, who teaches shy Nell Regan to trust her instincts—especially when they lead her into his arms!

Don't miss TYLER, the last of three gripping stories from Silhouette Romance!

ATTRACTIVE, SPACE SAVING BOOK RACK

Display your most prized novels on this handsome and sturdy book rack. The hand-rubbed walnut finish will blend into your library decor with quiet elegance, providing a practical organizer for your favorite hard-or soft-covered books.

Only $9.95

Approximately 16" x 8" when assembled

Assembles in seconds!

To order, rush your name, address and zip code, along with a check or money order for $10.70* ($9.95 plus 75¢ postage and handling) payable to *Silhouette Books.*

Silhouette Books
Book Rack Offer
901 Fuhrmann Blvd.
P.O. Box 1396
Buffalo, NY 14269-1396

Offer not available in Canada.

BKR-2A

*New York and Iowa residents add appropriate sales tax.

Silhouette Desire ®

CHILDREN OF DESTINY

A trilogy by Ann Major

Three power-packed tales of irresistible passion
and undeniable fate created by Ann Major to
wrap your heart in a legacy of love.

PASSION'S CHILD — September

Years ago, Nick Browning nearly destroyed
Amy's life, but now that the child of his
passion— the child of her heart—was in danger,
Nick was the only one she could trust....

DESTINY'S CHILD — October

Cattle baron Jeb Jackson thought he owned
everything and everyone on his ranch, but fiery
Megan MacKay's destiny was to prove him wrong!

NIGHT CHILD — November

When little Julia Jackson was kidnapped, young
Kirk MacKay blamed himself. Twenty years later,
he found her... and discovered that love could
shine through even the darkest of nights.

Don't miss PASSION'S CHILD, DESTINY'S
CHILD and NIGHT CHILD, three thrilling
Silhouette Desires designed to heat up chilly
autumn nights!

SD-445

Silhouette Special Edition

COMING NEXT MONTH

#481 CHAMPAGNE FOR BREAKFAST—Tracy Sinclair
Raoul Ruiz, Mexico City's most eligible bachelor, generously salvaged Lacey Scott's vacation. Then he passionately romanced her, proving as intoxicating—and elusive—as the bubbles in a glass of champagne.

#482 THE PLAYBOY AND THE WIDOW—Debbie Macomber
More earthy than beautiful, more wholesome than sexy, housewife and mother Diana Collins wasn't playboy Cliff Howard's type. So why did he find the plucky widow irresistibly enticing?

#483 WENDY WYOMING—Myrna Temte
That heavenly voice! Who *was* Cheyenne, Wyoming's sexy new deejay? Jason Wakefield pumped his pal, radio insider Melody Hunter—but suddenly he wanted Mel more than the answer!

#484 EDGE OF FOREVER—Sherryl Woods
Dana Brantley had sacrificed intimacy for refuge from a traumatic, haunting past. But insistent Nick Verone and his adorable ten-year-old son kept pushing. Would the truth destroy their fragile union?

#485 THE BARGAIN—Patricia Coughlin
Vulnerable Lisa Bennett kept pursuers at bay, so wily Sam Ravenal played hard to get. Intriguing her with pirate lore and hidden treasure, Sam freed her anchored imagination . . . and baited her heart.

#486 BOTH SIDES NOW—Brooke Hastings
To buttoned-down Bradley Fraser, Sabrina Lang was reckless, irresponsible . . . and dangerously alluring. Then, on a Himalayan adventure, Brad spied her softer side—and fell wholeheartedly in love!

AVAILABLE NOW:

#475 SKIN DEEP
Nora Roberts

#476 TENDER IS THE KNIGHT
Jennifer West

#477 SUMMER LIGHT
Jude O'Neill

#478 REMEMBER THE DAFFODILS
Jennifer Mikels

#479 IT MUST BE MAGIC
Maggi Charles

#480 THE EVOLUTION OF ADAM
Pat Warren